THE KILLING HOUR

(An Alexa Chase Suspense Thriller—Book 3)

Kate Bold

Kate Bold

Debut author Kate Bold is author of the ALEXA CHASE SUSPENSE THRILLER series, comprising six books (and counting); and of the ASHLEY HOPE SUSPENSE THRILLER series, comprising three books (and counting).

An avid reader and lifelong fan of the mystery and thriller genres, Kate loves to hear from you, so please feel free to visit www.kateboldauthor.com to learn more and stay in touch.

ISBN: 978-1-0943-7591-5

BOOKS BY KATE BOLD

ALEXA CHASE SUSPENSE THRILLER
THE KILLING GAME (Book #1)
THE KILLING TIDE (Book #2)
THE KILLING HOUR (Book #3)
THE KILLING POINT (Book #4)
THE KILLING FOG (Book #5)
THE KILLING PLACE (Book #6)

ASHLEY HOPE SUSPENSE THRILLER
LET ME GO (Book #1)
LET ME OUT (Book #2)
LET ME LIVE (Book #3)

PROLOGUE

Interstate 40, near the Arizona State Prison Complex at Kingman, northwest Arizona

9 a.m.

Robby Tyson could not believe his luck.

There, in the dry desert soil at his feet, lay a key.

It was the kind of key he knew all too well. It was a key to unlock his ankle restraints.

Tyson glanced around at the other orange-suited men on the work crew, and the armed prison guards who stood by watching them. Each convict, himself included, had a rake or a hoe in order to work on the landscaping at the edge of the highway. Crappy tools, every one of them. They made them flimsy so they didn't make good weapons. Not that it mattered. Every convict had a length of chain between their ankles that kept them from moving at anything faster than a shuffle. Even so, the guards gripped their pump action shotguns and watched them carefully, standing well back.

Who could have dropped this? They kept the keys on a heavy keychain on their belt. It didn't seem possible that one could have fallen off. The grip on the key wasn't broken or anything.

But Tyson wasn't going to second-guess the first bit of luck he had had in five years. He scraped at the ground near the key with his hoe, then bent over to pat the earth in place around one of the cacti the state had planted here. As he did, he palmed the key.

Knowing that watchful eyes were upon him, he held the hoe normally with both hands, continuing to work the gritty soil with the key jammed between his palm and the handle.

He waited, working for a full fifteen minutes before palming the key into the top of his sock on the pretext of sitting down and pulling out a handkerchief to wipe his brow. Believable enough. It must be ninety degrees already. It would top a hundred today for sure.

Tyson's mind raced. None of the screws had dropped that key. He was sure of it.

So who had? Mike, who had bragged he would bust out of here soon? Carlos, who never said a word but watched everything like a man with a plan? Someone else?

Didn't matter. The important thing was that he could get out of here. Trouble was, he'd have to get out of here now, this morning, because when you came back from an outdoor work crew there were random strip searches. If they found that key on him he'd get another three years for sure. If he told the warden "I just found it in the dirt," that dried up old turd would laugh his ass off.

So when would he do it? He'd have to time it just right.

All through that long, hot morning he thought about it. Through the first two-hour block of work, through his fifteen-minute break when they sat under a tarp out of the hard Arizona sun, and through the next two-hour work period all the way to lunch.

By then he had decided. He played it cool. Drank extra water to keep himself hydrated. Watched the guards out of the corners of his eyes. Saw which ones were bored, which ones couldn't take the heat.

Through all the afternoon he worked, head down, eyes open. He must have tended a hundred of those damn cacti the state planted by the roaring highway just a hundred yards away, as if there weren't enough cacti in the state. Maybe the tourists liked them.

Yeah, that's what he needed. One of those cars speeding by. Some happy family from California or Oregon. Innocent and helpless. If he could get one of their cars he'd be home free.

Easy now. First things first. Get those leg chains off. Get them off at exactly the right time. This kind of chance comes once in a lifetime. Hell, once in a prison's history. Do this just right, and he'd be a prison hero for generations. Mess up, and he'd be dog meat.

"Quitting time!" Officer Hanson shouted.

At last. It was always a bit slack at five o'clock, when the screws had been standing in the sun all day and were hot and tired and thirsty no matter how much water they had drunk. They all just wanted to get to some air-conditioned bar and down a cold one.

"Grab your gear and get in the bus!" one of the other screws ordered.

The prisoners, tired and hot too, moved slowly. Some stopped for a cigarette or a final glug from the big plastic jug of water they shared. Others sat down. The guards didn't hurry them too much.

Tyson moved closer to the prison bus, where a few prisoners were already filing in and getting their leg chains locked to the metal seats, and sat down on the dirt. He rubbed his ankle and grimaced as if he was hurt.

"What's the matter, Tyson?" one of the guards asked, his eyes wary.

"Scraped my ankle earlier today. The shackle has been rubbing on it."

"Should have said something earlier."

"Didn't think it would get this bad."

Another prisoner shuffled by and the guard's attention was distracted. As quick as he could, Tyson pulled the key from where he had tucked it in his sock and, pretending he was rubbing his ankle again, unlocked the shackle around it.

The soft click sounded like Santa Claus letting out a "ho ho ho" at Christmas.

"What are you smiling about?" Lavon, another prisoner, grumbled as he shuffled by.

"No more work today, what else?" Tyson replied, holding the shackle closed with his hand but taking care not to snap it shut again. He had already put the key back in his sock. That miraculous key. Until he had used it he couldn't believe it actually existed, that it must have been a mirage brought on by the searing heat.

Now for the risky part.

Tyson's heart hammered in his chest as he stood, holding the ankle shackle and wincing. He limped over to the prison bus.

"Go see the doc once we get back," a guard said.

"Good idea," Tyson replied. *But I got a better idea.*

He sat down at a seat right next to the door. Officer Hanson was going through the bus locking the leg shackles to the seats. He was one of the younger, tougher screws, with a buzzcut and a mean stare, although he said very little. Tyson noticed that the clasp on the utility knife he kept on his belt was unclipped. Just a quick pull and he'd have it.

It would be nice to have a knife again. He had had a lot of fun with one before he got caught.

Tyson tried to slow his breathing, clearing his mind.

Pretend this is one of your murders. Be calm. Move in for the quick kill. Get away clean. They never did stick but one on you. Take it easy and do it right. Control yourself, time it just right, and you'll be free.

Free to start living again.

Officer Hanson was moving down the bus, having started from the back. After a few moments he got to the man opposite Tyson, and by then the serial killer, charged and found guilty of only one case of manslaughter, was as serene as a Buddhist monk. He didn't even tense as Officer Hanson turned toward him, key ring in hand.

Tyson shook his ankle free and kicked him right in the nuts.

The guard doubled over with a loud *oof.* He tried to say something, but his words were drowned out by the cheers of the other prisoners.

Idiots, they just alerted the other screws.

Time to work fast.

He whipped out the knife from Officer Hanson's belt, opened it, grabbed him by the throat, and got him into a headlock, pointing the tip of the knife right at Hanson's eye. He'd learned people got more scared of that than a blade at their throat. Knowledge gained from long experience.

Hanson froze, hands in the air. Tyson let him out of his headlock and used his free hand to grab his gun. He half expected Hanson to fight at that point—he'd seen the guard give out beatdowns and he was plenty tough—but he didn't resist.

"Your eye is worth more than a guard's salary," Tyson said. "Smart man."

Movement just outside the bus. Tyson turned and saw three of the guards right outside, guns leveled.

"You can't kill me before I kill him," Tyson said, putting the gun against Hanson's temple.

The guards hesitated. Tyson grinned, knowing he had them.

"I'll make you a deal," Tyson said. "You let me walk out of here—"

"Not gonna happen!" one shouted.

"—and I'll let him go as soon as I'm away. I don't want a first degree on my record. If we continue with the Mexican standoff, I'll toss this key ring to the others and let them all free themselves. Then you'll have a hell of a problem on your hands."

The three guards looked at each other uncertainly.

"Do as he says," Hanson croaked. "He's only in for manslaughter. He won't kill in cold blood unless you force him. If he frees the other inmates, we're in deep shit!"

Pause. Tyson kept his breathing calm, regular.

The guards looked at each other.

"Please," Hanson pleaded. "He'll kill me if you force him. But I know this guy. He's smart. Real smart. A prison break will get him ten years. Killing me will get him a lethal injection. He won't risk that."

The guards looked at each other again and backed off. Tyson stood, keeping the gun to Hanson's head.

"Back off," he told them. They took a step back. "More. Hanson, grab that bag."

Hanson slowly picked up the large plastic bag they had brought their sandwiches in.

"All right, boys, you put your guns, phones, and walkie-talkies in this bag and I'll toss you these keys. I'm the only one escaping today."

The chorus of swear words from the other inmates almost drowned out the reply.

"No way, Tyson. Give yourself up."

Tyson pushed against Hanson's head with the barrel of the gun. "Give it up or he gets it."

One of the guards narrowed his eyes. "We'll give you the phones and radios but not the guns."

"Best you're going to get, Tyson," Hanson said.

"Shut up." Tyson thought for a moment. "All right. Toss them in."

Tyson stepped off the bus, Hanson just in front of him as a shield. One by one, the guards dropped their phones and radios into the bag and backed away. Their aim didn't waver for a second. Tyson tossed them the keys. They landed in the dirt with a loud clink.

The murderer turned and put a bullet through the bus's radio, making the guards and nearest prisoners jerk. Hanson didn't move a muscle.

He's a cool one, Tyson thought. *Watch out for him.*

Tyson studied the three guards, all pointing their guns at him. "OK, tell you what we're going to do. You screws are going to sit pretty in the bus while me and Hanson here go flag down a passing car. Don't worry. I'm not going to hurt any civilians. The poor bastard won't even be in his car for more than a second. Hanson will drive."

The guards moved into the bus, eyes alert for Tyson to make any mistake that would let them plug him.

But Tyson never made mistakes. The Southwest Slasher, that's what they called him, and as far as the police knew he had never been arrested. A bar fight with some thug had landed him with a manslaughter charge. The first time he let his emotions get the better of him. The first and the last.

The cops suspected he was responsible for a lot more murders than that, but they couldn't make the charges stick.

Once the guards were inside, Tyson pushed Officer Hanson toward the highway. A billboard was placed just right so Tyson could get behind it, out of sight of the passing drivers but still able to keep both Hanson and the bus in his sights.

"You know what to do," Tyson said.

"I won't give you any trouble," Hanson said.

"No, I don't think you will," Tyson said with a hint of admiration.

Hanson moved to the side of the road, waving at the passing cars. The vehicles kept speeding by. Some even sped up, not wanting to get involved even though all their drivers could see was a man in a prison guard's uniform asking them to stop.

But soon enough a car slowed and stopped.

Tyson smiled. He was home free.

He could get back to doing what he was meant to do.

CHAPTER ONE

East Jersey State Prison, Woodbridge Township, New Jersey
That same day

Deputy Marshal Alexa Chase had visited here before. It had been a bad idea then and it was probably a worse idea now, but she couldn't keep away.

She had to get some answers. She had to speak to the man she had put in here, the second-worst serial killer she had ever come across.

Bruce Thornton, otherwise known as the Jersey Devil.

She'd dealt with a few serial killers in her time. Some were dead. Others would never speak with her. Thornton was only too happy to. He was the only one who could tell her about the kind of animal she hunted.

As a hefty prison guard with a tattoo of a worm-eaten skull on his neck let her through the last door to Thornton's cellblock, Alexa tried to keep her cool. Last time she had lost it.

She had put many evil people away and forgotten about them as soon as the cell door slammed shut, but Thornton had gotten under her skin. The Jersey Devil, as the press had dubbed him, falling for his murderous marketing campaign. She couldn't help think of him by the same name. And while she had arrested him in the end, the things she had seen and the mental depths she had to delve had made her quit the FBI and not work for a whole year.

Because to catch him she had to think like him, bring out the aggressive side of herself in order to see the pattern of his thinking and figure out where he'd strike next.

In the end she had caught him and saved his last victim in the process, but the cost had been high. Once she had Thornton down and helpless, she had almost killed him. Almost. Only the presence of that little boy Thornton had intended on butchering had stopped her.

And she had regretted it ever since. An unworthy sentiment in an officer.

He was the devil, all right. But not of New Jersey. He was her own personal devil.

Alexa had worn her full uniform in order to assert some authority on the prisoners. That included blue slacks, blue shirt with "Deputy US Marshal" emblazoned in white across the back, and the famous six-pointed star. The cowboy boots and hat weren't regulation, but common enough in the Arizona branch she worked for. The only thing missing was the Glock automatic pistol that should have been in the holster at her belt. She had had to check that at the gate. Only prison guards got to carry arms in here, and every one of them did.

She walked slowly down the echoing concrete hallway, trying to control her ragged breathing, cursing the sweat that ran down her face, ignoring the curious stares and open leers of the men in the cells she passed.

Her pace slowed further as she approached the last cell on the left, the one where the devil dwelled.

But she did not want to embarrass herself in front of the guard, so she quickened her step again and sat down on a red plastic chair the guard had placed in front of his cell.

Thornton lounged on his bunk in his prison orange, grinning at her.

Every time she saw him, she was reminded of the old saying, "Never judge a book by its cover." He did not look like one of the worst serial killers of the last few decades. A pudgy five-eight, he had a receding hairline of thinning blond hair and a poorly trimmed moustache that looked like something from an '80s cop show.

Only the eyes showed the truth, beady little blue eyes that looked like a reptile's. No emotion, only hunger and calculation.

For a moment neither spoke.

Bruce Thornton set aside the book he was reading and smiled.

"So. Back for more?"

Alexa squirmed in her seat.

"What are you reading?" she asked, dodging the question.

Thornton patted the book. "*Bullfinch's Mythology*. Classic text. Of course I've read it before but it's worth rereading."

Alexa nodded. He had been obsessed with mythology and folklore from an early age, using it as an escape from an abusive household. As an adult he had become fascinated by the old folktales of the Jersey Devil, a beast said to lurk in the Pine Barrens of New Jersey. He had dug deep into the traditional accounts, and transferred old stories of monsters attacking children into real-life action.

"So ..." Thornton drew out the word, his smile widening.

"I got some questions."

"You had questions last time. I don't think you liked the answers."

"I have something different I want to know now."

"And you expect me to help you."

If I can goad your ego into doing so. Easier said than done.

The public thought that serial killers were mad geniuses. Most weren't. Many were of below average intelligence and got caught quickly. Others remained free to keep on killing because of police incompetence. Only a few combined the sharp intellect and low cunning the public generally assumed all serial killers to have.

Thornton was one of those few.

Alexa looked over her shoulder and saw the cell opposite Thornton's was empty.

"Where's your pal?"

Damn it, get to the point!

"My pal?"

"That rapist in the cell across from you. The one who kept interrupting our conversation with comments about me?"

"Oh, Rick. Yeah, that's a real tragedy. Got shivved in the rec room. Nobody saw who did it."

"Did he die?"

The Jersey Devil smiled. "Sure did."

"Why did someone kill him?"

Thornton keep looking in her eyes as he gave an exaggerated shrug. "Who knows? Probably disrespected someone important."

Alexa stared into those reptilian eyes for a long moment and knew the truth. She also knew she could never prove it.

It didn't really matter. He would never get out of here.

Time to get what she wanted before he got under her skin even more.

"I'd like to ask you about the people who write to you."

Alexa noted a tiny amount of tension break through the Jersey Devil's façade. "Look at the files. The guards read every one of those letters."

"I've read a bunch of them too. I'm not talking about their content. I'm talking about the people behind them."

"What do you mean?" he asked, although Alexa suspected he already knew.

Alexa let out a sigh and immediately regretted it. It was better to keep up a stony false front with his kind. So damn hard, though. And he seemed to see through everything anyway.

"The fans," she said. "Why do serial killers attract so many fans?"

"You worried about how Drake Logan is rising to superstardom?"

Alexa gave him a smug smile. "You worried he's outshining you?"

"Not at all. He's one of my heroes. I could only hope to be half as good as he is. He's become a legend. His breakout made him even more of a legend. When the state executes him, he'll be in the history books."

"So you're a fan. Tell me why."

"It's not the same thing when one of us is a fan."

Alexa's eyes narrowed. She didn't like the implication of the word "us." On her last visit, Thornton hinted that she was like him, someone who liked hurting those who were helpless, someone who liked beating down people who were weaker than she was.

She wasn't. Yes, she had wanted to gun down Thornton and Logan. Yes, she had regretted not doing so. But she wasn't one of them. The idea was obscene.

She tried to control her rage as Thornton went on.

"It's hard for people like us to understand. I have to admit it took me a while myself. For a long time when I was a kid, I thought I was one of them. The fans, I mean. Just a lonely kid with shit parents who got targeted by bullies and fantasized about lashing out at the world. It's funny, but I thought everyone tortured animals. I figured it was something everybody did but nobody talked about, like masturbation."

"Are you going to try and sexually harass me like your dead friend?"

The Jersey Devil made a dismissive wave. "He wasn't my friend, and I'm not trying to make any moves. I'm just being honest. That's what you wanted, right?"

"I wanted insights into why people become fans of animals like you."

"Short answer? Because people are animals. But let me give you a longer answer. You deserve it. It's nice having the company of equals."

"We are not equals. I'm out here and you're in there. And I'm the one who caught you."

"Could you have killed and gotten away with it for as long as I had?" Thornton shrugged. "Maybe. Maybe not. Hell, maybe you have and you're just not telling. Hiding in plain sight like so many of us do. Wouldn't that be great? A serial killer cop! Never heard of a cop becoming one. Well, not exactly."

"You were going to give me your long answer," Alexa growled.

"Touchy, touchy. Well, as I was saying, people get attracted to us because they're angry. They're misfits. Losers, usually. People who would never punch someone for picking on them, let alone go on a five-state killing spree. They live out their angry fantasies through us."

"Come on. This is Psychology 101 stuff. I thought you'd have some insights."

Thornton smiled. "You always were a sharp one. A real adversary. If I knew someone like you was on my case I'd have switched up my technique. Yeah, that is too basic of an explanation, although it covers some of the simpler drones who follow us. You can tell what they are from their letters. Boring as hell. I never answer them. It's the more refined fans that get a response from me."

Alexa had looked through some of his correspondence. The Jersey Devil got letters from all across the United States and as far away as Japan and Europe. He only responded to a very few. She hadn't had time to really delve into those letters. She was afraid if she spent too much time on them, the warden would alert her boss. She also worried it might corrode her soul.

But she needed to know. The U.S. Marshals Service was tackling an increasing number of serial killer cases and she and her partner stood at the forefront of that.

"Tell me more," she said.

Thornton got a distant look in his eyes and his voice fell as he answered.

"The interesting ones have this ... lack. The world's too dull. People are boring. There's no excitement, no challenge. Life is flat. It's a hell of a feeling, and once it gets into you, you can't shake it. Booze doesn't help, drugs don't help. Ever notice how few serial killers are addicts? Most of us try the stuff and end up feeling just as flat as when we're sober. No, it's only when we start to hunt that we find out the real thrill to life, find out what we're meant to be." Thornton shook himself, smiled a tight smile, and finished in a louder voice. "Anyway, Drake Logan said it all better."

"How many of these fans turn into killers?"

"All of them, I hope!" Thornton belted out a laugh, acting the brash criminal once again. Alexa glared as he tried to control himself. Finally the laughter faded away into a few chuckles. "But seriously, to answer your question I don't know. Very few. Even those who are awake usually don't want to risk it. Most of us get caught in the end, after all. No matter how careful you are, you're bound to slip up or get unlucky sooner or later. Or get a worthy opponent. And the smartest serial killers, or those who are fighting the urge, would never write to someone like me. Any idiot knows my mail is being opened and kept in a file. And even those who aren't so smart will stop corresponding before they work themselves up to killing. They distance themselves. All of us worry about getting caught. That makes us a tricky bunch to find, even if we're leaving a trail of bodies."

"But what about before that? How do we detect a serial killer in the making?"

"Ah, now that's the real question! I wondered when you'd get to it. I don't think you'll find it in my mail. I've had people who have written to me for years and years bragging about how they've planned the perfect murder, know just how to dispose of the body, write pages upon pages of description of just how they'd torture them, but they never do it. When a letter like that comes to me the writer's local precinct gets a call from the warden and they investigate. None of those people ever ended up getting charged. The ones who brag the most do the least. They're just seeking approval."

"So we have to look for the silent ones."

"That's right. Good luck finding them, though."

"But they're fans."

"Oh sure. I don't think there's ever been a serial killer who hasn't looked up to the men and women who came before them. Some even imitate the methods of some serial killer they get especially attached to. They'll know everything there is to know about their idol and try to reproduce their crimes exactly. Copycats are pretty rare, though. At least copycats who get it right. They really have to know the serial killer they're imitating as good as the serial killer himself. And kill more. Copycats may love their idols, but they want to be better than them too."

"So how to find them? You haven't really answered that."

Thornton cocked his head. "Why would I help you find them?"

Alexa leaned forward in her chair and looked him deep in the eyes. "Because you're a hunter, and stuck in here you can't hunt. You might get a cheap thrill by shivving someone and getting away with it, but it's not what you really want. You want the chase, the outwitting of your prey. You want to prove to a smart killer that you're smarter. And you want to shove that in their face when you get them."

The Jersey Devil nodded, a spark of admiration in his eyes.

"My, my, my, you really do know us. All right, Deputy Marshal Chase, I'll give it a think. It's a tricky problem, but there's not much to occupy my time in here so I'll try to have an answer in time for your next visit. By the way, when you come next I'd like some fried chicken and a large Coke, and we eat it in the prison yard. I wouldn't mind some extra time outside."

"I think I can swing that."

"Looking forward to the day."

Alexa rose. She had gotten a bit of what she wanted, and she knew that with patience she'd get more, even though it disgusted her to ask for help from someone like him. She should have left it at that, but she couldn't help turning Thornton's words back at him.

"Yeah, I do know you people. That's how I captured you, and captured Drake Logan twice."

She walked away, the clack of her cowboy boots echoing down the corridor. Tomorrow she'd be back in Arizona hunting animals and putting them in cages.

"Takes one to know one!" the Jersey Devil called after her.

CHAPTER TWO

Alexa arrived back at her house in the desert outside Phoenix late that night, and despite the exhaustion and creeping effects of jet lag, found she couldn't sleep.

And so she did what she always did when she couldn't sleep—she worked.

But she was between cases, and she knew she wouldn't make any progress on any cold cases before she drifted off.

That made her turn to a different sort of cold case, the murder of her partner's girlfriend when they were in high school.

The girl had been named Stacy, a name that made her shudder every time she heard it. Alexa's thirteen-year-old neighbor who helped out with the horses had the same name. That fact, and the anguished look on her partner's face as he told of finding her dead body, spurred her on.

The problem was, Stuart hadn't mentioned her last name or the precise location or date of the murder, so she ran a deep Internet search on Stuart, hoping to find her mentioned somewhere.

She quickly found his high school mentioned on his LinkedIn profile, and found that some of the yearbooks for that school were on a site called Classmates.com. There was a paywall so she bookmarked that site for later in case she couldn't find the information for free. Then she continued her search.

The next thing that came up nearly made her fall out of her chair. It was an online FBI newsletter with the title, "Agent Decorated for Saving Child's Life."

"Special Agent Stuart Barrett was commended by Director Wray in a special ceremony yesterday for his conspicuous display of bravery on the job. Agent Barrett, a veteran of two tours of duty in Iraq, where he earned the Purple Heart and Bronze Star, was one of a number of agents and members of local law enforcement hunting a suspect thought to be guilty of interstate trafficking of narcotics. The suspect was cornered in a vehicle in a rural area of Pennsylvania, where the suspect held the child of his girlfriend at gunpoint, demanding the agents withdraw.

"Special Agent Barrett, who had remained unseen by the suspect, managed to sneak around behind the vehicle, and when the suspect moved to retrieve something from the trunk, leaving the child at gunpoint a few feet away, Special Agent Barrett leapt in front of the child. The suspect fired and Special Agent Barrett took a round into the Kevlar vest he was wearing. He sustained only severe bruising while the other agents were able to shoot the suspect. The child remained unharmed and is now in state custody pending an investigation of the mother.

"Special Agent Barrett is to be commended for his bravery in the field and for showing the selfless sense of service we hope all employees of the FBI, indeed all Americans, will aspire to."

Alexa leaned back and stared at the screen. Her new partner was so self-effacing, he had never mentioned this, or the Purple Heart or Bronze Star. She was teamed up with a hero. A hero with flaws, sure, but who didn't have those?

Hopefully he won't have to show off so many heroics in whatever case we're getting next, Alexa thought.

* * *

Just like the last time she visited Bruce Thornton, Alexa felt a deep sense of relief to be going back to work the next day. She was a bit jetlagged from the journey, but getting into a case was the best way to wipe clean the words that dripped from that devil's mouth.

And like the last time, she met her partner in the lobby of a glass and steel high rise in downtown Phoenix, where the U.S. Marshals took up a whole floor, wedged between an insurance company and some tech firm doing something she didn't understand and didn't care to. They hadn't come up on Cybercrime's hitlist anyway.

Her partner, Special Agent Stuart Barrett of the FBI, had made it there before her. The way he drove, he was usually the first to get anywhere. He stood leaning against a marble pillar, watching something on his phone.

Stuart was the opposite of her in many ways, and his clothes showed it. He wore a conservative black suit, shades tucked into his pocket, and his dress shoes were freshly polished. Alexa smiled when she remembered how that city boy looked when he had made a jumping tackle of a fleeing suspect and ended up in a drainage ditch. He hadn't looked so spic and span then.

Got his man, though. So he wasn't completely Alexa's opposite.

Stuart was a bit short for an agent, but had the broad shoulders and compact muscles of the former college football player and soldier he was. He kept his blond hair cropped close, framing a round, youthful face that made him look several years younger than his actual thirty-three. At the moment he looked even younger, his blue eyes fixed eagerly on whatever video he had on his phone.

She walked up to him and looked at the screen. A bunch of strange, three-wheeled cars were racing around a mud circuit, bashing into each other and tipping over. A commentator with a British accent eagerly recounted the feats of each driver, whom he seemed to all know by name.

"What on Earth are you watching?" Alexa asked.

"Reliant Robin banger racing. It's how they do demolition derby in England."

One of the weird little vehicles got sideswiped by another and both flipped over several times. They landed on their side and both of their helmeted drivers got out, grinning.

"So these cars are called Reliant Robins?"

"They were big in the seventies and eighties. Because they only had three wheels they didn't count as cars and avoided vehicle taxes."

"They can't seem to avoid tipping over."

"Top heavy. That's what makes them so fun to race."

"The way you drive, you'd never stay upright."

"No, but it would be cool to do some banger racing over there. There's a demolition derby circuit here in Arizona. I'm thinking of joining."

"God help us. Let's go see the boss."

They went up a mirrored elevator with a pack of executives and got off on the fifth floor. Walking down a quiet, carpeted hallway adorned with photos of former U.S. Marshals, some dating back to the nineteenth century, they passed through a front office, signed in at the receptionist's desk, and went through to Marshal Hernandez's office.

They found Marshal Hernandez at his desk, talking on the phone. He waved them in and gestured to the seats in front of him. The head of the Arizona office was a stocky Mexican-American a bit past his middle years. His thick moustache was peppered with gray just like his close-cropped hair. Like Alexa, he wore cowboy boots, expensive ones hand tooled by a craftsman in Mexico City. "Buy the best and you'll have them for years," he would say when he put his feet up on a table, something he did when he was in a good mood.

He wasn't in a good mood right now. The deep worry lines on his weathered face looked deeper today.

"Yes. Thank you, Sheriff. And you said the Highway Patrol has the roadblocks set up already? Great. We're sending two of our people right away." His hard brown eyes took in the FBI agent and deputy marshal sitting in front of him. "Two of our best. I'll talk to you later."

He hung up, then turned his computer screen to face them. The browser was on the Arizona state prisoner database and showed a prisoner form. The mug shot of a remarkably handsome man in his early thirties gazed confidently at them. He had that rugged face, light brown crewcut, and muscular body a lot of women went for. The man also had something different than your ordinary convict—he had an open, friendly face. He even gave a little smile to the prison photographer. Alexa bet he was a smooth talker.

"This is Robert Tyson, goes by Robby. He just escaped from the prison at Kingman, where he was serving time for manslaughter. It was a bar fight the victim started, but Tyson was losing the fistfight so he picked up a bottle and smashed it over the guy's head. Severe concussion. Died in the hospital the next day."

"Does he have any prior record charges or convictions?" Alexa asked. She found herself surprised by her own question. With anyone else she would have assumed so, but this guy looked so unlike a criminal that she had a hard time believing he was guilty.

Unprofessional, she knew, but the feeling was hard to shake.

"None whatsoever," Marshal Hernandez said. "But he's suspected of killing three young women, luring them into his car or quiet areas, then knocking them out with a blunt object before carving them up with a knife. He actually got investigated for it because a fourth victim escaped and gave his general description and he was matched to a similar vehicle. He didn't get arrested, though, because the intended victim had been smoking marijuana at the time and couldn't pick him out of a police lineup when she sobered up."

Alexa shook her head. How many times had she heard similar stories?

"And the investigation didn't gather any evidence against him?"

"Not enough to bring charges. The original investigator felt strongly that it was him. No one else was ever found to be guilty of any of those murders, and no similar ones occurred after Tyson was put in prison on that manslaughter charge."

"We'll be bringing the original investigator on board, I presume?" Stuart asked.

Marshal Hernandez made a face. "We can't. He died of a heart attack two years ago. We have all his files, though."

"How did he escape?" Alexa asked.

"He was on a chain gang by the highway and—"

"A chain gang?" Stuart blurted. "A suspected serial killer was allowed to go out to work?"

"He has a slick lawyer who threatened a civil rights suit, saying Tyson was being denied his right to rehabilitation."

"Jesus!" Stuart said.

"That was my reaction when I heard," Marshal Hernandez grumbled. "It appears Tyson somehow got a hold of a key to open his leg shackles. Then he grabbed a guard, got his gun, and forced the guard to flag down a passing vehicle. Then he made his escape. It's all in the preliminary report. There was a sighting of him a few miles down the road from where he escaped. He went to a gas station, robbed it at gunpoint, and made the clerk exchange clothes. He's armed, extremely dangerous, and in civilian clothes."

"And if he's anything like Drake Logan, he'll kill as soon as he's able," Alexa said.

"That's what we're concerned about," her boss said. "We want you to go to his last known location and take up the chase. Local police and Highway Patrol are already on the job and there's a dragnet. But we need more boots on the ground. Cheryl will give you full printouts of the files on your way out."

Stuart and Alexa rose.

"We'll get right to it, sir," Alexa said.

"Coming so soon after the Drake Logan escape, you can understand how the media has exploded with the story. This is international news. We have to nab this guy before he starts killing. The governor has been on the phone with me three times already. He even got a call from the White House. The president got that new anti-crime bill through Congress after a huge fight last year and this is making the administration look bad. This is why I need you. You caught Drake Logan, and I need you to catch Robby Tyson ASAP."

They nodded, turned, and headed out. The marshals' receptionist handed them a box of files and they hurried to the elevator.

"How far is this Kingman place from here?" Stuart asked, lugging the box.

"About three hours. Two, the way you drive."

"Even so, the trail will be pretty cold by the time we get there," he said.

She hit the button and gritted her teeth with frustration to see the nearest elevator was still three floors up.

"Cold but not dead. And I'm not banking on the Highway Patrol dragnet to catch him," she said.

"Seems pretty smart the way he dodged those convictions and broke out of prison. I wonder if he had help."

"It's possible. Most prison breaks have help from the outside."

"Yeah, I don't see how he could have gotten a key otherwise."

The door finally pinged open and they got inside. Alexa hit the button and the doors shut.

"I'll drive and you read the files to me, all right?" Stuart asked.

"Sure. Just don't bash into other cars and flip over," Alexa replied with a smile.

"Spoilsport. And in any case the FBI only issues four-wheeled vehicles. Hard to flip over."

"Good."

"It's a major design flaw of most four-wheeled vehicles. Except the Suzuki Samurai. Remember those? Maybe I should buy one for my demolition derby career." Stuart hefted the box and grinned at her, eyes sparkling. "Good to be on the hunt again, isn't it? Makes you feel like you're useful."

"Sure does," she said, grinning back.

Then the Jersey Devil's words came back to her and suddenly she didn't have anything to grin about.

CHAPTER THREE

Barreling down State Highway 93 at a hundred miles an hour, Alexa and Stuart went over the case files. Alexa made sure to wear her seatbelt and felt grateful this car was fitted with airbags.

"Tyson has been a model prisoner ever since he got locked up," Alexa said. "That's one of the ways he got a work detail. He even goes to anger management counseling and expresses regret at killing the man."

"I don't believe that," Stuart said, passing a truck. They were in the open scrubland of western Arizona, and the state highway shot straight as an arrow for miles. There was nothing to block the view and the sky was vast, framed only by a few low, rocky hills. Her partner loved this kind of road. He could see for a mile ahead and go as fast as the vehicle could manage.

"I don't believe that either, but the prison psychologist did."

"So much for psychologists," Stuart grunted. "You'll never see me going to one of them."

Alexa didn't respond. She had been avoiding Joan, her therapist, since the end of the last case a couple of weeks before. She had been stuck in one unproductive meeting with the woman, where she had been instructed by her boss to "work through the trauma of losing your partner."

Talking to some well-meaning stranger who had never collared a criminal wasn't going to make her feel better about seeing her old partner and mentor get beheaded right in front of her.

"So what do you think?" Stuart asked.

"What do I think about what?" Alexa asked, realizing she had gotten so into her thoughts that she hadn't heard what he said.

"I asked where you think he'll go. You know this country way better than I do."

"The file says he doesn't have any close family. No ex-girlfriend either. He never got any visitors except his attorney, who is in Phoenix and has already been informed. So it's hard to say where he'll go. He's Arizona born and bred so he knows the area well. And he's already proven to be resourceful."

"His face must be on every TV channel and news site by now."

Alexa flipped through the files. "No known property either. He was renting at the time he was caught. And yet he worked as an electrician since he was eighteen. They make good money. Surprising he didn't own a house."

"Maybe he bought a little bolt hole somewhere that's not on the records," Stuart suggested, whipping past an SUV so fast the gleaming vehicle and its astonished occupants vanished in a blur.

Alexa nodded. "Maybe. He's been in jail for five years, though. Who knows if that bolt hole is still there."

"Did he have any known associates?"

"I've been checking that and he didn't have too many," Alexa said, flipping through the pages. "Neighbors described him as quiet, although several of them said he was popular with the ladies. He'd often hang out in one of the local bars and pick up women he'd bring back home. No complaints from the women, they all seem to have been willing. Oh." She stopped at a certain page as a line leapt out at her.

"What?" Stuart asked, leaning over and trying to read the paper.

"Jesus! Keep your eye on the road."

"Relax," Stuart said, but looked back at the road just the same.

"There's testimony from three different bartenders at bars where he was a regular. All of them said that he was a very light drinker. Would make a couple of beers last all night, or at least as long as it took to pick someone up."

"Wanted to keep his wits," Stuart said.

"Yeah," Alexa murmured, remembering what Bruce Thornton had said about serial killers avoiding drugs and alcohol.

Stuart flicked on the police radio. "We must be getting close to the roadblocks right now. Let's hear the chatter."

The airwaves were alive with communications back and forth between the local Highway Patrol base in the town of Wikieup just a few miles ahead of them and various units out in the field. It didn't take long for them to find out that Tyson was still at large. Stuart radioed in and found the command center was at Wikieup.

"They got a speed trap just outside of town," Alexa said, nudging Stuart. "Try not to get us a ticket, eh?"

"Will do." He slowed down to ninety.

"I'm serious. They hate feds in these parts."

"Don't they hate feds everywhere?"

"Not like in rural Arizona. Slow down."

Stuart shrugged and slowed down to seventy.

A mile later he had to slow down to a stop as they spotted a line of cars headed both directions stopped at a roadblock. Two police cars made a barrier across the road and police were checking every trunk.

Alexa pulled out a magnetic police light, opened the window, and thunked it onto the roof. She hit the little switch on the side and it lit up, emitting a loud wail. The cars edged to the side and Stuart drove along to the roadblock.

A cop stormed up to her side of the car, all scowls and dark sunglasses.

"Don't you know it's illegal for you to have one of those? You—" He stopped as he caught a glimpse of Alexa's uniform, gave a reluctant nod, and jerked a thumb at Stuart.

"Who's he?"

Stuart pulled out his FBI ID and waggled it in front of the officer's face. His scowl deepened.

He jerked his thumb in the direction of the roadblock. Alexa got the impression he jerked that thumb a lot.

"Get on through. You're holding up the line."

"Thanks, honey," Stuart said.

The cop gaped, and Stuart pulled off just as he sputtered something.

"Honey?" Alexa asked.

"Just wanted to see the reaction," Stuart said, snickering.

* * *

The little town of Wikieup, which according to the hand-painted wooden sign at the edge of town had a population of 137, was little more than a few ranch-style houses, a gas station, a convenience store, and a Highway Patrol base. Alexa was surprised to see several tents set up in the parking lot across the street. A crowd of men and women in the uniforms of various law enforcement agencies stood in pairs or in circles, yelling into cell phones or shouting at each other while waving their hands in the air.

Stuart parked on the street and they got out. The babble of voices annoyed Alexa and she glanced at her partner, unsure what to do next.

They decided to head for the tents. Each law enforcement agency seemed to have their own, except for Border Patrol, who had apparently come late and were just setting one up. The border was three hundred miles away, so Alexa wasn't sure why they were here at all.

Alexa stopped a BATF agent rushing by. “Where’s the command center?”

“How the hell am I supposed to know? I’m too busy getting my men to set up roadblocks.”

“Aren’t the roadblocks already set up?”

“Some are. But the local police departments and the Highway Patrol aren’t talking to each other, so I’m trying to fill the gaps. Gotta go.” He ran off.

“What the hell?” Alexa muttered. Then she remembered. There had been a case not long ago where the Kingman PD had collared a high-profile suspect but the Highway Patrol took the credit. Accusations and counteraccusations flew, and Alexa couldn’t tell how much each agency had contributed to the manhunt and eventual capture. What did it matter? The guy got caught.

To some people in law enforcement, eyeing next year’s budget requests, it mattered a lot.

“Over there,” Stuart pointed.

A tent not far off, surrounded by a crowd of uniforms, had a sign saying “Communications Center.” A satellite dish on a pole poked above the tent. They hurried over, Stuart nearly getting bowled over by another officer rushing through the crowd, a highway patrolman this time.

They got to the crowd surrounding the tent and pushed their way through to find several desks, each with a man or woman in a different uniform, talking a mile a minute on phones. Everyone in the crowd was talking too, shoving papers in front of the people on the phones and shouting to get their attention. Alexa had no idea how the people on the phones could hear anything.

A local highway patrolman Alexa had met before by the name of Vanders stepped in front of Stuart.

“No civilians. Get back to the street.”

“I’m FBI.”

“Oh God, you people are here too? I’ll try to get you a table.”

“A table for what?” Alexa asked.

Vanders turned, and Alexa saw recognition on his face, then a struggle to remember her name. His gaze flicked down to the name patch over her star, then he said, “Oh, hello, Deputy Marshal Chase. You need a table too?”

“For what?” she repeated.

“Press communications.”

"Press communications? We're just trying to find the ops center."

"Which one?"

"What do you mean which one?"

"We got ours in the base across the street. Don't go over there. The boss already kicked everybody out. The Kingman PD set one up in their town. They're trying to get everyone to set up over there. And the BATF just set one up in the tent over there and—"

"Who's in charge?"

Vanders blinked. "I don't know. Are you?"

They turned and walked away.

"This is a total circus," Alexa said, looking around for something, anything that looked like a place where they could get information on the investigation.

"Why would they ban civilians from the press tent?" Stuart asked. "Isn't the whole point of a press tent to accommodate civilian journalists?"

"You got me there."

"And where's the press anyway?"

"Who cares? Maybe Kingman. Maybe somewhere here in Wikieup. Maybe on the moon. Just be thankful they're not here."

Her sister-in-law Melanie worked for Action News in Phoenix. She was a real ambulance chaser and Alexa would bet a month's pay that she was up here somewhere. She was the last person Alexa wanted to see.

Stuart and Alexa stopped, looking around at the chaos. The street between the field of tents and the Highway Patrol base was rapidly become clogged with cars. Their honking added to the noise.

"Let's get out of here," Stuart said. "There's nothing for us here."

"Sure, and go where?"

Her partner shrugged. He had no answer. Neither did she.

Then an officer with some local police department caught their attention. He was standing on top of his patrol car in the middle of the traffic jam and waving his hands in the air.

"We got him! We got him!"

Alexa felt some hope for the first time since they had gotten there. Had Robby Tyson been stopped at a roadblock?

They ran for the patrol car and saw everyone else within earshot running for the car too. It looked like a riot. The cop on top of the car gaped at the converging mob and probably wondered if he should have worn riot gear.

As they got closer, Alexa could see from his shoulder patch that he was from Bullhead City, a small city thirty miles to the west of Kingman and in the opposite direction from the way Tyson had fled. She wondered why he was here and not setting up roadblocks with the nearby state line with California.

"We caught him! Caught him in Golden Valley!" the officer shouted with glee. Several people cheered. Others shouted at him.

"No way he took off in that direction!"

"You make a positive ID?"

"Did he resist? Did you shoot him?"

The officer made a calming gesture and smiled, obviously enjoying the attention.

"We got him and are bringing him to the Bullhead City jail. He's probably already there. We'll release a full report once we get some things cleared up."

"Where's Bullhead City?" a Border Patrol officer asked.

"How the hell should I know?" a woman from the Treasury Department replied. Both took out their phones and pulled up Google Maps.

"Let's go," Alexa said.

They ran to their car and found it blocked in. Stuart cursed and began honking, adding his own contribution to the din. He didn't have to honk long, though, because everyone else rushed to their cars too. The cars began to pull away, one going in the wrong direction.

"Up State Highway 93 to Interstate 40, then head west," Alexa told him.

"I'll try to break free of this crowd," he said.

"Good luck with that." Alexa switched on the siren again so no one would pull her "civilian" partner over for speeding.

They got onto the state highway, a four-lane divided highway that was thankfully not too busy this time of day. The few civilian vehicles on the road moved to the shoulder as a phalanx of official and unmarked cars, motorcycles, vans, and four by fours, all with sirens blazing, sped north.

It took some time for Stuart to weave his way through the vehicles. Most refused to budge. Some even tried to cut him off. Stuart muttered something about "interagency cooperation, my ass" and focused on the road. Within a few minutes he broke free, and they sped for Bullhead City.

Alexa found herself wondering how many people Tyson had killed in the short time he was free.

CHAPTER FOUR

The bad news started coming in as they got within radio range of Bullhead City, driving along the cracked and worn State Road 68 through terrain that had gotten hillier and drier. It reminded Stuart of some of the places he had seen in al-Anbar Governate in Iraq. A good place to hide; not such a good place to survive.

They had passed three different roadblocks manned by three different local police departments. None of them had any clear information about what was going on in Bullhead City. The guys at one roadblock hadn't even heard that Tyson had supposedly been caught.

Supposedly. Because Stuart was beginning to suspect these yahoos couldn't catch bedbugs in an Iraqi hotel.

The first faint crackling transmissions from the Bullhead City police frequency mentioned they had detained a "suspect." That made Stuart and Alexa trade a worried glance. The guy back at Wake Up or whatever that hick town was called had sounded 110% sure they had caught Robby Tyson. Now they had "detained a suspect."

As the miles sped by and the transmission became clearer, the guy at the radio degraded the "suspect" down to a "person of interest."

"We're wasting our time," Stuart said.

"Yeah, I'm beginning to think so too. In fact, I thought so as soon as I saw that mess back in Wikieup. Now I—"

The radio crackled again, and the dispatcher from Bullhead City announced, "We have determined that the person of interest is not Robert Tyson. Repeat, the person of interest is not Robert Tyson. A witness spotted someone in an orange jumpsuit in the desert near here and called nine-one-one. The suspect was carrying a rifle. That person was detained after a brief standoff and has now been determined to be a hunter wearing orange hunting gear. A background check determined he was a local man."

Stuart groaned. "It took them that long to figure it out? Now what?"

"Back the way we came. We'll go to that gas station Tyson robbed and start from there. We should have gone there in the first place."

The highway here was divided. Rather than wait to find one of the infrequent paved access routed between the two sides, Stuart slowed to twenty and turned off onto the gritty soil. Rocks thumped against the undercarriage and the car jolted. He pulled onto the other side just as a semi carrying a load of natural gas crested a nearby hill.

"Watch out!" Alexa shouted.

"I got it. This is the last of the old police interceptors. It would be a shame to blow it up."

"Huh?"

"*Road Warrior*. Classic movie. Never mind."

He hit the gas and the FBI-issued vehicle tore down the road, the semi dwindling into the rearview mirror.

"I love these desert highways!" Stuart shouted.

"You love them too much," Alexa replied, checking her seatbelt for the third time this ride.

"Don't you like driving fast? Annette loves it. Sometimes we go to the desert and haul ass. She's got as much lead in her foot as I do."

Annette was a genius CSI expert he had met on his last case. They had only been going out a few weeks but they saw each other all the time. They'd gotten far closer, far quicker, than any relationship Stuart had ever been in. He had felt a whole lot better about the move to the desert now that he had met her.

"Enough about your girlfriend," Alexa grumbled. "Just get us to that gas station."

"That's what I'm doing," he said in a quieter tone. Alexa got way too focused on these cases. Sure, you had to be focused, but they had at least half an hour of driving to do. She could lighten up for a second or two.

They crested another rise and saw a long line of law enforcement vehicles still headed for Bullhead City, going almost as fast as Stuart had been.

"Didn't they hear the dispatcher?" Alexa wondered out loud.

"Maybe they're still on the interagency channel," Stuart replied.

She switched to that channel and the radio nearly exploded with countless voices all talking over one another.

"Jesus," Alexa muttered. "I'd try and warn them, but there's no way they'll hear me."

"There's going to be a hell of a riot in Bullhead City."

"Damn. All this bumbling and Robby Tyson is still out there somewhere. It won't be long before he starts up his killing spree again."

* * *

Cassandra Fox hummed happily to herself along with the car radio as she drove along the lonely Highway 93 on her way to Prescott National Forest in the Arizona uplands. She had two days off, and she liked nothing better than to do some hiking all on her own, communing with nature and pushing her body to climb the rugged mountains.

Her mother and father always worried about her going to the mountains alone, but she could take care of herself. She was careful and always had a bottle of pepper spray clipped to her belt. Besides, in the places she went, she hardly ever saw anyone anyway. And she had been out of college for five years! She didn't need her parents fussing over her so much.

She should probably call to check in. Even though her mom and dad could be annoying, their hearts were in the right place.

Opening her phone, she saw there was no signal. Of course not. She tossed it back on the passenger's seat. She'd call when she got to the entrance to the park. There was a cell phone tower there.

A car was parked by the side of the road up ahead, the first vehicle she had seen in twenty miles. The hood was up and a man stood bent over the engine. A tool box was balanced on the edge of the front end next to him. His image wavered in the rising heat.

Cassandra slowed and took a better look. The man stood up, a young handsome guy who gave her an open smile and a wave.

That was all she saw as she passed by at forty miles an hour.

She put her foot on the gas and got back up to seventy, and then started to feel bad. That guy was stuck out there in the middle of nowhere. There was no signal, no emergency phone box, and the heat was topping a hundred degrees. If he didn't have any water he'd be in serious trouble. A lot of people didn't carry water in their cars. Amazing, but true. She always carried a pair of two-gallon jugs. Even if he did have water, he was still marooned in the desert.

I should go back there, she thought.

As soon as she thought it, all the old lectures about not trusting strange men came back to her.

She kept driving, but the feeling of guilt began to increase.

A predator wouldn't be out here in the middle of nowhere. He'd be in some bar somewhere, spiking a woman's drink.

And she could take care of herself. She was a good judge of character. She'd drive back the way she came, slower this time, and take a better look. Maybe he had a family with him. She hadn't had time to take a look inside the car.

If the situation seemed wrong, Cassandra promised herself, she'd drive on.

She slowed, did a U-turn in the middle of the empty road, and headed back to the man with engine trouble.

Driving at a sedate thirty, slow enough to get a good look but fast enough that she felt more than safe, she approached the man. He was hunched over the engine, fiddling with something. The sun flared on the windshield and Cassandra could not see if anyone else was in the car.

The man heard her, stood, and turned. He smiled and held up a hand as Cassandra drew close. A young, handsome guy. Well dressed with a blond buzzcut.

His bright eyes sparked with recognition. His smile widened and he waved more energetically.

He had recognized her.

That decided it. For some reason that recognition made her too embarrassed to drive on. She pulled over on the opposite side of the street, about a hundred yards down the road.

He stood waiting for her by the car.

Cassandra felt a little tug of doubt, then buried it, checked her pepper spray was on her belt, and got out.

"Car trouble?" she called out. Stupid question. Of course he had car trouble.

"Yeah," he called back. He didn't try to approach and that made her feel more confident. "I stopped to take photos of some birds over on that cactus and it wouldn't restart. Old battery. I should have replaced it months ago. I have some jumper cables if you don't mind pulling up."

"Um, sure," she said, looking around.

"Thanks. I've been here awhile and I won't lie, I was getting worried."

Cassandra got back in her car, turned around again, drove up, and parked facing the stranger's car nose to nose. The man had opened his trunk and was just pulling out some jumper cables. Leaving the engine on, she got out.

"Sure am glad you stopped. I was trying to coax it back to life but of course that didn't work. A quick jump is all I need."

He clipped the red clamp to the positive terminal of his battery and held up the cables, waiting for her.

"Just a sec." Cassandra turned to pop her hood. She kept an eye on the stranger, who smiled at her reassuringly. He seemed like a nice guy. She shouldn't be so suspicious. Most people were good, after all.

The hood caught, and she had to turn and look at what she was doing. After a little jiggle, the hood lifted up.

There was a clatter of metal on concrete behind her. For a second she didn't turn, busy as she was propping up her hood.

By the time she did turn to check on that odd sound, it was too late.

The stranger had dropped his jumper cables and reached into his toolbox. Cassandra turned just in time to see him pull out a wrench.

"What are you—"

The stranger rushed her.

Cassandra screamed, backing off and reaching for her pepper spray, already knowing it was too late.

The wrench came down on the side of her head. To Cassandra, it felt like she was at the center of an exploding star. She saw a brilliant white light, a shock of pain, and then nothing.

She must have blacked out for a moment, because the next thing she knew she was lying on the pavement, the stranger over her.

He grinned, and as if from a great distance she heard his mocking voice say, "Let's get to work."

Then she saw the knife.

CHAPTER FIVE

"Did the man who robbed you say anything?" Alexa asked. "Did he give any indication as to where he was going?"

Alexa was at the gas station interviewing the man who got held up and had his clothes stolen. Several officers from that mob of law enforcement had already done the same thing, but she wanted to hear his testimony for herself. Meanwhile, Stuart was trying to get them organized. She wished him luck.

The station was at the intersection of State Highway 93, heading south, and Interstate 40 heading east/west. The robbery had happened hours ago, and Tyson could be anywhere by now. If he had looped back the way he had come and driven back west or northwest, he could even be in California or Nevada.

"He didn't say a word except to hold me up," the man said. He was a grizzled older guy with the deep tan of an Arizona native. He lit a cigarette from the end of his previous one, his hands shaking slightly. "You seen the security camera video. The guy pulls up, rushes out in his prison jumpsuit, and sticks me up. No one else was in the station. Took the money and made me trade clothes with him."

The victim was back in regular clothes now. His wife had come with a spare set. The Kingman police had taken away the orange prison jumpsuit as evidence. It had all been on the security footage. Tyson, after getting a new set of clothes, had also grabbed a couple of jugs of water and some snacks. He hadn't even looked at the big glass-front refrigerator of beer next to the front counter.

Once again Alexa was reminded of the Jersey Devil's comment about serial killers avoiding drugs and alcohol. They wanted to stay in control, of themselves and everyone else.

Part of the duties of a U.S. Marshal was to hunt down escaped prisoners, and Alexa had done that several times in her career. One of the things they almost always did was grab some booze as soon as possible. A lot of cons were heavy users of substances, and as soon as they escaped custody that craving kicked in.

Not Robby Tyson. He was being practical.

“And you didn’t see which way he headed?” she asked the gas station attendant.

“Nope. Sorry. He made me lie face down in the back room and count to a thousand. Told me if I came out before that he’d shoot me. I know he was only saying that so he could take off without me seeing which way he took, but I wasn’t about to peek.”

“I don’t blame you.”

The gas station attendant shrugged. “Sure wish I could help you more. You should have seen the look in his eyes. Like a shark’s eyes. No life to them at all.”

He shuddered and took a long drag from his cigarette.

Alexa sighed. “Well, thank you for your time. I—”

Stuart’s FBI vehicle screeched to a halt outside. Stuart leapt out of the car, leaving the engine running. Alexa met him at the door.

“There’s been a murder. State Route 96,” he said breathlessly.

Just then a stream of law enforcement vehicles began to pass by.

“Tell me as you drive,” Alexa said, running out to the car.

Despite the harsh Arizona sun, the world seemed to grow dark. They had already failed. Tyson had already killed someone.

They hopped in, tore out of the gas station parking lot, and cut off a Border Patrol four-by-four. The Border Patrol officer behind the wheel honked and gave Stuart the finger.

“A highway patrolman got the call on his phone,” Stuart said, ignoring him. “Told the rest of us, only *after* he had a five-minute head start.”

“In. Credible.”

“Yeah, we have a mess on our hands with these guys. So the details are sketchy. Appears a young female was found dead by the side of the road. Middle of nowhere. No witnesses. That’s all I know. Got the location on the GPS already.” He tapped the screen.

Alexa looked at it and zoomed in. Stuart swerved into the oncoming lane to pass a pair of police cars before cutting back to the right just before an oncoming van would have obliterated them.

“I know this road,” Alexa said. “There’s nothing out there. Looks like it happened not far from Bagdad.”

“Bagdad?” Stuart glanced at the GPS, nearly rear-ending a BATF vehicle. “Huh. That’s weird. But you hicks misspelled it.”

“Maybe the Iraqis misspelled it,” Alexa suggested.

“Maybe we need to get the hell out of this traffic jam.”

Stuart swerved into the opposite lane again, gunned the engine, and shot past a few more vehicles.

"It's fifty miles away," Alexa said. "By the time we get there, Tyson will be long gone."

"At least we might get a marker for which direction he headed."

"It won't help much. Prescott National Forest isn't far down the road. That's in the mountains with more than a million acres of forest. If he's gone in there, we're going to have a hell of a time finding him."

* * *

The crime scene was what Alexa imagined it to be—an utter mass of chaos. Despite Stuart's maniacal driving, several agencies had made it there before them because they happened to be much closer to the scene.

At least the Highway Patrol had been professional enough to block off the area of the crime with police tape and traffic cones, leaving all the officers with an all too clear view of the ugly aftermath.

A pretty young woman in her early twenties lay beside what Alexa presumed to be her car. She had been hit on the head with some sort of blunt object and then, as she lay on the ground, cut open, her belly slit from one side to the other.

She was entirely clothed and showed no sign of sexual assault.

The exact same MO as the three killings Tyson had supposedly committed but had never been convicted of.

Alexa studied the car from beyond the police tape, having to move side to side to peek between the cluster of men and women in front of her. Yes, definitely her car. The victim wore hiking boots, and there was a backpack in the back seat. The bumper had stickers for the Rainforest Alliance and the World Wildlife Fund. The car's front hood was up, the engine still running.

Stuart nudged her and pointed to the gritty dirt by the side of the road in front of the victim's vehicle. Tire tracks. Someone had turned a car there. Judging from the way the dirt was moved Alexa could tell that the vehicle had been facing the victim's and done a three-point turn before heading east toward Prescott National Forest.

She looked around. They stood on the Arizona highlands, the breeze not as hot here although the sun shone just as strong. The rocky surroundings were dotted with Saguaro cacti, those famous sentinels of the Sonora Desert, and Joshua trees, the indicator plant of the Mojave

Desert with their strange, branching trunks and spiky tufts of leaves. She also saw mesquite and cholla, prickly pear cacti, and palo verde shrubs. They were at the transition between the two deserts here, a high point close to the border between Arizona and California, with the bottom corner of Nevada not far to the northwest. The land continued to rise further to the east, the way Tyson had headed, rising high enough to support proper forest and standing water and vast stretches of land preserved untouched by the federal government. A good place to hide.

But also a place full of hikers like this poor woman, so it was also a good place to hunt.

"He pretended to break down," Alexa said. "He waited by the side of the road for a victim to come along, then asked for a jump start. That's why the hood is open. Once she turned her back to open her hood, he clubbed her and cut her open."

"The exact same MO," Stuart said, reading her thoughts. "But why not steal her car? Why not change vehicles when he had the chance?"

"Maybe he's already switched vehicles from the one he initially stole," Alexa suggested.

"He didn't take any of her gear," Stuart said, standing on tiptoe to peek through the car's back window. "She looks like she was off for a big hiking trip, but I'm seeing a backpack and a Sterno stove and a tent all there for the taking. You'd think he'd want that where he was headed."

"That's strange," Alexa murmured. "Yes, that's very strange."

Why wouldn't he take camping gear if he was heading to a national forest?

Maybe because he wasn't heading there at all. Maybe he was going somewhere else. This road didn't have any turnoffs for miles. It was either Prescott National Forest, and the roads and highways beyond it, or going back the way Tyson had come, straight into the jaws of the manhunt.

So those mountains to the east might not be his final destination.

So what was? She had no idea. They would let the ground troops swarm over the forest while she and Stuart got back to digging into Tyson's past and his associates. Hopefully they'd find a clue as to where he had gone.

They'd better. Because if they didn't, some other poor woman would end up with her belly slit open.

* * *

The cops would never find him here. Prescott National Forest was the perfect place to hide.

The desert upland dirt crunched beneath his boots as he strode through the dimming late afternoon light for his destination.

He was far from any roads now, far from roadblocks and police vehicles. There was no one around to ask who he was or where he was going. He felt free.

The air, which he breathed deep into his lungs, carried the smell of green and damp, a rare pleasure in the Desert Southwest. He was nearly to the tree line, climbing up and up, further away from civilization and closer to his destination.

Old Virgil Yeager, Tyson's great-uncle, had a cabin up here, one he had built with his own hands the year he got home from World War Two. He had been in the Navy, surviving kamikaze attacks and slugfests with Japanese battleships.

"I never want to see the sea again in my life," he had said. And he never did. He had moved from his home state of California to Arizona and never looked back, living for the rest of his ninety-eight years in relative isolation here at the edge of Prescott National Forest, making a simple living taking city folk on hunting and fishing trips.

Now old Virgil Yeager was dead, passing on during the second year of his great-nephew's prison term. Few people knew the two were related, or even remembered the isolated shack that had been unoccupied for three long years.

It would be the perfect place to hide from the world, rest up, and figure out his next move.

The perfect place to kill.

CHAPTER SIX

Stuart never thought he'd ever be in Baghdad again.

Or "Bagdad."

He sat with Alexa eating dinner and going through Tyson's files in a battered old diner, the only business in town besides a gas station. Bagdad was a scattering of houses along a hillside. There couldn't have been more than two thousand people living here, but it looked like they all had plenty of work. At the other end of town loomed several large tan heaps of tailings from a giant copper mine.

"If you're willing to live in the middle of nowhere," Stuart had said as they pulled into town to have lunch, "it looks like you can get a well-paid job."

"This isn't Nowhere, this is Bagdad," Alexa had replied. "Nowhere is just down the road. It's a ghost town now."

Stuart didn't have a reply to that, so they ordered some food and got to work. All meals were working meals when Alexa Chase was around.

Alexa sat opposite him, going through Robby Tyson's files. Stuart had his laptop out and was going through stolen vehicle reports while digging into a chicken fried steak. Investigators had determined that the tire tracks came from Goodyear tires on a four-door vehicle, almost certainly a sedan instead of a Jeep or pickup, and yet no such vehicles had been stolen in the past twenty-four hours in that part of the state. Three pickup trucks, a coupe, and a golf cart of all things, but no sedan. Strange.

So maybe Tyson hadn't changed vehicles? The one he had stolen was a sedan. Or maybe he ditched the car he stole when he got away from the chain gang and it hadn't been found yet?

The most likely possibility wasn't one Stuart liked to think about—that Tyson had killed the owner of the vehicle, dumped the body, and thus the vehicle hadn't been reported as stolen.

He checked missing person reports. No one had been reported missing for the past twenty-four hours, but of course someone generally has to be missing for twenty-four hours before you can report them missing, so that didn't help. There were exceptions, and the records for the area showed two such exceptions—a small child and a senile old man. Neither of them would have had a car to steal.

So Stuart and Alexa didn't have much to go on. At least the police had gotten a bit better organized. The communications were getting untangled and Stuart began to see a better picture of the response. Local police departments and the Highway Patrol had set up roadblocks all over the region. On some roads, different agencies had set up their own roadblocks, leading to there being more than one on some roads. A total waste of manpower, but at least the roads were all being watched.

For a time, not all roads had been, including the one Tyson had fled down.

The one where he found someone to kill.

The Forestry Service had been notified and was checking Prescott National Forest, but it was so large that if Tyson had fled there it would take a long time to find him. A helicopter was buzzing the area, trying to see through the tree cover and spot the fugitive. Stuart didn't put much faith in that working out.

Stuart supposed this disorganized overresponse was thanks to Drake Logan. That serial killer had escaped from a prison transfer bus, getting broken out by a team of his followers. Alexa's old partner had been killed in the attack, and Logan had let her live because he had some twisted idea that she was a serial killer in training. Stuart knew she was still haunted by it.

The whole state was haunted by it. Reports on him still appeared in the news and social media, especially now that preparations were being made for his new trial, one that might see him get a lethal injection. Stuart supposed all these bumbling officers were just panicked that there might be another killing spree like Logan had perpetrated.

But Logan had been different. As soon as he got released, he tore through the state, killing as many people as possible. Tyson appeared to be more controlled. As far as they knew, he had only killed once. He hadn't killed the prison guard he had taken captive or the guy he carjacked. He ditched the driver immediately and the prison guard a few miles down the road. And he hadn't killed the guy in the gas station either.

Why not? Perhaps because they didn't match his victim profile. Tyson got off on killing young women he could charm into a false sense of security. The other three people he had interacted with had all been men, and had been means to an end. He had even refrained from hurting the prison guard. Most cons wouldn't have been able to resist at least beating him up, but Tyson hadn't done a thing to him.

No, he only wanted young women, and now he was after them. Like before, he was going after victims of opportunity. Maybe he really had had engine trouble and Cassandra Fox had just been unlucky enough to come by and stop to offer help.

The question was—where had he gone? He looked at the map. The roadblocks encompassed a huge area, cutting off Interstate 40, State Highways 93, 95, and 60, and several smaller state routes. There were also roadblocks at the state lines with Nevada and California. Assuming Tyson hadn't slipped through the net, a big assumption given his lead time and intelligence, he still had an area about two hundred miles to a side to hide in. How the hell were they supposed to find him?

When he kills again, but then it's too late.

Stuart bit his lip and stared at the map.

Think! Where could he go? We still haven't found any records that he owned property, and all the sightings coming in have proven pretty thin. So where could he go?

Then something from the Drake Logan case came back to him. Early in his career as a serial killer, one victim had survived. When Logan had broken out of prison, he had gone straight for her.

Tyson had let someone survive too.

"Alexa, what's the survivor's name and current address? You know, the woman who failed to identify him in the line-up?"

His partner looked up from her work, eyes wide, immediately realizing the significance of his question.

She hunched back over the files, flipping through them until she found the page, then turned it so Stuart could read it.

He already had his phone out.

Punching in the number, he fidgeted as the phone rang and rang until it beeped.

"Hello, this is Angelina Cruz, please leave a message."

Stuart groaned just in time for it to be caught after the beep. Clearing his throat, he said, "Ms. Cruz, this is Special Agent Stuart Barrett of the FBI. The man who probably attacked you several years ago, Robert Tyson, has escaped from prison. He is somewhere in the Kingman, Wikieup, Prescott National Forest Area. Please call me back at this number as soon as you can."

He hung up and turned to Alexa. "What's the—"

Her finger was already pointing to the number of the victim's local police precinct in Peoria, a suburb of Phoenix. He called them and filled them in on the situation, thinking how well he and Alexa worked together. Stuart had had a few partners in his years in the FBI, and while they had all been good officers, none could match this cowgirl. It felt a bit like being back in his platoon in Iraq.

"We'll keep an eye on her," the woman at the police precinct told him. "Once we track her down, that is. She's well known to police as a habitual drug user. Ms. Cruz has several priors and was forced to enroll in a drug rehabilitation program. As soon as she finished it she was back to using. She's not going to want police protection."

"At least get her to stay with family at a different address," Stuart said.

"We'll try." She did not sound hopeful.

"Now that that's taken care of," Stuart said, digging into his chicken fried steak again, "how about I try to organize this supposedly interdepartmental response into a team that might actually achieve something, while you keep investigating into Tyson's past."

"Sounds like a plan," she said, munching on a fry and not taking her eyes off the files.

"Find anything yet?"

"Not much. Tyson has the typical bad upbringing you find in serial killers. Alcoholic and abusive father who went to jail for beating his wife, and a mother who ran off with every guy in town, leaving Tyson to fend for himself. He got in trouble with the law a bunch of times for criminal trespass and vandalism but somehow never ended up in juvenile detention."

"Did he ever go to jail as an adult?"

"No, and that's interesting. He left home when he was sixteen and seemed to turn his life around. Got his GED and managed to get a union scholarship to enroll in vocational training. That's when he became an electrician. He never spoke to his parents again and never got into trouble with the law until that bar fight went wrong. He seemed to have turned his life around."

"Seemed," Stuart grunted. "I've seen this with serial killers before. They get sneaky, quiet. I wonder how many women he attacked before he escalated to murder."

"The first murder attributed to him happened when he was twenty-eight, so that's a long build-up period. There are a few unsolved murders of young women dating to before this first victim that don't fit the MO."

"As you know, that's also typical. He could have been finding his way. I had this one sicko who started beating people to death from behind before moving on to strangulation. So some of those might have been him, and then of course there are the missing persons."

"True, but he never hid the bodies of the first three victims, or the one today. He left them on display in places isolated enough that he'd have time to get away but busy enough that they would eventually be discovered."

"Any other murders come close?" Stuart asked.

"A few, but no evidence to tie him to them. The evidence tying him to the other murders is all circumstantial. That and Ms. Cruz being such a poor witness is what got him off."

"Until he slipped up and killed a man who was only using his fists. And he's slipped up again with Cassandra's murder. We can nail him once we get him." Stuart popped the last bit of chicken fried steak in his mouth and stood. "Speaking of, I better get to the crime scene. You all right just working here or do you want me to take you back to Wikieup?"

"Back to that riot scene? No thanks. It's quieter here, and closer to the crime. I got all I need. This will be my office for the moment."

"OK. They got free refills on coffee. You're going to need it. So will I, as a matter of fact."

He left the diner and drove alone back to the murder scene, speeding along the little-used road, his mind going over the possibilities. Tyson was proving to be smart and elusive. Most escapees got caught within hours. Tyson had been out for more than a day, and seemed to be getting further and further ahead of his pursuers.

It didn't take long to get back to the location of the killing, and when he did he found a total mess. Now that the horde of law enforcement had made it to the scene of Cassandra Fox's murder, along with a few television crews, the scene was even more chaotic than before. As he surveyed the scene of yelling officers and nosy reporters, he shook his head.

I'm in for a long night, he thought. *And meanwhile, Tyson is out there somewhere, getting further away from justice and planning his next move.*

CHAPTER SEVEN

Alexa was at the tail end of a long night. She still hunched over the files at the diner in Bagdad, which had decided to stay open all night to serve the unexpected windfall of law enforcement officers taking up most of the tables.

She sipped yet another cup of coffee poured by a waitress who looked as sleepy as she felt, and focused her tired eyes on the files to track down the latest line of inquiry. Over the many hours of night she had traced Tyson's relatives, coworkers, and few friends and come up with nothing solid, but now, at last, she had found something.

A long shot, but something.

Tyson's great-uncle, whom she hadn't found earlier since he was on the maternal line with a different last name and had since died, had taken Robby Tyson on a few hunting and fishing trips after he fled his parents' home. This she had learned from a mention by one of the guys he used to work with. The coworker recalled that it was one of the few good things Tyson ever said about his past. Apparently he recalled those days with fondness, his eyes lighting up with a happiness unusual to him when he talked about those trips.

He had mentioned a cabin in the mountains somewhere. Unfortunately, the coworker couldn't remember where, just that it was in Arizona somewhere. Maybe it was the mountains around Prescott National Forest? There was a fair amount of private land surrounding the public land.

The problem was, the land registry office didn't open until nine. She had started calling at eight, hoping someone would arrive early.

She was dialing again just as Stuart came in.

"How's it going?" she asked.

He slumped down in the seat opposite her. The waitress immediately came over with a cup of coffee.

"Thanks," he said. "Bacon and scrambled eggs, please." Then he turned to Alexa. "No trace of Tyson. Park Service is looking for him and put up his mug shot on all park entrances. They found that the tire marks at the murder scene don't match the car Tyson stole, so as we suspected, he's changed vehicles."

"Did you—" Alexa stopped as the land registry phone line, which had been ringing while Stuart was talking, got picked up.

"Arizona State Land Registry, this is Joan, how may I help you?"

The woman at the other end of the line reminded Alexa of her psychologist, who had the same name. Alexa had ignored her calls for the past couple of days. She reminded herself to reply. When she had the time. If she had the time.

"Hello, this is Deputy U.S. Marshal Alexa Chase. Can you look up any property owned by Virgil Yeager? Social security number 078-84-8462. Deceased."

"One moment, please. I'll check the computer files but if he's been deceased for more than twenty years it will be in our paper records. That will take some time."

Of course it will. Everything is taking time on this investigation, and we don't have time.

Out loud she said, "Thank you, I'll hold."

"What's up?" Stuart asked, looking at her with bloodshot eyes over the rim of his coffee cup.

"His great-uncle used to take him hunting and fishing in some mountain cabin when he was a teenager. I'm trying to find out where that is."

"When he was a teenager? So I presume the great-uncle is dead? The cabin may not even exist anymore."

"Yeah, it's a pretty thin thread to follow."

"Better than nothing."

Joan's voice came over the phone again. "Hello, Deputy Marshal? You're in luck. I found the property. It was owned by Virgil Yeager until his death in 2015. The property has not been sold or claimed by any family member. Apparently Mr. Yeager didn't make out a will. I have no records of it being demolished or marked as a hazardous building."

"Where is it?" Alexa asked, suddenly a lot more awake.

"There's no street address, but it's on a parcel of twenty acres owned by Virgil Yeager right next to the Prescott National Forest. I'll text you the grid coordinates."

"Thank you," Alexa said, standing and gathering her things with her free hand. "This helps very much."

Stuart got up too. "Guess I'm not getting my bacon and eggs."

"No, we need to go."

Stuart glanced at all the other law enforcement officers sitting around having breakfast and didn't say anything until they were in the privacy of their car.

"So is this cabin close?"

"Less than an hour from here."

"Half an hour with me at the wheel," he said with a grin. "Just point me the right way and we're there."

"Take a right out of the parking lot."

"I suppose you don't want to tell that mob back there?"

"No."

"Neither do I. The only interagency cooperation that seems to be functioning on this case is you and me."

Alexa checked her gun. Tyson was armed, and would be desperate if cornered.

"It's going to be dangerous trying to get him, but more dangerous if those idiots swarm in with sirens blaring. Who knows? Tyson might even have a hostage. We need to sneak up there and assess the situation."

Stuart tapped the police radio on the dashboard. "We'll call them when we're almost to the cabin. They can serve as backup."

"Fair enough."

Because if Tyson manages to take us out, someone will need to take our place.

* * *

The dirt track led over a rise and out of sight, cutting through a pine forest that felt cool and shady after the exposed sun of the mountain road. They were high up in the mountains now, and Alexa breathed deeply the fresh, sharp air. After all those long, fatiguing hours, it revitalized her a little. As much as she loved the desert, she enjoyed coming up to Arizona's few, precious "sky islands" of woodland.

Alexa wasn't going to enjoy this visit, though.

She checked a handheld GPS. They had parked the car and turned off the engine a mile back. They didn't want even the faintest sound of their approach to reach Tyson's cabin.

Assuming it still existed. It didn't look like anyone had been on this track for years. While the ground was still rutted from frequent passage of a vehicle, plants had grown up all around it, the grasses and shrubs found in these temperate uplands.

"The GPS says we have another quarter mile to go," Alexa told her partner in a low voice.

Stuart scanned the track. "I wonder where he ditched the car. No one has driven along here for ages."

"In this region there are a million little tracks. He could have driven down any one of them, parked out of sight, and come here on foot."

Stuart pulled out his gun. So did Alexa.

"Let's get to it," he said.

They quietly followed the faint path, keeping spread out on either side of the track. Alexa noticed Stuart's eyes took in everything. The joking stopped, and he walked in a hunched posture that made him less of a target. His gun followed his gaze wherever it went.

Alexa had seen this before. His old war instincts had kicked in. She wondered about his service. He hardly ever talked about it except to joke about it. He never spoke about anything serious.

She wondered about that Purple Heart and Bronze Star too. Just what was this man capable of?

That might get tested pretty soon. As they came over the rise, they both instinctively crouched behind trees. For there, past a swale and up another rise, barely visible through the greenery, stood a small wooden cabin.

Stuart gestured to her, pointing to her right and then looping his finger around. Yes, the slope rose at that point. Not that she could get a clear view of the terrain, but the treetops further on were higher than the ones at their location. As much time as she spent in the wilderness, it had taken the ex-soldier to spot that.

Alexa nodded. Stuart held up his hand as if to tell her to wait, and retraced his steps back down the way they had come until the terrain put him out of sight of the cabin before crossing the track to her side and coming up to join her.

She went downslope a little too, and together they cut to the right, walking steadily up the incline until they felt they could flank the cabin and come at it from above.

The swale rose up to a ridge connecting the two high points, and they crossed this, crouching low because the ground was rocky, thinning out the foliage. They couldn't move to the opposite side of the ridge and move along out of sight because the slope was steep and eroded with loose stones everywhere. They'd make too much noise, assuming they didn't slip and sprain their ankles first.

Alexa kept darting nervous glances down at the cabin, which passed in and out of sight behind various trees and bushes. It looked small, perhaps only two modest rooms, with a tin pipe for a chimney. Weeds had grown up around it, and the roof had a noticeable sag, but it still looked habitable.

Was there anybody in there? No smoke came from the chimney, and no one appeared at the window.

They passed the cabin and came down the slope behind it, keeping enough distance that the structure was all but invisible. Now they paused, spread out to make less of a target, and began to move with care toward it. They heard nothing but birdsong and the wind rustling the pine needles.

Slowly the cabin emerged into view. Now that she could see it better, she noticed it was worse than it had looked when up on the ridge. The boards were rotted at the bottom, and a few were warped. The window facing them still had its curtain, but the window itself was dirty and spattered with bird droppings. A thick carpet of pine needles lay on the little porch.

The cabin faced downhill and Alexa and Stuart circled to come around the back. They pressed close against the wall, listening. They heard nothing. The window on this side was just as dirty as the other one they had seen. This, too, was covered by a curtain.

Alexa nodded, and she crept around one side of the cabin as Stuart made his way around the other.

They came to the front at the exact same time, peeking around their respective corners of the cabin to look at the porch and front door.

What they saw made Alexa grip her gun harder. From a distance they had seen the porch covered by pine needles, twigs, and other windblown debris. Now they could see footprints in that mottled green and brown carpet, and a couple of snapped twigs from the weight of someone stepping on them.

Alexa looked at Stuart and nodded. They had already decided they would not announce themselves for fear that Tyson had a captive. They had also decided to go right in as soon as possible. They had radioed back to the emergency response units on their way up here and knew they didn't have much time before the mountainside was swarming with law enforcement.

The time to surprise Robby Tyson was now.

Stuart crept up the stairs, wincing as the old wood creaked under his weight. Alexa got behind him and slightly to the left, gun aimed at the door, ready to fire into the cabin. He took another step, the boards creaked louder, and then he rushed the door, obviously deciding he had made too much noise already.

He kicked hard right where the lock of the door met the door jamb and the door flew open, the weathered wood splintering.

Alexa and Stuart both angled their guns down at the man on the floor. Alexa almost pulled the trigger, thinking the man was prone, ready to fire.

But no, he wouldn't fire or do anything ever again.

Robby Tyson lay on his back just inside the door, a purple bruise on his temple and his belly slit open.

CHAPTER EIGHT

Even after a couple of hours of watching the Flagstaff CSI team working on the interior of the cabin, Alexa couldn't keep her eyes off the corpse on the floor.

Someone had killed Tyson using his own MO.

He had been dead for only a few hours. A sleeping bag was spread out on the old army cot. The knife and gun he had stolen were on the dusty bedside table. A jug of water and a plastic convenience store bag full of snacks lay on the card table in the rusty and cobwebbed kitchen. No fingerprints other than Tyson's had been found inside the cabin.

At the end of a dirt path a couple of miles from the cabin, park rangers had discovered a Jeep that had been reported stolen in Wikieup the previous day. Robby Tyson's prints were all over it.

And that told Alexa what she had suspected ever since seeing the fugitive lying dead on the floor of his great-uncle's cabin. He had not killed Cassandra Fox. Someone else had done it.

The same person who had killed Robby Tyson.

But who?

No one had any idea.

They had found no prints or traces of hair, and so far no witnesses had come forward saying they had seen anything.

Considering how remote this cabin was, she didn't hold out much hope of that happening.

Amid the babble of conversations around the cabin, Alexa overheard something of interest. She pushed through the crowd to listen in.

A Highway Patrol officer was talking to a couple of DEA agents. Why the Drug Enforcement Agency had decided to hop on this case was beyond her. She had stopped trying to understand this lemming-like rush to the Tyson manhunt, just as Stuart had stopped trying to organize it. "It's like herding cats," he had said. "Feral cats."

The state trooper was saying, "... so we got a positive ID from the guy. Same MO as the convenience store. Gun out, give me your keys, see you later."

"Are you talking about Tyson stealing the Jeep?" Alexa asked.

“Yeah, it happened in front of a Walmart Superstore by the highway. I guess Tyson picked it because it had a big parking lot and no witnesses would get a closeup of him. He waited at the edge of the parking lot until the guy with the Jeep parked, then parked right next to him. Got out, held him up, took his keys and money, and took off. The on-ramp to the highway was just three minutes away so by the time the guy got a nine-one-one response Tyson was long gone.”

“Did he know it was Tyson robbing him?”

The officer laughed. “No, he didn’t. When he learned he nearly had a fit. He sure feels lucky he got through that in one piece. And now he’s even getting his Jeep back, minus half a tank of gas.”

“Was anyone with Tyson at the time?”

“No. No mention of that. CSI is going through the car he left. That’s the one he stole when he first broke off the chain gang.”

“Interesting. Thanks.”

Just as she moved away, her phone rang. Marshal Hernandez.

“Deputy Marshal Chase, I heard the news.” He sounded his usual businesslike self, uplifted with a note of triumph.

“Yes, Tyson was killed by his own MO,” she said, glancing at the cabin. Stuart stood outside, talking to a member of the CSI team. Stuart had been griping that the Phoenix team, run by his new girlfriend, hadn’t responded to the call. They had been too busy with a gang shooting, so the Flagstaff team had come instead.

“Well, it looks like you’re all finished there. Come on back to Phoenix and take the rest of the day off. You’ve both earned it.”

Alexa hesitated. “Um, sir, I think it would be best if we stayed on another day.”

“Deputy Marshal, your assignment was to hunt down a prison escapee. Now that he’s dead, local law enforcement can find his killer.”

“I understand that, sir, it’s just that the situation is a bit chaotic at the moment. We’d like to stay to tie up loose ends on the case and perhaps find some leads to assist the local precinct.”

She heard her boss let out a low chuckle. “Just like a pit bull. You never like to let go. All right, Deputy Marshal. You stay until tomorrow morning. Then come back to Phoenix. We don’t have any urgent cases but there’s some background work on cold cases that you can get to once you’re back.”

“Thank you, sir.” She hung up.

So that was it. They were off the case. All that work for nothing.

But there was a new killer out there, someone clever enough to get the drop on the likes of Robby Tyson. And if this new guy killed that woman by the highway, then they had a copycat serial killer on their hands.

She trudged up to Stuart, suddenly dead weary. The FBI agent turned to her.

"Oh, hey. This is Dr. Takashi," the agent said. "He's friends with Annette. He's going to call me if there are any developments."

"Thank you, Dr. Takashi."

The bespectacled man nodded. "You're welcome. Any friend of Annette's is a friend of mine. Hope you can handle her," he said, punching Stuart in the arm.

The FBI agent laughed. Annette had quite the reputation. Alexa felt a flicker of annoyance. Not only was this conversation borderline unprofessional, but Stuart was always going on and on about his new girlfriend. It got irritating.

"The boss is giving us another day," she told her partner. "While the team wraps things up here, let's go to Tyson's prison up in Kingman and look through his correspondence and talk with the guards a bit more. Maybe we'll come across some clues about who did this."

"All right. It's a bit of a long shot but it's better than nothing. From what the doctor here says, the killer was careful not to leave any traces. And there's no sign of forced entry. Tyson must have been at ease with his killer because he didn't even grab his weapons."

"Yeah, that's why I'm thinking it might be a longtime correspondent, a friend on the outside, or maybe an ex-prisoner he made while he was incarcerated."

Stuart smiled. "You're frustrated you didn't get to catch Tyson, so now you want to solve his murder."

Alexa smiled back. "Damn right."

* * *

That didn't prove so easy. While the warden at the Kingman prison was accommodating, he didn't have any leads as to who might have killed the escapee. Alexa interviewed all the guards who were present at the prison break to get the full story. The only one who wasn't there was Officer George Hanson, the man he had kidnapped. He had been given sick leave for a week to recover.

"I don't know who might have killed him," Officer Hanson told her over the phone when she called. "You might want to check on Kaine Patterson or Spike McCallum. They both hung out with him a bit. Both finished their sentences and left a while back. Not sure if they would want to kill him the way he was supposed to have killed those girls, but they might have something for you."

"Did he ever talk about the serial killer investigation?"

"Only if someone asked. He always maintained his innocence, but of course all these guys claim they're innocent. The questions pissed him off, and because he was in on a murder conviction people didn't want to cross him."

"I understand."

There was a hierarchy in prison. Murderers were on the top. People knew they were capable of killing and gave them respect. Below them came the violent offenders, then robbery and drug offenses, the white collar criminals, and at the bottom rapists and child molesters. That last category often ended up beaten or worse.

Not that that bothered Alexa.

"You were assigned to his cell block, so you knew him better than the other officers present at the breakout. Did he ever mention anyone on the outside?"

"No. He hated his family like a lot of guys in Kingman. You know, if parents just learned to be parents, I'd be out of a job."

That made Alexa think of Stacy, her teenaged neighbor with the alcoholic parents. She spent more time at Alexa's house than her own.

"So he never mentioned outside friends or family at all?"

"I got the impression he was a bit of a loner. Kept to himself in the pen too, as much as you can, anyway. He did mention some uncle with a cabin somewhere. You might want to track him down. Sounds like the only family he got along with."

"Thank you, Officer Hanson." *Too bad no one thought to interview this guy when we were still on the manhunt.*

"No problem. If I think of anything I'll call you. And you got my number. I'm taking the week off, but call me anytime." He paused, then in a voice so quiet Alexa barely heard him, said, "It's a hell of a thing looking down the barrel of a gun. I was in the Army, learned all about that stuff, but I was never deployed. Never had to deal with it for real. Seeing death up close … well … it's a hell of a thing."

"Thank you, Officer Hanson. Take care of yourself."

Alexa hung up and went back to the conference room where Stuart sat going through Robby Tyson's prison correspondence.

"How's it going?" she asked.

"Not too good. I haven't looked at the legal correspondence yet because I figure he probably wouldn't let anything slip there. And besides that there's not much else. From his first year in prison he got a few letters from friends, one reminding Tyson that he owed him fifty bucks." Stuart chuckled. "Probably didn't get his money back. There was also a letter from his sister asking about the case and what happened. After that, the letters dry up. I've seen this before. A lot of criminals don't have any close personal connections and they soon get forgotten on the outside. Sure doesn't help their rehabilitation once they're released."

Alexa sat down, suddenly feeling very weary. Neither of them had gotten any sleep the night before.

"Well, let's get through everything. None of the officers had anything helpful to say. Once we read all these letters we'll call it a night and get a motel somewhere. The boss wants us back in Phoenix tomorrow."

Back in Phoenix. Defeated.

Alexa hadn't felt this low since Robert Powers had gotten killed.

CHAPTER NINE

That night in the motel, after a long day of finding nothing in Tyson's correspondence and no new clues out in the field, Alexa curled up in bed, ready to go to sleep even though it was only nine at night.

But not yet. She wanted to do a bit of reading first.

Her old partner, Robert Powers, had left her a diary in his will. It had already helped her a great deal. Not only did it give her a connection to her mentor, something to remember him by other than that last terrible moment when he got decapitated right in front of her eyes, but it had also given her a lot of sound advice.

So she had been reading a day or two of entries every evening before bed as a way to unwind, remember, and learn.

Alexa opened the diary and set aside the place marker, a photo of the two of them together in front of a field office in Bisbee, and read. She was especially interested in the journal now, because she had reached the part where she had become his partner.

Alexa still doing well. Needs to work on her self-confidence. The Jersey Devil case really spooked her. Poor kid. Alexa smiled. It had been a long time since anyone had called her "kid." Powers had never called her that to her face, but of course compared to him she was, in so many ways. She read on.

We're following the trail of a serial killer. A bad one. He's killing across state lines and in the back country of Arizona, so it comes under our jurisdiction. A long line of suspects is getting shorter as we eliminate them one by one. What really bothers me is that one of them is Drake.

Alexa blinked. Why was he calling Drake Logan by his first name? And why would his being on the suspect list bother him? She read on.

At the time I knew he was a bit off, but we all looked up to him. The cool older guy who bought us beer and could get us weed, even though I never wanted that. Some kids thought it was cool that he had dropped out. I never understood why he liked me. I was so different. No drugs, not that he took much of that stuff himself, and I was a straight-A student. He seemed to see something in me. He always wanted me around and that made me feel cool. Big.

I remember one time we were all out in the desert partying. I felt kind of unsure of myself because of the people there—the tough kids from my school, other dropouts, and some older guys. There were even a couple of bikers. Drake put an arm around me and announced to everyone, "This little square is going to go far, as far as any of us. Well, not as far as me." Then everyone laughed. That's how he was back then, always generous with people he liked but always saving the limelight for himself.

Could he really be the guy we're hunting? The evidence sure is mounting, and now, looking back, he had all the traits of a developing serial killer—terrible home life, rebellious nature, and a cruel streak I only saw once but I'll never forget.

It was at another party a short time after the one I just wrote about. Another big bonfire in the desert, far away from parents and the law. One of Drake's followers (I can't call them anything else) had brought along a friend, a real thug. He was the oldest guy there. Must have been nearing thirty when I and a lot of the others were still in high school. He was swaggering around, bragging about this and that. Really intimidating.

Drake was holding forth as usual, spouting stuff about being your own man and going your own way like he always did, when this guy comes up to him. Gets right in his face. "You think you're the shit, you little twerp? I could break you in half."

Sure looked like he could. Drake was small. Slight. This guy was almost twice his size and you just knew he could fight.

Drake didn't bat an eyelid. Just gave an exaggerated bow like he was submitting to him but saving a bit of face by making a show of it. The thug got a surly smile like he'd won the pissing contest.

That smile didn't last long. As Drake bowed, he picked up a rock and slammed it into the guy's knee. The man went down with a howl, and Drake hit him again, on the head this time. Then he stomped on him at least a dozen times. Everyone was stunned. Even the thug's friend was so shocked that he just stood there. Didn't lift a finger.

When Drake finally finished and the guy lay there bloody and half conscious, Drake turned and looked right at me. Me of all people. He had this weird look in his eye. Defiance, like he was challenging me to object. There was something else there too, something I had never seen before, and something I could hardly believe.

A search for approval. Every teenager knows it when they see it, because their friends and younger kids are looking for approval all the time. Drake never did. Except this once.

I remember I nodded to him, too scared and confused to do anything else, and his face lit up. He went over to the cooler, cracked open a beer, and handed it to me. That was the only time I ever saw Drake Logan serve someone.

I never gave him a chance to do it again. I avoided him after that. The beating made me feel sick, but what made me feel even sicker was that it kind of turned me on. A smaller man beating down a bigger one, beating him down to the ground and humiliating him in front of his peers. It was an image that entranced me, and it repulsed me at the same time. Or more accurately, I was repulsed at the idea of being entranced. The actual beating didn't repulse me at all. I didn't want to see something like that again. I didn't want to feel that conflict of emotions a second time.

Alexa set the journal aside, stunned. For a full minute she could do nothing but stare at the wall, her mind in a chaotic turmoil of half-formed ideas and conflicting emotions. She felt shocked, and a bit betrayed. Powers had never said anything about this in all the years they had worked together.

A host of questions came up in her mind, and she had answers for none of them. Had Robert Powers really known Drake Logan when they were younger? Even though it was right there in black and white, it was hard to believe.

And why hadn't Powers said anything? Because he was embarrassed? She thought back on the investigation. He had never let anything slip, but she did remember that he became increasingly sure that Logan was the killer even before they had disproven the other suspects. She remembered that at the time she felt unsure why he was gunning for Logan, but kept her mouth shut because she assumed the more experienced officer had figured out something she couldn't see.

Now she knew that was true.

But why not say anything? It had never come out, not even after years of being her partner. That didn't make any sense.

But in a way it did, because she had that cruel streak in her too. She had only ever hurt people in self-defense, and yet she had always felt a dark little thrill at doing so. She had never admitted that to anyone.

Powers had learned to control that. How?

She wished she knew.

But she couldn't figure that out now. She was too exhausted. The fatigue of the day dragged her down.

Time for bed. Perhaps they'd land on some new developments on the Tyson murder tomorrow. Just quitting this case like this bothered her. She wanted to finish what she had started.

CHAPTER TEN

Juana Vazquez jogged through El Rio Park in the outskirts of Phoenix. Even though it was night, she wasn't nervous. The route along the wash, a channel that only saw water during monsoon season, was well lit. A fence ran along the edge of the wash so creeps couldn't jump up from down there and kids couldn't go down there to take drugs or get drowned in a sudden rush of water from some storm upstream.

On the land side spread a manicured lawn with a few bushes and some mesquite trees leading up to a road a couple hundred yards away. Nowhere for a creep to hide. Besides, she wasn't the only person along here. Couples walked their dogs, and there were other joggers too on most nights.

Except tonight. Tonight it seemed strangely quiet. Was that because of that prison breakout? They must not have watched the nightly news, because that guy had been found murdered in some cabin in the woods.

Juana Vazquez jogged along, her arms and legs keeping a steady rhythm. She wanted to keep slim for the wedding. Only three months away and her *abuela* kept trying to stuff her face anytime she came over.

"You're too thin, Juanita. Eat something! What is Marco going to think on your wedding night? He's going to think he married a scarecrow."

Well, Marco already knew what she looked like naked, but there are some things you don't tell a Mexican grandmother.

So she decided to jog another mile further than she usually did, just to offset the enormous lunch her *abuela* had cooked for her.

She had never been this far down the riverside park. Not that it mattered. It all looked the same after a while.

Juana kept up a steady pace. Another mile and then she'd turn back. She shouldn't stay out too late, even in a safe park like this. Besides, she had a long day at the office tomorrow and yoga in the evening. She loved yoga. So relaxing after a day of columns and figures. An accountant's job paid well, but it wasn't exactly exciting.

The path was quiet here. Juana, despite her focus on her pace and her dreams of the upcoming wedding, kept her wits about her and looked around.

No one, except for a hunched man with a cane a hundred yards ahead of her limping up the grassy slope toward the road.

They really should put more paths to the road. Look at how much trouble that guy is having.

He didn't look old, although it was hard to see since his baseball cap shaded his face from the streetlight. Maybe he had a sports injury. Juana had sprained her ankle once while jogging and had to skip exercise for a whole two weeks.

As she got closer, the man slipped on the grass and fell to his knees, letting out a cry of pain.

"Are you OK?" Juana angled off the path toward the man, who looked around him and tried to rise.

"This damn knee," he muttered. "Had to have restorative surgery on it last month. Ow!"

"Let me help you."

Now that she stood over him, she could see he was only in his thirties, a bit older than herself.

Juana grabbed his free arm and, as the man pushed up with his cane, got him to his feet.

"Did you hurt yourself?" she asked.

The man gave her a strange look that made her let go of his arm.

"No, thank you," he said in a calm, even tone. "I'm just fine. Never been better."

Then he swung his cane at her head, connecting with her temple. She saw a flash of light, the world spun, and the next thing she knew she was lying on her side in the grass.

Through the roaring in her ears, she heard him chuckle and say, "No good deed goes unpunished."

Strong hands grabbed her ankles. Juana felt herself getting pulled along the slope.

She tried to scream, but only managed a groan.

"Shut up," the man snapped. There was a pause, and again the cane smacked down on her head.

Juana Vazquez didn't see or hear anything after that. Ever.

CHAPTER ELEVEN

Alexa's phone woke her from a deep sleep. She lay in her motel bed a minute, trying to get her bearings. From the lack of light peeking around the curtains she could tell it was still dark out. She fumbled on her bedside table for her phone, found it, and answered. This early in the morning it could only be bad news.

"Hello?" Her voice came out mumbled, fuzzy.

"Is this U.S. Deputy Marshal Chase?"

The voice sounded official. Yes, it was bad news. She woke up a little more.

"Yes, it is."

"This is State Trooper Fletcher. We met on the Tyson investigation?"

"Oh yes, right." She had no recollection of that.

"I just heard that a woman was killed in El Rio Park last night. Same MO as the suspected Tyson killings and the same MO that was used on Tyson himself. Thought you'd like to know."

"Thanks. I'll look into it." She was fully awake now. As she threw on her uniform, her mind, dreaming just two minutes before, now raced with questions and possibilities. El Rio Park was in Phoenix. Why go to an urban area where there was more danger? Tyson never killed in built-up areas. Why would the copycat change his method?

And if he was changing his method, that meant he'd be twice as hard to predict.

Still buttoning her shirt, she hurried to the room next door and knocked.

It took a minute, but Stuart came to the door, rubbing his eyes and wearing only boxer shorts. He had a muscular body, marred by a jagged scar on his shoulder that must have taken a hundred stitches, and a smaller one on his rib cage that had probably needed ten or fifteen.

"There's been another murder, hasn't there?"

He said this more than asked it.

"Yeah. How did you know?"

"Because there's always another murder with you. Who is it this time?"

"A woman in Phoenix. Same MO."

Suddenly Stuart was a lot more awake.

"Damn. We really do have a copycat on our hands. OK. I'm going to take a shower, pack, and get changed. I'll meet you outside your room in five minutes."

"You can do all that in five minutes?" Alexa asked, dumbfounded.

He smiled. "A skill earned in active service." He closed the door.

Those scars were earned in active service too, but you aren't going to tell me about those, are you?

Alexa hurried back to her own room, packed, washed her hands and face, and managed to get out the door in a little over five minutes. Stuart was waiting for her with an air of impatience.

"Come on, slowpoke. I want to get there before rush hour."

"What time is it, anyway?"

"Six-thirty. Oh, and we need to stop at a drive-through and get a double espresso. Annette likes double espressos when she does early morning cases."

"Um, all right."

They headed to the car.

"You know, this really isn't our case," Stuart said.

"No, it isn't."

"But we're going to check it out and find the guy." It was not a question.

"Yes, we will."

Stuart laughed. "I think I'm beginning to like living in a flyover state."

* * *

Stuart always got a little flutter in his chest when he caught sight of his girlfriend.

Annette Guevara looked like a university graduate student, even though she was thirty-two, almost as old as he was. She was a petite Mexican-American with long brown hair, an oval face, and the biggest, darkest eyes Stuart had ever seen. He could get lost in those eyes. Or that hair. Or … other things.

Looks weren't enough for Stuart, and luckily Annette had way more than looks. She was more than qualified to run the CSI team of Arizona's biggest city. A certified genius, she had a PhD in biology, several years of experience, and when she was on the job, she was off in her own world.

That took some getting used to.

When he and Alexa arrived at the crime scene, a strip of municipal park land by the side of a dry wash, she was on her hands and knees just inside the police tape, staring at a blade of grass.

"Hi, Annette, I brought you some coffee," Stuart said.

"Oh, hi," she murmured. Stuart shifted on his feet and glanced at Alexa, who gave him a cheeky smile. Stuart gave it even odds that Annette hadn't even processed who was speaking to her. That information was, for the moment, irrelevant.

"Mud," Annette said. "Dried mud."

"I beg your pardon?" Stuart asked.

"Not generally found in the Desert Southwest." She turned and beamed him a smile, those big brown eyes sparking as they sized him up. "A snowbird like you probably wouldn't know that."

Stuart laughed and handed the plastic cup over the police line. "Double espresso?"

"I've already had two."

"I know you like three."

"That's why I keep you."

"So what have you discovered?" Alexa asked, sounding impatient. Hardly a surprise. On a case, Stuart's partner always sounded impatient.

"The body is over there," Annette said, nodding to a white tent erected about twenty yards away. Such tents were put up at crime scenes to preserve the body from any more contamination as well as to hide it from public view. A bit of decency and respect for people killed in the most indecent, disrespectful ways. "The guys are processing it. Blow to the head with a narrow, blunt object, done by the left hand. Then her belly was cut open with a medium-sized knife, seven inches long, using the right hand. Jogger out at night. That streetlamp over there is broken, the only broken streetlamp for a mile. The guy scouted out this location, planned it through. Waited on the pavement just about over there." She pointed down to the path. "There's a faint trail up the grass to here and a bit further up."

Stuart stared at the places indicated. He didn't see a damn thing. He was convinced she was right, though. Annette Guevara didn't make mistakes, and was scientific enough to admit when she didn't know something or wasn't sure for lack of evidence. Unlike a lot of geniuses, she wasn't arrogant.

Well, not much.

"He walked with a cane," she said. "The gait shows the limp was fake. Too long of a space between these impressions of the cane."

She pointed to several spots on the grass. Now that she mentioned it, he could kind of see faint little round spots where the grass was pressed down. The blades had almost entirely risen back up in the ensuing hours. He would have never spotted them if she hadn't pointed them out.

"So he faked having a limp so the victim came and helped him?" Stuart asked.

"Yep. Pretended to fall just up there," she pointed. "The footprints are faint, but a male size ten or eleven, female size about eight or nine. The victim was eight and a half. He struck her on the temple with his cane, then struck her again on the top of the skull when she was down, then dragged her over behind that bush, which would have been in shadow, where he cut her up."

"So what's this mud you found?" Alexa asked, peering over the tape.

"Don't get too close. I still have to collect it. See it right there? Dried bit of mud. Looks like imported soil like they use on all the lawns here. The lawns you're always complaining about that waste water. Looks like he placed the end of his cane into the soil of an overwatered lawn, perhaps while he was practicing his crippled act. So I'm thinking he was doing this in the privacy of his own yard. That's just a hunch, though. What I do know is that it couldn't have happened more than an hour or so before he killed our victim."

"Why not?" Stuart asked. While he agreed with the saying that "smart is sexy," listening to his girlfriend when she was on the job always made him feel a bit lost.

"Because given the weather conditions last night, the mud would have dried sooner, and thus would have flaked off while he came here, or further down slope as he set his cane in the grass. It took some time for the mud, which was still damp, to flake off right at this spot. I didn't find any other bits of mud in any of the other spots where he set his cane, or in the victim's hair, so this half-dried bit of mud flaked off as a single piece right here."

"I don't suppose there are any witnesses," Alexa said.

Stuart nodded. That might prove a bit more useful than a dried bit of mud. Annette sometimes had trouble seeing the broader picture.

"Nope. A dog walker found the body at five-thirty this morning. Shall we go see the body?"

"Sure," Stuart said without enthusiasm. He hated this part of the job. People thought soldiers and law enforcement officers got used to seeing dead bodies. They did not. Or at least they shouldn't. There had been a couple of hard cases in his regiment who acted all brash and unconcerned around corpses. He knew for a fact that at least a couple of them were hiding their pain. He knew that because they ended up having nervous breakdowns.

He and Alexa walked around the big square of police tape while Annette cut across the interior, weaving between spots of interest invisible to their eyes. They met at the tent, where Annette took a slug of coffee and motioned for them to join her.

She entered. They, out of courtesy for the pair of men working inside, stood at the entrance.

Juana Vazquez lay on her back, her arms splayed wide, her legs slightly apart. Stuart could clearly see the livid bruise on her temple from where the killer had hit her with the cane. Her could not see the wound to the scalp and did not look for it long.

His attention was drawn further down, to Juana Vazquez's belly, which had been ripped open from one side to the other by a knife. Blood had soaked her Phoenix Suns T-shirt and her black Lycra jogging pants. A gold cross on a chain was around her neck, and a diamond engagement ring on her finger.

As with the previous victims, she hadn't been robbed and no souvenirs had been taken. There was also no sign of sexual assault.

They were dealing with a copycat. No doubt about it. Some sick individual who looked up to Tyson, believed he had committed those other killings, and wanted to walk in his footsteps.

But why would a copycat kill his idol in the exact same way he admired?

Stuart had no idea.

He turned to Alexa, who had grown pale. She walked out of the tent, calling someone.

"Hello, Marshal Hernandez? This is Deputy Marshal Chase. We have a copycat on our hands. A murder in El Rio Park last night exactly fits the MO of the killings Tyson was accused of, and the murder of

Tyson himself. We'd like to continue our investigations… We can? Thank you for your understanding, sir."

Stuart nodded in approval. Marshal Hernandez was a good guy.

Alexa hung up and turned to Stuart. "Now we need to figure out who this guy is. Looks like he's too careful to leave the CSI team anything solid to go on."

Stuart nodded. "Don't worry. I know just where to look."

CHAPTER TWELVE

Once again, Alexa felt grateful that she had been teamed up with Special Agent Stuart Barrett. He had delivered, and had delivered in less than an hour.

The FBI kept a watchlist of people who bragged online about wanting to be serial killers. There were a remarkable number of forums dedicated to serial killers, including some that not only documented and discussed these criminals, but expressly glorified them.

Alexa had come across this herself during her time at the Behavioral Analysis Unit, the same FBI unit that Stuart was in now. Every time she delved into those forums she wanted to clean out her brain with soap. She was glad that Stuart was going through it and not her.

It didn't take long. Sitting in the booth of yet another diner, having the breakfast they should have had five hours ago, Stuart turned his laptop around so the screen faced her.

"Check this out. This is a list of individuals who idolized Robby Tyson online. I've left out the women and people living overseas and organized it in order of the highest number of violent posts. The FBI scores each post on the basis of how explicitly it advocates violence. It's done automatically via keywords, so it isn't perfect, but I've found it to be pretty accurate. And there's one man who scored way above the rest."

Alexa stared at the screen, which contained a profile of the user, who went by the handle ThrillKiller.

"How do we know he's a man?" Alexa asked.

"He said so in some of his posts. Has a deep hatred for women."

She continued looking at the profile the FBI had constructed. The computer was in a home right here in Phoenix. Alexa took in a sharp intake of breath.

"We got him," she whispered.

"Not yet. According to census records, there are three people living at this address. A married couple and a college-age son. Last name Ogilvie. There are enough posts over a long enough period of time that it's doubtful they're made by a visitor, but it could be any resident in the home so we'll have to interview all three. Including the woman, just in case."

"Shouldn't be too hard to pick him out."

Alexa clicked on the posts and skimmed through them. While they covered a wide variety of serial killers, or had subject lines such as "Best knives for cutting bitches," there was a preponderance of posts about Robby Tyson.

She delved deeper. They ran from when Tyson was first accused of being the Southwest Slasher back when he got arrested right up to a couple of weeks ago. Like the police, ThrillKiller believed Tyson and the Southwest Slasher were one and the same.

"Fooled them all," said one of the posts. "Too bad he got caught for smashing that punk in that bar. Bad luck for a brilliant mind."

Another post read in part, "He has a great technique. Charms them into a false sense of security, proving the superiority of the male mind over the female, then knocks them out but not dead so he can cut open those child-bearing bellies they're so damn proud of. I hope one day some male genius can figure out an efficient way to make test tube babies so we can rid the world of these whiny parasites."

Alexa pushed the computer away. "I've read enough. Let's go."

Stuart put away his laptop and stood. "We'll call backup on this one. It's a residential area and we don't want him to slip away and hurt someone. What I find significant is that he stopped posting a couple of weeks before Tyson broke out. That makes me wonder."

"Yeah, I'm wondering about that too," Alexa mused on the way to the car. Had this copycat helped his hero break out of jail? And then did they fall out for some reason and ThrillKiller killed him? Or had the whole plan been to kill Tyson and prove himself to be the better murderer?

"ThrillKiller is a movie reference," Stuart said.

"It is?"

"*The Thrill Killers* is an early film by Ray Dennis Steckler."

"Who?" Alexa asked, buckling her seatbelt for another crazy ride across town.

"*The Creeper*? *Devil's Little Acre*? *The Incredibly Strange Creatures Who Stopped Living and Became Mixed Up Zombies*? How can you not know Ray Dennis Steckler?"

"Sue me."

“You miss all the high culture out here in the desert,” he said as he tore out the parking lot and cut off a semi. “You ever see the music video for Jefferson Airplane’s ‘White Rabbit’?”

“Once, I think.”

“Steckler did that too.”

“Um, OK.”

“Annette loves those kind of movies. The gorier the better. Dario Argento is her hero. Every Wednesday is movie night. You should come over sometime.”

“I think I’ll paint my nails instead.”

“You paint your nails?”

“No, but I’ll start. Could we focus on catching the serial killer?”

“All work and no play makes Alexa a dull cowgirl.” He reached for the radio as he drove on the median line to zip between cars going two different directions.

Alexa snatched the handset from him. “Focus on the road! I’ll call for backup.”

They sped through town as Alexa arranged the backup at the address of interest. She made it clear to the local police that she and Stuart were going to make the collar, however.

She wanted this scumbag for herself.

* * *

The house looked much like every other house in this residential neighborhood. A ranch-style dwelling with white stucco facing to imitate adobe, and a green lawn like you’d find in some northern state, entirely ignoring that the residents lived in the middle of a desert. A new Lexus was parked out front next to a beat up old Honda. The windows were framed with peach-colored curtains. No one was in sight.

In fact, no one was in sight in the entire neighborhood. There were no sidewalks here. The residents drove everywhere and did not interact with their neighbors. Alexa hated places like this, neighborhoods that weren’t neighborhoods.

But considering the monster who lived in this house, it was better that no one interacted with anyone else.

They studied the house for a moment from their car parked across the street.

"No windows by the door," Alexa observed. "If I stand away from the peephole, they won't see my uniform. You knock. Maybe they'll think you're an insurance salesman or a Mormon or something."

"I thought we wanted them to open up."

"If they don't, we can identify ourselves. I'd like to get the door open before we do that."

Stuart nodded, then picked up the handset to the police radio. "Everyone in position?"

"Car 34 in position," came the response. They were parked a block down the street, watching the only street exit to this dead-end road.

"Car 65 in position," came another voice. They were parked in the next street over, in case someone ran out the back way and cut across the neighbor's yard on foot.

Alexa took a deep breath. "Let's do this."

They got out, moving swiftly for the door. Alexa kept her eyes on the windows. She did not see any curtains twitch.

Stuart placed himself in front of the door and Alexa stood a little to the side, her hand on her holstered pistol. She would have liked to kick down the door and rush in guns leveled, but she reminded herself this was still only a suspect. This wasn't Tyson's cabin in the woods.

Then she noticed the beat up old Honda had four doors and dirt and pebbles stuck into the grooves of the tires. Her grip on her pistol tightened.

Stuart knocked.

Sound of movement within. The peephole darkened.

"Who is it?" a mature male voice asked.

Stuart looked at her and she shrugged. When asked, a law enforcement officer had to identify themselves unless they were undercover. Stuart pulled out his ID and held it up to the peephole.

"Stuart Barrett of the FBI and Deputy Marshal Alexa Chase of the U.S. Marshals Service."

"What the—?"

"Could you please open the door, Mr. Ogilvie?" Stuart asked in a polite but authoritative tone.

A lock snicked and the door opened to revealed a confused-looking middle-aged man with a large bald spot. He was slight, with a pot belly, and wore a polo shirt and slacks.

"Is there some sort of trouble?" he asked, glancing back into the house.

Probably not with you, but I'm betting there is with your son, Alexa thought.

"Can we come inside?" Stuart asked.

"Come on in." The man sounded resigned.

They entered.

"Bob, what's wrong?" a woman's voice called from somewhere in the house.

"The police."

"Police!" The sound of hurried steps, then a plump woman in her late forties appeared. She greeted them with a worried stare and a waft of gin.

"It's something to do with the Internet, isn't it?" Mr. Ogilvie said.

"Why would you say that, Mr. Ogilvie?" Alexa asked.

"Our son," he grunted, gesturing vaguely toward the back of the house. "He's on that computer eighteen hours a day."

"He works," his wife objected.

"At a 7-Eleven. Never did finish college." Mr. Ogilvie grunted again. Alexa got the impression he grunted a lot.

Alexa studied the man in front of her for a moment. Slight of build and out of shape. Plus he had a defeated look to his eyes. He had greeted them with resignation, and perhaps a bit of satisfaction that his son was finally getting in trouble.

No, this wasn't a serial killer. But the son …

"What's your son's name?"

"Gus."

"Was he working yesterday?"

"Yeah, he had the night shift."

"And the day before that?"

"Went off to one of those stupid video game tournaments all day."

"Are you sure he worked and went to that tournament?"

Mr. Ogilvie blinked. "Um, well, he said so."

"Can we speak with Gus?" Stuart asked.

"Sure, if you can stand the smell," Mr. Ogilvie said.

"Would you two like a drink?" Mrs. Ogilvie asked. "I was just fixing one."

She made to move away. Alexa held up a hand. "I'd prefer if you stayed with us, ma'am."

Alexa didn't think this woman capable of clubbing a burly serial killer over the head and then slitting his belly open, but she wasn't going to take any chances.

For the first time, her husband got a worried expression. He looked between Alexa and Stuart.

"Just what has my son done?"

"We'd just like to talk with him, sir," Alexa said.

"It's not porn, is it? I caught him looking at that stuff."

There had been no note about illegal porn being accessed from this address, but Alexa decided to keep that to herself.

"Could we speak with him now?"

Mr. Ogilvie gestured for them to follow and they passed through a living room fitted with an easy chair, a couch, and a huge flat-screen TV. A mantelpiece held various photos. Alexa noticed one showing a younger Mr. and Mrs. Ogilvie together with a little boy and two teenaged girls.

"Do your daughters live with you?" she asked.

"No," Mr. Ogilvie said. "They both graduated and made something of themselves."

They passed out of the living room and down a carpeted hallway to the end, where a door was closed.

"This is our son's room," Mrs. Ogilvie said.

"If you can call it that." Mr. Ogilvie grunted. "They shouldn't have sent the FBI. They should have sent the EPA."

Alexa paused. The young man on the other side of this door had praised Robby Tyson to the skies, and had fantasized about murdering women in just the same way.

Even worse, he had the right kind of car, had been absent at the time of Tyson's murder, and had gotten dirt on his tires. In the middle of Phoenix.

Alexa motioned for Mr. and Mrs. Ogilvie to back away. They glanced at each other nervously and took several steps back. Alexa nodded at Stuart.

He opened the door.

CHAPTER THIRTEEN

Alexa wasn't sure what to think about what she saw on the other side. The bedroom was a disaster area, at least what she could see of it. The blinds were drawn, the lights off, and the only illumination came from a computer screen with some first-person shooter video game. A heavyset figure sat slouched in a special lounge chair Alexa had heard called a "gaming chair," a comfortable and adjustable seat favored by hardcore video game players. He had his back to them, busy blasting away at computerized cops. Blood sprayed on blue uniforms. Alexa frowned.

A horrible funk fouled Alexa's nostrils. She took in the unmade bed and heaps of dirty clothing on the floor. On the bedside table lay several old McDonald's wrappers and a plastic Big Gulp cup. Posters of video game characters and heavy metal bands adorned the walls. Her neighbor Stacy was a neat freak compared with this guy.

The man at the computer didn't move. Alexa saw he was wearing headphones, and probably didn't notice that they had entered.

She was wrong.

"Mom, could you close the door? You're shining too much light on the screen. How many times do I have to tell you that?"

The voice came out in an adolescent whine, but with the deep tones of an adult.

"Oh, but bring me a soda, would you? I'm out."

He gestured at the computer desk, which was a mass of empty Mountain Dew cans and candy wrappers.

Alexa and Stuart traded confused looks, then went up on either side of the youth in the gaming chair.

As they flanked him, he looked up at Alexa and practically leapt out of his seat.

"Jesus! Who are you?" He tore off his headphones, allowing Alexa to hear the sounds of battle. Gus Ogilvie looked in the other direction and saw Stuart looming above him. "Gah! What's going on?"

"I'm Deputy Marshal Alexa Chase and this is my partner, Special Agent Stuart Barrett. We have some questions for you."

"It's not about the porn, is it? The websites certify they're all eighteen."

Alexa resisted the urge to smack him upside the head.

"No, it's not about the porn, not yet. Could you stand up and keep your hands where I can see them, please?"

He stood, his mouth open in confusion. Alexa took a step back. Although fat and unwashed, wearing only a stained T-shirt and underwear, he had a menacing presence, standing a head taller than both Stuart and Alexa. And there was bulk behind that fat. If he exercised more he could have been a linesman on a college football team.

Gus Ogilvie was naturally hefty, naturally strong. He would be capable of beating Robby Tyson unconscious. Maybe not chasing him very far, but if he knew the killer and had been allowed inside the cabin, he could have gotten the drop on him.

"Put your hands on your head and interlace your fingers," Stuart said.

"Huh? Am I being arrested?" He did as he was told.

Stuart patted him down with a noticeable look of distaste. On the screen, the cops had finally caught up with him and his character died in a red haze.

"He's clean," Stuart said. She could hear the irony in his voice.

Alexa moved to the light switch and flicked it on. Mr. and Mrs. Ogilvie stood close together a few steps down the hallway.

"Can you confirm your whereabouts last night?"

"Yeah. I was working at the 7-Eleven from six in the afternoon to two in the morning."

Alexa bit her lip. If that was true, there was no way he could have committed the murder.

They could check that easily enough, and he knew it. So would he lie?

"And the day before?" she asked, more doubtful now.

"I was at Gamerfest. I won a silver medal for RPG."

"You got the medal around here?" Stuart asked, still standing behind him.

Gus looked over his shoulder at him. "It's a virtual medal."

Stuart raised an eyebrow. "You played all day for a virtual medal?"

"Street cred, bro. What's all this about?"

"You go by the name ThrillKiller?" Alexa asked.

Even in the dim light she could see Gus go pale.

"Wh-what?"

"Did you not hear me?" Alexa asked, leaning in half an inch. It was an intimidation technique Robert Powers had taught her. The suspect generally doesn't even see the movement, but he unconsciously picks it up. It tended to make a weaker suspect get nervous.

And it sure worked on Gus Ogilvie. He started to tremble.

"W-wait. I didn't mean any of that stuff."

"'I'd like to slit a bitch open with a knife just like Tyson. That man is a hero to men everywhere,'" Stuart recited.

There was a gasp from Gus's mother out in the hall.

"That was playacting, letting off steam," Gus said, waving his arms around.

"Hands back on your head," Stuart snapped. Gus put his hands back on his head so fast he slapped himself.

"Calm down, please," Alexa said. "Sit."

Gus slumped in his chair. He looked less threatening that way. In fact, now he looked like an overgrown schoolchild sitting in the principal's office.

"Tell us more about your online activity," Alexa said.

Gus shrugged, not meeting their eyes. "I just … needed to let off some frustrations. I can't get a girl. Makes me mad. It's all just fantasy, though. I would never do anything."

"You stopped posting a couple of weeks ago. Why?"

"Got to be too much. I was having these dreams. Nasty dreams. I never really meant any of those things I said online. But in my dreams I was really doing them. That made me scared. So I stopped. Went cold turkey. Gaming is more fun anyway."

The screen read, "Cop Kill Count: 437."

"What did you think when you heard Robby Tyson escaped?" Alexa asked.

Gus's eyes went wide. "Huh? He escaped?"

"Don't you watch the news? It's all over the place. And he's been killed."

"Oh." Gus looked down, his face softening. In a voice so quiet she barely heard it, he said, "That's too bad."

Guess you haven't given this stuff up entirely, have you?

"You mean to tell me you haven't heard Tyson was killed in the same method he was accused of killing those girls with several years ago?" Alexa had a hard time believing that.

"No, I hadn't heard. I don't watch the news and no one on my social media mentioned it. They don't know I was into serial killers. I kept that separate. And you think I killed him? Check my manager at 7-Eleven. Check the guys at Gamerfest."

"We will," Alexa said. As much as this guy filled her with a mixture of loathing and pity, she did not think it was him anymore. He was all talk. An Internet fake. Another dead end.

They had to be on the safe side, though. With all of them.

"Why is there dirt on your tires?" Stuart asked.

"The guys at Gamerfest had all the medal winners drive out to the desert for a photo shoot. Google it."

Damn. We've struck out, Alexa thought.

Alexa got on her radio and called the backup units. "Please send a couple of patrolmen to the house. We need to process three suspects."

"Three?" Mr. Ogilvie said from the hallway. He walked to the door. "Why three?"

"Just routine, sir."

Yes, just routine. Looks like we've hit a dead end.

* * *

As Alexa suspected, the Ogilvies were all innocent. Gus's alibis for 7-Eleven and Gamerfest were proven with time-stamped videos and several witnesses. His father was at work one of the days, meaning he couldn't have been in Prescott National Forest to kill Robby Tyson, or on the road to kill Cassandra Fox. While he didn't have an alibi for the night Juana Vazquez was killed in El Rio Park, if he was innocent of two murders he was innocent of the third. Mrs. Ogilvie was out to dinner with friends and a bar for most of the night Juana Vazquez was murdered, and didn't have access to a car the day the other two were killed. Not that she had been much of a suspect anyway.

So there they were, stuck without a solid lead. Again.

Several calls to the continuing interagency mess-up in Wikieup and Kingman revealed that no new cases had been found there either. Not that that surprised Alexa. They had been searching for Tyson, who had slipped through the net and ended up dead. Now every agency was launching their own separate investigation into who killed him and where he might have gone. There was a general consensus, with which Alexa agreed, that the killer probably hadn't stayed in the Phoenix area after he killed Juana Vazquez. The location was too dangerous.

That killing struck Alexa as odd. Both previous murders had been in remote locations. El Rio Park was more built up. It had been extremely risky to hunt for a woman there. So why do it?

That little dollop of mud might hold the answer. Annette Guevara had said it had most likely come from an over-watered lawn, and someplace close. That hinted that the killer lived in the Phoenix area. Had he needed to return home for some reason?

If so, he was escalating. A smart killer wouldn't have committed murder so close to his base. He would have gone elsewhere, because he must have seen the news that Tyson's body had been discovered, and thus the police were searching for him. Killing someone in El Rio Park was a bad move, and showed a lack of control.

They needed to find out more, so hoping for a few more clues, they visited Annette in her CSI lab in downtown Phoenix.

It was housed in the basement of a local police precinct, a large but unobtrusive structure of red brick. It looked like many other police stations, and no one would suspect the horrors that were kept in the basement.

Although Alexa had been here several times, it always gave her the creeps. She didn't know how Annette could work with body parts all day and still remain so chipper. But being a genius, Annette didn't think the way other people thought. Maybe that helped.

They checked in at the front desk and passed through a busy office where police officers were processing suspects or making calls to witnesses on the phone. A hallway lined with photos of decorated officers led them to a set of stairs leading down.

A door with a key card lock blocked their way, but the lab knew they were coming and one of Annette's assistants opened up for them.

They found themselves in a large lab. Brilliant white lights shone down on microscopes, computers, and a variety of scientific equipment Alexa couldn't name let alone describe the purpose of.

Annette stood at the far end of the room, holding a test tube up to the light as the fluid inside turned from a pale pink to a deep yellow.

She set it into a steel holder and turned to them.

"Did you bring me a double espresso?" she asked Stuart.

"Um, no."

"It's over between us."

Stuart's face fell. "What?"

"It's a joke, FBI boy. There's an espresso machine over by the corner. Go make me one, but keep your ears perked. I got some news for both of you."

As Stuart dutifully went off to get the coffee, Alexa stifled a smile. The forensics expert had this war hero wrapped around her finger. Annette continued in a slightly louder tone so he could hear.

"To answer the question you were about to ask, yes, we've made progress. First off, the general timeline of the crime has been confirmed by a more detailed look at the ground. Also, we found a hair on the victim's body that wasn't hers. Blond. Cut very short like a buzzcut. It was on her shirt. Considering the type of fabric it is unlikely to have been on there very long. Probably fell on her from the murderer as he was bent over her doing his business."

The espresso machine began to hiss as the water steamed up. Annette raised her voice.

"The root wasn't attached. It used to be you needed that to get a DNA sample, but a couple of years ago a team at the University of California at Santa Cruz managed to pull it off. It's still a new technique and a good defense attorney will cast doubt on it in court, but it will certainly add to the prosecution's case, once you get someone to prosecute."

"Plus there's the hair type match," Stuart called over his shoulder. "That's been admissible for decades."

Annette shot him a smile. "Focus on making my coffee."

"Wow, you're getting bossy lately."

"You're on my turf. When we get back home, you can boss me around, studmuffin."

Studmuffin? Alexa thought. *Good Lord.*

"But I have more," Annette declared. "Remember that little glob of mud? I found a seed in it. A marigold seed."

"Did it have the name and address of the murderer written on it?" Stuart asked as he walked back and handed Annette her coffee.

"No, but it's another piece of the puzzle. I'm afraid that's all I have for you crazy kids. Now if you'll excuse me I have to pick through two hundred thirty-seven hairs and separate the golden retriever hairs from the human ones. I hate it when dog owners get murdered. Their homes are so contaminated with extraneous material. Run along now."

Run along where? Alexa thought as they left the building. It was the end of another long, frustrating day. Another day where a copycat killer roamed free.

"Marigolds sound pretty domestic," Stuart said. "Like married couple or little old lady domestic."

"Yeah. I can't see a loner psychopath planting marigolds," Alexa said.

"Maybe he was staying with someone? A mother or an aunt maybe?"

"Could be. Maybe even a wife. There have been married serial killers. We caught one ourselves."

"Yeah, but they're rare. Let me drive you home. We'll start fresh in the morning."

Alexa was too tired to object. The sun had set a couple of hours before, and there was little more they could do today. They got in the car and headed north.

As they passed through Phoenix, she used her flashlight to look through some more files, trying to find something, anything that might hint at who had killed Robby Tyson. If he was Phoenix based, he must have left pretty soon after Tyson escaped to make it up to the cabin in time to murder him. if he wasn't based in Phoenix, the question remained—why would he come here?

Alexa nodded off the passenger's seat as Stuart drove out of the city on U.S. Route 60, headed northwest. Her forehead rested on the files.

They passed through Morristown. A few lights, a lonely gas station, and it was gone.

Almost there. Alexa roused herself and opened the window to breathe in the fresh desert air. The highway and the city were well behind them. She was almost home. That always made her feel better, even when preoccupied with a case.

"I think we should go back to Kingman and check the prison records again," Alexa said. "Start from scratch. Maybe we missed something. We never did get through it all."

"All right," Stuart replied.

"That means an early start. You got your overnight bag?"

"Sure. We never stopped at home all this time, remember?"

"Oh, right. How about you stay in my guest bedroom? Then we can hit the highway right after breakfast."

"Sure, if you don't mind."

Stuart slowed. The road to her ranch house hadn't been repaved for years, and was more cracks than pavement. Alexa's porch light shone in the distance. She perked up. She had left it off and that meant only one thing. Stacy was staying the night.

There had been trouble at home.

CHAPTER FOURTEEN

Alexa got out of the car after Stuart parked under the corrugated steel awning she had built to protect her vehicle from the sun. Ironically, her own car had been baking in the sun in the U.S. Marshals parking lot since the beginning of the case. Too much of that treatment and her paint would fade.

Stuart popped the trunk and she got out her overnight bag.

In the distance, in the direction of the trailer half a mile away owned by Stacy's parents, she could hear laughter from a number of people and the sound of loud classic rock. Mr. and Mrs. Carpenter had decided having a bunch of their drunk friends over for a party was more important than Stacy getting a good night's sleep on a school night.

"Could you wait out here for a minute?" she asked Stuart.

Her partner glanced in the direction of the trailer and nodded. While he had never been to her house, he knew the situation with Stacy.

Alexa went inside. Stacy sat slumped on the couch. A slim girl with her blonde hair tied back in a ponytail, she watching TV and texting at the same time. Thirteen-year-olds never seemed to do just one thing at a time. Except, in Stacey's case, take care of horses or ride. When Stacy was with a horse, she was all attention.

"Hey," Stacy grunted, still texting. She didn't even look up. No cheerful greeting or news about Alexa's horses, Smith and Wesson.

"What's up?" Alexa asked, dropping her overnight bag and sitting down on the sofa next to her. Stacy turned her phone so she couldn't see the screen.

"Nothing."

"Have you eaten?"

"Yeah."

"Got any homework?"

"Done it."

"How was school?"

"Fine."

She still hadn't looked up from her screen, and her fingers still hadn't stopped typing.

"Staying the night?"

"What do you think?" Stacy snapped. Then looked up at her uncertainly. "Sorry."

Alexa put an arm around her. The girl stiffened, but did not pull away.

This was bad. Stacy loved hugs. She sure never got any at home.

"Stuart's here. Remember my partner? He came up to my family's ranch once."

"The city guy who can't ride?"

Alexa smiled. "At least he didn't fall off."

Stacy's mouth tweaked with the hint of a smile. "He almost did, and he didn't mount right. Had to swing his leg over the horse's head. I thought he was going to get bit."

"Well, you can remind him all about it. He's outside."

"Why did you leave him outside?"

To see how you were first, but of course I can't remind you of that.

"He had to make a call. You know how weak the signal is out here."

Stacy rolled her eyes. "Big time." Then she looked at Alexa with a serious expression. "You're hunting the guy who killed that escaped prisoner, aren't you?"

"Since when did you become a news junkie?"

"Since you spend half your time running around the desert hunting bad guys."

Alexa gave her a squeeze. This time the girl didn't resist. "Sorry I haven't been around much."

She decided not to tell her she had to leave first thing in the morning. Stacy was only just beginning to cheer up. It didn't take much, just an adult who paid attention to her.

Good thing the girl found the right type of adult.

"It's OK," Stacy said. "It's what you do. Oh, Melanie texted me, asking about you."

Alexa groaned. Her sister-in-law was still trying to get an interview with her, and had used a family reunion as the chance to wheedle her way into the kid's confidence.

"Honey, I asked you not to talk with her."

"What could I do? She texted me. I just told her I was at school and didn't know when you'd be back."

"She texted you during school hours? God. I'll talk to her."

"Thanks. It's annoying. Did she try to call you?"

"She knows better than that. I never answer. You do the same."

"OK. You look hungry. You want me to make Hamburger Helper?"

Alexa smiled. It was a trap. If Stacy cooked one of the five or six recipes she knew, then Alexa would be stuck cleaning the dishes, and she suspected there was already a heap of unwashed dishes in the sink. There usually was when the kid was around.

"Sure. Cook some for Stuart too."

"You guys dating now?"

"No! He's my partner."

Stacy grinned and made air quotes. "Partner."

Alexa gave her a playful bap on the back of the head. "Partner as I'm working with him partner."

"You should date him. He'd chill you out and you could teach him how to ride."

"Enough of that."

"Well, he sure won't date you if you leave him standing outside all night."

"Oh, right!" Alexa sprang out of the couch and went to the front door. She looked through the screen and was surprised not to see Stuart.

Curious, she stepped out onto the porch, looking around. Stacy followed.

After a moment, they spotted him standing away from the light in the desert, staring up at the sky.

Stacy elbowed her. "He's wishing upon a star that you'll like him."

"Go make the Hamburger Helper."

Stacy giggled and went inside.

"Come on in when you're ready, Stuart," Alexa called out.

He turned and nodded, but made no move toward the house.

"Sorry, but you're getting the couch tonight," she said.

He waved.

"Think I'll stare at the stars for a bit."

"OK. We're making some Hamburger Helper."

"Wow. I haven't had that since I was a kid. You go be a mom and call me when you're done."

Alexa smiled, then went back inside.

* * *

By ten the next morning, they were back at Kingman prison. They had woken at the crack of dawn and stayed at Alexa's home just long enough to make breakfast and make sure Stacy got on the school bus. She liked to skip school when she was feeling down, a bad habit Alexa was trying to cure her of.

But now Alexa had to focus on the task at hand and hope Stacy could fend for herself today. The kid was pretty resilient, and thanks to her parents was accustomed to taking care of herself.

Alexa and Stuart sat in the same conference room as before, going over the letters and visitor logs. They were going back to the earliest ones, dating to when he was just put in prison, the ones they hadn't had time to search through.

And they had found something interesting. Very interesting.

Someone named Ryan Deanfeld had written him a few times right after his incarceration, when the news said he was a suspect in the Southwest Slasher murders.

"Listen to this," Alexa said. "This is from Deanfeld's second letter to him. 'Mr. Tyson. Thank you so much for insights into the criminal mind. It will be a great help in my book. I hope the cigarettes and chocolate got to you without any trouble. I found our discussion on your theories of certain events to be very revealing. I can't thank you enough. It's so interesting to correspond with a man who is in such close contact with his animal nature.'"

Stuart leaned forward, interested. "'Theories of certain events'? That sounds like code for the killings he was never convicted of. Looks like Deanfeld was just as convinced he was guilty as the prosecution."

"And Tyson was talking to him about it." Alexa held up a photocopy of a letter Tyson had sent. "It's vague, speaks in generalities, but it's there. He always says 'the murderer' this and 'the murderer' that. But it's pretty clear."

"What did he say his motives were?"

"Nothing profound. Just a feeling of power. Says 'the murderer' slit the bellies of women because women are so proud they can bear children and men can't. Tyson wrote, 'It's the one thing they can do that we can't do ten times better.' So it's a form of humiliation."

"I'm amazed the prosecution didn't pounce on this," Stuart said.

"Oh, the Southwest Slasher is only one of a dozen cases they discuss. They hide it in plain sight so they can have some plausible deniability."

"What's the date on that letter from Deanfeld?"

"September third."

Stuart held up the visitor's log. "Guess who visited him on September fifteenth?"

"Really? Did he come see him again?"

"Three more times."

"Why didn't the guards mention that?" Alexa said, frustrated. "They all said he never got visitors."

"As far as I can see he hasn't had visitors in the last two or three years, so they probably forgot. Hell, most probably weren't even around five years ago. There's a lot of turnover on a job like this."

Alexa nodded. She'd known a fair number of prison guards. A lot joined thinking it would be an easy job, or were attracted by the thought of bullying a pack of lowlifes. They didn't realize just how stressful it could be having to be constantly on the watch, constantly having to look over your shoulder. It burnt people out. The bad pay didn't help either.

"What's the return address on those letters?" Stuart asked.

Alexa flipped the envelopes over. "A post office box in Flagstaff."

"From five years ago. It's probably not being used anymore. The post office will have records, but what do you want to bet it's a fake one?"

Alexa bit her lip. Her partner had a point. When you wanted to rent a post office box, they made you fill out a form, but you could always lie and they never checked.

Then she remembered something Bruce Thornton had told her when she had gone to visit him a second time. Serial killers were careful to avoid talking to their objects of their admiration. They didn't want to leave clues. Deanfeld and Tyson's correspondence was typical of what the Jersey Devil called his "interesting" contacts on the outside, people he could speak intelligently with about the motives for murder. And Deanfeld obviously enjoyed the discussions too. He said so several times. Looking through the letters, she found several instances where the aspiring author had sent the prisoner gifts.

But after a few months of back and forth, Deanfeld stopped writing. Why? They hadn't argued. Alexa suspected Deanfeld wanted to graduate from fantasy to reality and decided to distance himself from the prisoner first.

"We need to talk to this guy," she said out loud. *I can't believe Thornton is actually turning out to be useful.*

Stuart got on an FBI database to check his name.

"There are fifteen Ryan Deanfelds in the United States. Only one in Arizona. At a place called Paulden. Where's that?"

"I'm not sure."

Stuart grinned. "The geography master finally falls down! Must be a seriously hick town for you not to know about it."

Alexa stood, her face grim. "Whatever it is, we're going there."

CHAPTER FIFTEEN

Paulden turned out to be a scattering of homes spread out in the desert uplands to the north of Prescott National Forest. Alexa had been through this land before, but hadn't remembered Paulden.

Not that there was much to remember. They had left the pine-topped mountains behind, the road tabling down to a flat, open plain that resembled a desiccated Kansas more than it did Arizona. The land was mostly flat, with dry grass and the occasional scrub. Ranch-style homes stood scattered here and there, each seeming to want the most space it could get from its neighbor. Some had a few scraggly trees around them. One or two homeowners had even made a heroic attempt at flower beds, adding a rare flash of color to an otherwise dreary landscape.

"Why the hell would anyone live here?" Stuart asked.

"Solitude."

"You got that at your place, but at least there's something to look at."

"You liked the stars, eh? I saw you staring up at them."

"Don't get that kind of a view much back east," Stuart said quietly. "Kind of puts a perspective on things."

"It does," she replied, giving her partner an appreciative glance. Maybe he would adapt to the Southwest after all.

"Oh, Stacy came out to the living room and talked to me last night after you went to bed."

"I hope you were wearing more than your boxer shorts."

Stuart laughed. "With one and a half ladies in the house? Of course! I was tempted to wear my suit but I didn't want it to get wrinkled."

"What did she want to talk to you about?" Alexa asked, curious.

"Asked about me, mostly. We didn't talk much that weekend up at your dad's place. Asked all about my family. My mom and dad. I also told her about Gunther. Remember I told you about him? My older brother's girlfriend's kid?"

"Yeah, the one who was like your little brother."

"Yeah, he didn't have a big brother or a dad and I didn't have a little brother, so it just kind of worked out that way. Stacy really liked that. Asked me all about him."

"Really? That's sweet."

Alexa settled back in her seat, a warm feeling inside her. She wondered what Stacy thought of her as. A big sister? A mother? A friend? A bit of all three? They had never really discussed it. Alexa decided they didn't need to. Stuart and Gunther probably hadn't either. It was better just to go with it and enjoy having someone be important to you, and for you to be important to them.

"I'd like to meet Gunther," Alexa said.

"I really want him to come down here now that I'm settled. We're talking about it."

"Great. We'll teach him how to ride."

"He'll probably be a natural, just like I was."

Alexa put a hand over her mouth to hide her smile.

Then she grew serious. "See that dirt track on the right? Ryan Deanfeld's house is down at the end."

They looked into the far distance and saw a single-story white prefab. It stood a good mile from any other house, in plain sight but so far from the road and neighbors that no one could see what went on there.

Hiding in plain sight, just like Thornton told me.

"I don't see how we can sneak up on that place," Stuart said. "We're just going to have to drive on up and hope for the best."

Alexa took a deep breath. "I don't like that."

"Neither do I. Shall we call for backup?"

They were drawing closer now, Stuart having slowed on the dirt road. A gleam of sunlight off a windshield told them someone was home. Alexa hesitated for a moment.

"It would take ages to get here and this is only a hunch. Let's do this ourselves," she said.

She could already see Stuart's gaze roving, looking at every shrub, every fold of the terrain, searching for hidden dangers. He was poised, tense, but not overly so. The only time she had seen him get jittery was when a bomb planted by Drake Logan's minions had nearly taken him out. That had been too close to his experiences in Iraq, and it had rattled him.

Although, to be fair, it would have rattled anyone, and he had gotten over it quicker than most would have.

I bet you really earned that Bronze Star.

Stuart slowed more as the car trundled over stones and pot holes. Ryan Deanfeld obviously didn't maintain this track very well. Probably because he didn't want visitors.

And he didn't need to maintain it. Now that they were only a quarter of a mile away, they could see a large black four by four parked in front of the house.

That made Alexa nervous. Given the flat land hereabouts, if Deanfeld wanted to take off, he wouldn't have to stick to the track, while they in their city car would have to.

There seemed to be no sign of him making a break for it, though, or even any sign that he had noticed their approach. From the glare of sunlight on the windows, she couldn't see if there were curtains or not, but there was no sign of life from the house or surrounding land.

Alexa noticed that Stuart had hunkered down in his seat to make less of a target. She did the same.

No shots came at them as they got to Ryan Deanfeld's front yard. Stuart parked right in front of the four by four, putting it in between them and the house. He had found the only cover for miles, and had gone straight for it.

I really wish we didn't keep needing his combat skills, Alexa thought.

Both of them got out, keeping low and keeping behind Deanfeld's vehicle.

They paused for a second, watching and listening. She could now see that both windows facing them had the Venetian blinds down and shut. No sound came to their ears except for the rustle of the dry grass in the wind.

"Let's go," Alexa whispered.

They bolted for the front door at the same time, keeping a distance between each other.

Alexa's heart raced as fast as her legs. She felt terribly exposed, fully expecting the muzzle of a rifle to smash through one of the windows and start firing.

God, Stuart had to deal with this every day for years.

They got to either side of the front door and looked at each other for a second. Stuart reached over and tried the doorknob. It turned slightly.

Stuart looked at her, a question in his eyes. Alexa nodded. Regulations required that they identify themselves if there wasn't a crime obviously in progress, but regulations didn't mean much when you were in the middle of nowhere at a serial killer's front door.

Stuart flung the door open and ducked back behind the frame. They paused for a moment. No shots and no other sounds.

Alexa dared a quick peek around the corner. An empty living room with a cheap set of furniture. She ducked through, going low and left. Stuart came right behind her, going to the right.

From the living room they could see into the kitchen and a small hallway leading to two more rooms. Quickly they cleared the house. Bedroom. Home office. Bathroom. Nothing else.

Where was he? She opened a slat on the Venetian blinds of a back window and saw a large prefab shed standing in the back yard. The door stood open a crack.

"There," she whispered.

Without another word they went back out the front door and circled the house.

Just as they did, they heard a woman's scream come from the shed.

They rushed across the back yard, the sound of their hurried footsteps drowned out by another scream, followed by a plaintive plea.

"Don't cut me! Oh please, don't cut me!"

Alexa made it to the door a step before Stuart and kicked it open.

Inside they saw a scene of horror. The large shed was fitted out like a dungeon. A small cage stood in one corner. A rough wooden table with arm and leg restraints stood to one side. Along one wall ran a series of hooks from which hung whips, goads, and other instruments Alexa couldn't name although she knew they were all made to inflict pain.

In the center of the room, suspended by her arms from a pair of heavy iron shackles, hung a naked young woman. A livid bruise blossomed from her temple, leaking a bit of blood. Standing before her was a tall, wiry man holding a knife.

He was brushing it against her bare hip, slowly moving it up her flesh toward her neck.

At the sound of the door bursting open he spun around, his face twisted in rage.

CHAPTER SIXTEEN

"Freeze!" Alexa shouted. "Drop the weapon!"

The man let out a cry and moved to get behind the woman.

Alexa aimed for the head, about to squeeze the trigger …

"Don't shoot!" the woman shouted.

As the last instant Alexa noticed the man's hair.

Black. Not blond.

Too late, her finger was already going through the motion. Her wrist flicked up and the bullet sang through the air to punch a hole in the far wall.

The man flinched, dropped the knife, and backed away with his hands in the air.

"It's not what you think!" the woman shouted.

Stuart, standing right beside Alexa, rushed into the room, kicked the knife away, and kept his gun trained on the man.

"Don't hurt him! Ryan and I are just having sex play!" the woman said.

"What the hell is going on here?" Alexa demanded. She paced toward Ryan Deanfeld, focusing on his hair, her gun not wavering for a moment. No, it did not look dyed. His eyebrows were black too, as was the hair on his arm.

"We're swingers!" Ryan said, backing up to the wall and with his hands still in the air.

"Into the BDSM scene," the woman said.

Stuart put away his gun and, while Alexa covered him, went over and cuffed Ryan.

"What are you doing?" the woman said, twisting a bit in her shackles. "We just told you this was consensual."

"Just until we figure out what's going on," Alexa said. She turned to the woman hanging from the ceiling. "How do I get those shackles off?"

"The key is on the rack," she replied.

"The what?"

"That table over there," the woman said, nodding toward the table with the arm and leg restraints.

Now that she got a better look at it, Alexa could see each end was actually a drum that could be rotated with a crank. She imagined a victim tied to it, their body being pulled painfully taut. Another turn of the crank and the joints would strain. Another turn and the joints would pop.

Bruce Thornton wouldn't be so smug tied to that. No, the Jersey Devil would scream and scream ...

Alexa shook herself to snap out of the ugly fantasy, let out a little shudder, and retrieved the heavy brass key lying on the rack.

Looking around, she found a low stool and grabbed it, putting it under the woman so she could stand on something as Alexa unlocked her.

Meanwhile, Stuart was interrogating Ryan Deanfeld.

"What is your relationship to this woman?"

"She's a play partner. We met at a swingers party."

"How did she get that bruise on her head?"

"She wanted it!"

"Answer the question!"

Stuart's tone made Alexa glance over. His face was red with rage, and he leaned close in on Ryan, glowering at him.

"We always go over our sessions in detail before we start," Ryan said quickly, sensing the danger. "The bottom tells what she's willing to have done to her and her limits. Then we go through with it."

"It's true," the woman said as Alexa got the second shackle off. She rubbed her wrists, which were badly chafed. "Pain turns me on. So does dominance. It was all completely consensual."

"He's in cuffs and in custody," Alexa told her in a reassuring tone. "He can't hurt you anymore."

"You idiot," the woman snapped, making Alexa blink in surprise. "Normos like you can never understand."

She walked over to where Ryan sat in cuffs, knelt on the floor, and kissed his shoe.

Alexa and Stuart exchanged a look. Stuart looked as disgusted as she felt.

"Get up and get dressed," Alexa ordered.

The woman stood, shot Alexa a contemptuous look, and walked out of the shed into the yard.

"What are you doing?" Alexa called after her.

"My clothes are in the house. Part of the play was for him to strip me and then drag me naked across the yard." She walked off toward the house. Then called back over her shoulder. "He drags me by the hair. You should try it sometime."

"Un. Believable," Stuart said.

Alexa walked up to Ryan Deanfeld, who was struggling to get a hold of himself.

"You nearly shot me," he said breathlessly. "Why?"

"What do you know about Robby Tyson's escape and murder?" Alexa demanded.

Ryan turned a lighter shade of pale. "Oh God. It's about those letters, isn't it?"

Alexa nodded, her eyes hard.

"Look, I'm a writer. I go by the pen name Anton Black. I write BDSM novels. That's how I make my living. I've interviewed lots of killers and criminals. They give me so much insight, so much inspiration." He began to get animated. "They're such a treasure trove of information. For a few dollars' worth of candy and cigarettes, they open up to me and launch ideas for an entire series of novels."

"Why did you break off your correspondence with Tyson?" Stuart asked.

"Because I got what I needed. I wasn't going to waste any more time with that scumbag."

"Scumbag?" Alexa asked, surprised.

"He hurts people without their consent. That's wrong."

Alexa's doubts grew. They had started when she had seen his black hair, got worse when that weird woman defended him, and now solidified into a certainty.

Ryan Deanfeld wasn't a killer, just a sad, twisted individual playing out his fantasies in a house in the middle of nowhere.

* * *

Stuart drove them back up into the pine forests of Prescott National Forest. The sun was setting, turning the pine needles golden, but Alexa had no eye for natural beauty at the moment. They kept coming up on dead ends.

Ryan Deanfeld's story checked out. They had searched on his computer with his consent and found timestamped emails that showed he wasn't anywhere near the scenes of the murders. He also proudly showed his profile on a popular BDSM hookup site where he had a

Gold Star ranking for "his technical skill as a master and his contributions to the community through his literature."

The "literature" included such titles as *Chained and Loving It*, *Kiss the Whip*, and *Bondage Beatdown.* Alexa wouldn't be adding any of those to her Kindle anytime soon.

When they left, they had decided to return to Tyson's cabin, where the CSI team was just finishing up, hoping they'd find something.

That was a bit of a long shot. It would have been quicker to bypass the mountains and national park and go straight back to Phoenix, but they had no overriding reason to return to the big city. In fact, they had no idea where they should go, but something she had read in Powers's journal had made her decide to give the cabin a second look.

"When you get stuck on a case and aren't sure what to do next, it's always good to go back to the beginning. Try to see the case as if you're looking at it for the first time. You might see something you missed."

And so this desperate return to the place where the prison escapee met his end.

As Stuart drove carefully up the rutted dirt road that passed close to the cabin, Alexa radioed ahead.

"Calling any unit at the Tyson cabin, this is Deputy U.S. Marshal Chase. What's the situation there?"

"This is Officer Rogers of the Arizona Highway Patrol. The CSI boys are wrapping up. They went through everything. You come to talk with them?"

"Yes. We're hoping to find some more leads." She decided not to announce on air that all their other leads had gone bust.

"All right. I'll tell them to wait."

Stuart stopped the car when the trail got too rough, parking next to a Highway Patrol vehicle.

"Looks like we're walking the next half mile," he grumbled.

"I thought you'd be used to marching," she said as they got out.

He clicked the button on his keychain to lock the car. The electronic *bloop bleep* sounded jarring in the quiet, cool forest.

"I've been on marches so long I lost two or three inches of height in a day," he said with a smile. "I used to be six-five."

"Well, that didn't stop your heroism," Alexa said as they walked the same faint forest trail they had crossed a couple of days before.

"Oh, none of that. Every man and woman in uniform is a hero, especially those who saw active service."

"Don't be so modest. They don't hand out Bronze Stars and Purple Hearts in cereal boxes."

Alexa did not expect the reaction she got. Stuart's head snapped around and he gave her a suspicious look. "Who told you that?"

Taken aback, Alexa shrugged. "I read it."

His frowned deepened. They had stopped now, facing each other.

"Read it where?" he demanded.

"Geez, Stuart. I don't know why it matters. I read it in an FBI newsletter in an article about you getting that commendation."

Stuart put his fists on his hips. "Why the hell are you researching me?"

"Whoa! Calm down. I just wanted to know more about who I'm working with."

"You're working with an FBI agent. That's all you need to know. Now let's get going. We have a psycho to catch."

He stalked off down the path. Alexa followed along in silence, utterly confused. Why would this bother him so much? It's not like she was digging up dirt on him.

Unless there's dirt to dig up.

Alexa pushed that thought aside as unworthy of him. Stuart was a war hero and had shown an equal degree of heroism in law enforcement. If he didn't want people looking into his past, it was for some other reason.

The war?

Whatever it was, she didn't dare ask. He looked furious, and they walked the whole way in silence until they clambered over a ridge and saw the Tyson cabin on the next eminence.

And then all thoughts about Stuart's odd reaction vanished, because she had something more to think about.

An Action News film crew had gathered not far away from the cabin, and Alexa's sister-in-law Melanie stood speaking into a microphone with the cabin as a backdrop.

CHAPTER SEVENTEEN

Alexa wanted to turn right back around and head for the car but she didn't want to explain that to Stuart, not in the mood he was in. Plus she had a job to do.

Taking a deep breath, they descended the far side of the ridge, walking along the broad grassy swale and up the other ridge to the cabin, keeping well away from the camera crew.

That didn't work.

Melanie rushed over, her camera crew hurrying to keep up. Despite Alexa's annoyance, she had to admire her sister-in-law for being able to run through the woods in heels. Alexa could barely walk along a sidewalk in them.

"Don't worry, Alexa!" Melanie shouted just as she was opening her mouth to tell her to go away. "We're not on the air. We couldn't carry the satellite uplink all the way out here."

"We don't—"

"So I'm not asking for a recorded interview, but if you could just give some comments about the case."

Stuart cursed and pushed away a camera shoved in his face.

"I don't have time for this, Melanie," Alexa said.

"So you're saying this investigation is a race against the clock, that the copycat killer might strike again soon?"

"I didn't say that. We're following some leads and now I need to consult with the CSI team to go over the evidence."

"So you're saying some evidence was missed."

Stuart glared at Alexa's sister-in-law. He looked even angrier than Alexa was.

"I'm not saying that at all," Alexa went on, struggling to keep her voice level. "It's just that CSI investigations take a long time and we need to consult with the team to find out what they've discovered."

"So you're saying you're frustrated with the investigators dragging their feet?"

"I'm not saying anything except no comment," Alexa snapped.

She and Stuart walked up the ridge, Melanie and the camera crew following them and only stopping when they got to the police tape. As

Alexa and her partner ducked under the tape, finally making it to safety, Melanie called out,

"Would you be available for an interview after you catch the killer?"

Alexa rounded on her, raising an angry finger to point at her. "No, I would not. And don't misquote me in your story. Don't quote me at all. And leave Stacy alone."

Melanie flicked her perfectly teased hair, a habit Alexa knew she did when she was nervous. "She's a good kid. I'm glad you're helping her. I think it would be a great human interest story. Tough cop helps out troubled daughter of alcoholic parents. That trailer they live in—"

Alexa ducked back under the police tape and strode up to within an inch of her sister-in-law. Melanie flicked her hair again but did not retreat.

"You've been sniffing around the Carpenter home?"

Melanie snorted. "If you can call it that."

"When?"

"Oh, I wanted to give Stacy a gift. Remember how she told us over dinner she liked musicals? The station got a couple of tickets to *The King and I* and she might—"

"Then you talk to me. You don't go sneaking behind my back. What did the Carpenters say?"

"Well, Stacy was in town with friends, and they didn't say much. They were pretty far gone. Judging from the inside of that trailer that sounds like their usual state."

"But their being drunk didn't stop you from interviewing them, right?"

Another flick of the hair. "I was concerned about Stacy's welfare. We all are. You saw how big of a hit she made at the ranch. You don't have to do this alone, Alexa. You—"

"You're only doing this to get some story for your own damn career. Back off!"

Alexa felt a hand on her shoulder. Stuart. His eyes smoldered and his forehead was furrowed in a deep frown. She couldn't tell if he was still angry at her, had shifted his anger to Melanie, or was just angry at everything.

"Let's go. We got work to do," he said.

"Don't arrest any more hunters just because they're wearing orange," the cameraman snickered.

Stuart shot him a look and he and Alexa turned, went back under the police tape, and up to the crime scene.

Alexa didn't dare look back. She didn't want to know what her sister-in-law was up to now.

What could she do about this? Melanie had been acting all friendly to Stacy, hoping for an angle to a story, but she should never have approached the kid's parents. She had gone way over the line.

The most frustrating thing was that Alexa couldn't do a damn thing about it. Not right now. She had a murder scene in front of her.

The CSI team was in the final stages of packing up. A highway patrolman and a park ranger stood nearby.

Alexa collected herself and walked up to the Flagstaff CSI team. One of them turned to her.

"They told me you wanted to know if we found more evidence."

"That's right," Alexa said, her voice coming out in a low growl despite her efforts to control it. Melanie really got under her skin.

The forensics expert made a little frown, probably wondering why this deputy marshal was angry at him. "We found a hair sample. Blond. We spoke with Dr. Guevara down in Phoenix and compared the sample with the one she got off the body in El Rio Park. Perfect match."

"Good," Stuart said. "That doesn't get us any closer to the murderer, though."

The CSI man spread out his hands. "Sorry, but most of what we get helps convict, not catch."

"Got anything else for us?" Alexa asked, managing to put a better tone into her words this time.

"No. We couldn't get a good footprint match. Approximately a men's size ten or eleven, just like in El Rio Park. No idea what kind of a shoe it was, but it was a shoe and not a boot. We would have gotten a clear print off of the forest waste on the porch, that leaves perfect prints, but you guys walked all over it."

Alexa did not hear any criticism in that statement. They had been bursting in thinking they were going to apprehend a fugitive, after all. Still, it was a bit embarrassing.

"Sorry," Alexa said, as much for her previous tone as for destroying evidence. "I suppose no fingerprints?"

"None, except on the plastic bags, but we already matched those to the guy Tyson stuck up. So no help there. And we didn't find any unusual items. Nothing that Tyson didn't either bring himself or that hadn't been sitting in this cabin for years. And there wasn't much of that either. Some old pots and pans. Some canned goods way past their sell by date, an orange hunting jacket, and some issues of *Field and Stream* from 2011."

Alexa bit her lip. So another dead end. She had tried to go back to the beginning and she had come up short.

Except something tickled the back of her mind, something Melanie's cameraman had said. She had ignored it as a stupid comment at the time, but the CSI guy had jogged her memory.

The orange hunting jacket in the cabin … the cameraman joking how they grabbed a hunter thinking it was Robby Tyson. He had been wearing an orange hunting jacket that some citizen had mistaken for a prison jumpsuit.

The Bullhead City police saw the mistake immediately but kept him all the same because he had been out in the desert with a gun at night. He had claimed to be hunting, but people generally don't hunt at night and so that aroused suspicion.

But if this guy was up to no good in the desert, why bring attention to himself by wearing bright clothing? Or did he want to bring attention to himself?

Did he want to be brought in to distract the police while the real escapee snuck off?

Her excitement mounting at the half-formed idea in her head, Alexa took Stuart by the elbow and led him away from the cabin a little, getting out of sight of Melanie and her camera crew, who waited patiently to harass them once they left the crime scene. Alexa wouldn't put it past them to zoom in with their camera and try to read their lips.

Stuart looked at her curiously as they stopped behind the cabin. She could still see the annoyance stamped on his features, but that was being replaced with a professional level of attention to what she was about to say. She'd have to make up to him about her slip later. Right now they had a murder to solve.

"We have never answered the question of how Robby Tyson got the key to his handcuffs," she said. "Prison officials checked and there were no missing keys. The guards certainly didn't loan Tyson a key, so where did it come from?"

"From an outsider, or a fellow prisoner," Stuart said.

"Except a fellow prisoner doesn't make any sense. Why let Tyson go and not release yourself?"

"True enough."

Tyson had made few friends on the inside. He had kept to himself. He hadn't been a charismatic figure like Drake Logan who could command respect and obedience.

"So an outsider then," Alexa went on, an idea growing in her mind. "Someone who had somehow made a copy of a key. Someone who knew that Tyson was on the work crew and where that work crew would be."

"And he also knew about this cabin," Stuart said, looking at the remote little structure.

"Anyone who would go through all that trouble to get Tyson out would want to make sure he got clean away."

"So he could kill him later and take over his role as the Southwest Slasher. This is getting way too convoluted."

Alexa grunted in agreement. "That's for sure. But who distracted the police and made them go in the wrong direction?"

Stuart's brow furrowed. "You're not thinking of that hunter in Bullhead City?"

"Why not? Is that behavior any stranger than breaking out a serial killer just to kill him?"

Stuart stared off into space for a moment, and began to murmur the very words that she had been thinking a moment before. "Why hunt at night? So as not to be seen? Then why wear a bright hunting jacket? Damn, that's a stretch but we should look into it!"

He pulled out his phone, his previous anger vanished now that he had another lead. Alexa immediately felt better. This man was a good partner, and whatever landmine she had inadvertently stepped on would not kill their working relationship.

He frowned at the screen, held the phone high in the air, and frowned again.

"No signal. Why is it I never get a signal working in this state?"

"You're in a national forest. Some places shouldn't have phone coverage."

The joke fell flat. Stuart put his phone away and said, "Let's get to the park entrance. You mentioned there was a cell phone tower there."

"All right, but we need to avoid that camera crew. If we cut along that ravine there, we can get on the other side of that ridge and work our way around them and get back to the car."

"That's a waste of time," Stuart objected.

"Not as much time as my sister-in-law will make us waste."

"Good point," the FBI man grumbled. "They might even follow us. We can't have that happen. Let's go."

They hurried off through the woods, their sense of urgency giving them speed. Alexa wasn't sure if this hunter had anything to do with it, but he was another piece of the puzzle that hadn't been put in its place.

And anyone sneaking around the desert in the middle of the night with a gun was obviously up to no good.

CHAPTER EIGHTEEN

As soon as Stuart drove them close enough to the park entrance for her to get a signal, Alexa called the Bullhead City police department. The officer who answered put her through to his chief.

"Hello, Chief Gregors, this is Deputy U.S. Marshal Chase. I was wondering if you could tell me about that hunter you detained a couple of days ago on suspicion of being the escaped prisoner Robby Tyson?"

"Now wait a minute, Deputy Marshal," Chief Gregor snapped without bothering to say hello, "The media twisted that whole story into a pretzel. We did not detain that man on suspicion of being an escaped prisoner. We arrested him on suspicious behavior and suspicion of illegal hunting at night."

Alexa remembered the Bullhead City cop standing on top of his car joyfully shouting, "We got him! We got him!" She decided not to mention that.

"Could you tell me more about the suspect and what led you to detain him?"

"Gladly. I want to set the record straight. We never, I repeat never, thought that man was Robby Tyson."

"I never thought you did, sir," Alexa replied, rolling her eyes.

"Good. Now the suspect's name is Keith Hutton. He lives out near Oatman in a trailer. Works part time as an odd jobs man, roofing and such like. Also does some repaving for private and state folks. Works as little as he can, as far as I can see. His trailer is falling apart and he drives an old banger of a pickup. We've cited him three times for broken taillights or expired insurance."

"Does he have any other charges on his sheet?"

"What, haven't you heard?" Police Chief Gregors sounded surprised.

"No."

"It's all over the media."

"I don't pay attention to the media when I'm on a case."

The officer laughed. "Good girl! They never get anything right anyway. Doesn't matter which channel you listen to, they all got an axe to grind and even when they don't, they still make mistakes by accident instead of on purpose. Keith Hutton got charged for assaulting a woman with a knife a couple of years back."

"What?" Alexa said this so loudly Stuart turned to look, almost missing the turn on the winding mountain road they were descending at seventy miles an hour.

"Bar fight. We get a lot of them around here. He got into an altercation with some fellow. At first it was just fists. Keith Hutton knocked the guy down. He's a big guy and the other man must have been pretty drunk to think he could take him on. Well, the guy decided to even the odds. Picked up a beer bottle in each hand and charged Hutton. So Hutton draws a hunting knife he had on his belt. Self-defense, the way I see it. Just then the other man's girlfriend, who is drunker than both of them put together, leaps on Hutton and tried to claw his eyes out. She gets cut and goes down. Not cut too badly, but she pressed charges."

"Did he do time?"

"He claimed it was an accident, that he brought up his arm to protect his face and didn't mean to cut her. The defense made a lot of the fact that he got a lacerated eyeball. The prosecution made a lot of the fact that he laughed at her as she lay bleeding."

"Sounds like a charming individual."

"Oh yes. He's a model citizen around these parts. He ended up winning the case because she's even more of a model citizen. She's lacerated three other eyeballs in the past five years. The boys around here call her the Killer Kitten."

"And the media picked up on this and compared it to the Southwest Slasher murders?"

"That's right."

Alexa thought for a moment. The media might have been saying more than they knew. What if Hutton got a taste for cutting female flesh from that incident, and a resentment against women after having his eye scratched? Or maybe that had been building before and he let it slip at the bar.

Then Police Chief Gregors said something that made Alexa wonder even more.

"He's taken to stalking around the desert at night. Been getting a lot of complaints about him the past few months. When we talked to him he always denied it was him, and because it was night the neighbors couldn't say a hundred percent it was him, but we all knew it was."

Alexa didn't ask how they knew. In these small towns and rural areas where everyone knew everyone else, people got to understand each other's behavior. Often you didn't even need a witness to know who had committed a crime.

"But you finally caught him the other night," she prompted.

"That's right. The whole state was going crazy about the Robby Tyson escape, and that night at about two in the morning we got a call about someone out in the desert in an orange jumpsuit. That's what the media jumped on as being a description of the escapee. We never believed that." Once again, Alexa said nothing. "So we go out and catch Keith Hutton sneaking around the desert."

"Doing what?"

"He said he was hunting coyotes but we held him on a charge of illegal hunting. As you probably know, coyotes are one of the only animals you're allowed to hunt at night, and with all the other crimes he's committed, we wanted to check his property for evidence of illegal hunting. Didn't find any. Also got him on criminal trespass because he cut across the witness's land, but the witness didn't want to press charges so we dropped that."

"And where's Hutton now?"

"I guess he's at his trailer or one of his repaving jobs. I'll text you the address if you want it. I need to look it up."

"Please do. Thank you."

Alexa hung up. For a moment she watched the scenery go by. They were going around a curve in the mountain road. The last of the pine trees had given way to shrubs and cacti as they descended, and over a guardrail and cliff she could see the desert spread out before her, a mottling of browns and yellows with the distant green specks of mesquite and cacti. She allowed herself a serene moment to absorb this beauty before getting back on the phone.

This time she called Kingman Prison. She had a hunch.

It took some time to get the head supervisor. Once she did, she asked if Keith Hutton had ever worked for them.

"Sure did," the man said. "A lot of folks around here have bad things to say about Keith but he's good at repaving work. Some of the boys who work here hang out with him. That's how he got the recommendation to do the repaving earlier this year."

Alexa gripped the phone a little tighter.

"Inside or outside the wire?"

"Both."

"How long did that job take?"

"Not sure. A couple of weeks, I guess."

"So he had access to the inside of the prison."

"Yup. Don't worry, our security is pretty tight."

Alexa blinked. This man just said those words the same week a suspected serial killer escaped from a chain gang?

"You mentioned Keith Hutton was friends with some of the guards?"

"Most of them. Oh, I know what you're thinking, why would prison guards hang out with someone with a record? Well, good old Keith is a really nice guy, and never did anything really bad. Everyone's had a broken taillight at one time or another, and the Killer Kitten? That bi—I mean woman—had what was coming to her."

Alexa, struggling to control her irritation, asked, "So when was this job Mr. Hutton did?"

"A few weeks ago."

"And had he worked for Kingman prison before?"

"A couple of times. Paving work like before. State regs say we got to maintain it good, but they don't give us enough budget. Hutton works cheap."

"Thank you."

She hung up, and found the police chief of Bullhead City had sent her Keith Hutton's address. She also saw that the signal in her phone was almost gone. They were rapidly getting out of distance of the cell phone tower at the park entrance and there wouldn't be another one for a while. Before she lost the signal, she texted back to the police chief asking for the locations where Keith Hutton had been spotted on his nighttime forays.

Then she settled back to think of the possibilities. It was a long way to the little town of Oatman, and she was glad for Stuart's quick driving.

There was something pretty damn suspicious about Keith Hutton.

* * *

Like a lot of towns in rural Arizona, Oatman barely qualified for the term. With a population of just over a hundred, it was mostly a single street of real or fake Old West buildings and similarly themed tourist shops with false fronts and names such as the Lucky Strike Old West Jewelry Shop and the Shoot 'Em Up Saloon. The old mining town had nearly gone extinct like so many others, but had reinvented itself. Now the small band of locals made a living by reliving the past.

Stuart chuckled as they passed through the town. "How are you on your fast draw, Marshal?" he asked in a fake Western drawl. "We might have to fight some banditos in these here parts."

"We might at that," she said, feeling relieved that he had finally cracked a joke. He had been pretty quiet for the past couple of hours. "Keep your eyes on the road."

"Why? We've already passed through town. Not that it took long. Whoa!"

Stuart slammed on the brakes as a wild burro wandered out from behind a sign and right into his lane.

"That's why," Alexa said.

"What the hell was that?" Stuart asked, driving around the animal, which looked nonchalantly at the passing car.

"A wild burro. Didn't you see the sign saying 'Beware wild burros'?"

"Yeah, I thought it was a joke."

"Nope. They're the descendants of the burros that used to haul loads for the prospectors. They're all over the area."

"Jesus. It nearly killed us."

"Maybe you should drive slower."

"Maybe this state should be more friendly to human beings. I'll tolerate getting killed by some maniac. I'll even accept getting offed by a scorpion or a rattlesnake. But I will absolutely not stand for getting killed by some wandering donkey."

"Burro. A donkey is domesticated. Nowadays the Spanish term *burro* is applied to wild donkeys."

"OK, Merriam-Webster, where's this guy's trailer?"

Alexa checked the GPS while Stuart kept his eyes on the road for once.

"Next left, then a mile down."

The narrow two-lane Oatman Highway was flanked by rough rocky hills dotted with cholla cacti and low shrubs. The rough terrain made it hard to see far. Here and there they caught a glimpse of a trailer or prefab home half hidden behind some hill. The people here liked their privacy.

So did Keith Hutton, apparently. As with so many suspects Alexa had chased, he lived at the end of a dirt road that had no other houses and thus no reason for stranger to drive down it. Stuart took it slow, his gaze once again darting here and there. This was a more dangerous approach than some others. The terrain here was perfect for an ambush, and Hutton was a hunter. No doubt he had a high-powered rifle and probably a scope. Both Stuart and Alexa sat low in their seats.

They came around a bend and suddenly they were there. A small trailer stood in an open graveled lot. On top of it was a solar panel, and a water pump beside it no doubt led to the water main that paralleled the highway. To the side stood an asphalt layer machine and a pallet stacked with bags of material. Alexa also spotted a flatbed but no pickup or other vehicle.

"Looks like Hutton isn't home," Alexa said.

"Let's take a look around."

Stuart parked, and despite it appearing that no one was home, still got out hunched behind the door, hand resting on the gun in his shoulder holster. Alexa followed suit.

For a moment they listened. All they head was a faint *clack clack* from the water pump that obviously needed adjusting, and the distant swoosh of a car passing along the Oatman Highway.

Satisfied they were probably alone, they took their eyes off the trailer and surrounding hills and looked at the tracks on the ground. A pickup truck had passed by here numerous times. There didn't seem to be any trails heading anywhere else, or even a place for a pickup truck to go except along the track on which they had come. So Keith Hutton really was gone.

Alexa felt a mixture of frustration and relief.

They headed for the trailer. The weathered door was locked and the curtain on the one grubby window drawn. Circling around it, they noticed a prefab building about ten feet to a side tucked in a little ravine. They couldn't see it from the drive. Alexa had no doubt that was deliberate.

Alexa and Stuart exchanged glances. Without a word they headed for it.

Halfway there, Alexa stopped, cocking an ear as she heard another vehicle on the highway. It passed.

They moved to the prefab. It had no windows, more like a large storage shed than an outbuilding.

Hope we don't find another bondage scene. One was enough for a lifetime.

Alexa tried the door and found it unlocked.

She opened it, then stepped back and gasped at the sights and smells that came out at her.

CHAPTER NINETEEN

Alexa gagged. The interior of the prefab was filled with carcasses.

Hanging on meat hooks attached to the ceiling were at least a dozen coyotes in various stages of decomposition. The nearest one was crawling with maggots.

Alexa took a step back, covering her nose and mouth.

Stuart took a step forward and peered inside.

"No people, just wolves," he said.

"Coyotes," Alexa corrected, retreating a little further. "How can you stand the smell?"

"Ever come across a mass grave? I mean a mass human grave?"

"No."

"Once you've smelled that, you can take anything short of that."

Alexa grimaced. The smell of a decomposing human being was the worst smell imaginable, hitting hard against a person's most basic instincts. She had smelled that more times than she cared to count. But a mass grave? No, she had never had to endure that.

"What the hell is he doing?" Alexa wondered out loud.

"Psychopathic behavior," Stuart said. "Collecting dead things is a classic symptom."

Alexa held her breath, stepped forward, and took a closer look. After a long moment, she stepped back to take another breath.

"No signs of torture, though," she said. "Psychopaths like to torture animals as a stage in the escalation to killing humans."

Stuart closed the door. "Is shooting coyotes legal in this state? I've been studying Arizona state law but I haven't gotten to hunting laws yet."

"Yes, it is."

"What about hunting them at night?"

"That's legal too. Hunting some animals at night is illegal, though. And remember he was spotted on private property at least once."

They started walking back to the trailer.

"Well, I'm sure that mess in there violates some health codes, so I think we have probable cause to enter the residence," the FBI man said.

"Agreed."

They passed the trailer and returned to the car. Stuart popped the trunk, and Alexa pulled out a crowbar and walked back to the trailer, setting the end between the door and the doorframe. A quick jerk snapped the door open.

Alexa and Stuart peered inside and saw a cramped space. There was a dirty kitchenette, an unmade bed, and a little sitting area with a TV.

"You can get reception out here?" Stuart muttered. He stepped back from the trailer and looked at the small satellite dish on top. "Bingo! He's got an illegal descrambler. At a stretch we can hold him on that."

"I'd rather prove something a bit more serious," Alexa said, stepping in to the trailer. Stuart joined her.

There wasn't much inside and it didn't take long to search. They found a couple of boxes of .30-06 rifle ammunition, a hunting knife, and little else.

"No women's clothing or jewelry," Stuart said, going through the dresser. "But our guy didn't take any obvious trophies."

"Yeah, Tyson and this copycat killer both hate women. They probably don't want any female items in their house."

Alexa moved over to the kitchenette and looked through the small cupboard. Besides a few canned goods, there were several bottles of bottom-shelf whiskey and vodka, and a large bag of cat food.

Wait, cat food?

She had seen any cats. She looked closer at the cheap carpet on the floor. Mixed with the dirt and sand, she saw hairs from at least two cats, a tabby and a white-haired cat.

"You seen any cats around here?" Alexa asked.

"No. It's too hot for any cats to be out right now. They're probably hiding in the shade until the sun gets lower."

"That's just it. There's no shade around here except for under the trailer, and there was nothing under the trailer."

"I'm a little more worried about our missing suspect than a missing cat," Stuart said.

"Sure. But it's still odd. My old partner always said, 'If any detail about a scene strikes you as odd, keep it in your mind, no matter how trivial it seems.'"

"Wise words. I wish I had met him." Stuart said this softly, and with obvious sympathy. Alexa recognized an olive branch when she saw one.

She put her hand on his shoulder. "Let's go take a look around the surrounding desert."

Stuart smiled. "Great. Tromping around the desert in the heat. Seems like it's all I do these days."

Alexa checked her watch. Another hour until sunset. Twilight would give them a good forty-five minutes after that of decent visibility. Time enough to search the area.

Alexa left the trailer and made a wide circle around the lot. She spotted two faint trails of boot prints going off into the surrounding hills, both headed away from the highway. She picked one at random and they walked along it.

The trail led them along a gritty swale between a pair of rough hills, their steep slopes covered in loose stones. Alexa spotted the tracks of jackrabbits and javelina and coyotes as well as the human ones.

About three hundred yards from the trailer, as the trail curved around behind a hill, they came across their first body.

The rotted corpse of a coyote lay on the ground, baked almost to leather by the sun. It barely smelled it was so dried out. Since most of its flesh had been picked away by buzzards, it took some time before she noticed the bullet hole in its flank.

Alexa looked around. The caw of a buzzard gave her a clue where to look next.

Following the sound over a low hill and down into a ravine, they found the next coyote.

This one was riper, with flesh still on it. Half a dozen buzzards stood around it, picking away at the remains.

"This guy's got something against coyotes," Stuart said.

Alexa only nodded.

They made a wide circle around the lot, and found coyotes lying dead all around. Some were nearly skeletons. Others looked like they had been dead only for a short while. They also found bits of flesh and fur nearer to the lot, and traces of where Keith Hutton had dragged the bodies to their positions.

"Strange," Alexa muttered as they returned to the lot. The sun was low on the horizon now. "From what it looks like, he's hunting them elsewhere, then keeping them in that prefab for a bit to let them rot before dragging them out around his property."

"Everyone's got to have a hobby," Stuart said with a shrug.

"Very funny. I think he's marking his territory. Keeping the coyotes away by putting down bodies. Every species avoids the dead of their own species. It's primal avoidance of danger."

"But why? To protect his cats?"

"Maybe." Then Alexa snapped her fingers. "No! It's revenge."

"What? The coyotes ate his cats?"

"They're known for that. They'll eat small dogs too."

"Filthy animals. I might start hunting them myself."

"Lots of people do. Keith Hutton seems to have taken it to another level."

Stuart looked around. "I don't know much about hunting, but I'm thinking he couldn't have bagged so many coyotes just in this area. After taking out three or four they probably cleared out. So he's wandering around at night shooting them and bringing them back here. That's … weird. Like really, really weird."

"Makes me wonder what else he's doing."

"Big time."

Alexa sat in the car and turned on the GPS. She had entered all the locations where Hutton had been seen hunting at night. She had also instructed the local police to inform them if they spotted Hutton anywhere. So far, no word. He hadn't been seen in a couple of days.

And that made Alexa nervous.

She noticed from the dates of the sightings that Hutton was slowly moving westward, cutting across the hilly desert in his quest for more coyotes to kill.

Alexa traced a finger along the route. Stuart, sitting next to her out of the heat, nodded.

"Looks like we have a pattern, but how is he getting there? That's a long way to walk and the police chief says he's got a crappy old pickup. No way he could get over this terrain. You'd need a Hummer or at least a Jeep."

Stuart reached for the GPS. Alexa hit it first, changing it from a map to a satellite view. A faint track ran right through Hutton's hunting areas.

"Great minds think alike," Stuart said. "Let's go get something to eat at Oatmeal—"

"Oatman."

"—and then head out once it's dark. No point trying to hunt the hunter until he's out there."

"Right," Alexa said. Her brow furrowed in a worried frown. "What I'm wondering is where he is now."

* * *

The night air was still. No wind rustled through the dried shrubs, and no animal sounds disturbed the silence. Alexa looked around with an increasing amount of unease. Silence in nature was a sign of trouble. When animals got quiet, it was because they were scared. And if they were scared, that meant they sensed a predator.

Humans didn't generally have that effect, unless they caught the scent of a human they knew was dangerous.

Had Keith Hutton killed so much that the local wildlife had learned to fear him as much as a mountain lion or a bobcat?

It was possible. Another possibility was that one of Arizona's large felines was on the prowl. A bobcat would be no great danger, they avoided humans, but a mountain lion would jump on a person just as readily as on a rabbit.

Alexa decided she didn't need to warn her partner, who was pacing through the desert more alert than anyone she had ever seen. She wondered if this brought up bad memories of Iraq. She suspected so, given how he reacted to her mention of his medals.

But he got just as mad when she mentioned the commendation he got at the FBI. Strange.

The two of them walked on either side of the rough track they had spotted on the satellite view. It was little more than two ruts in the sandy grit of the desert floor, and a few crushed cacti. The whole desert was crisscrossed with such trails, shortcuts for off-road vehicles. They ruined the desert habitat, but it was impossible to stop people from making them.

This track ran along a relatively flat area of desert between two chains of hills visible only as black silhouettes against the starry dome of the sky. Alexa figured Hutton could get his pickup truck along this route with little trouble.

But where was the pickup, and where was Hutton? They had parked a mile back and hadn't seen any sign of life.

They continued to pace forward, eyes and ears alert. Stuart had brought along a pair of army surplus desert boots ("I'm sick of scuffing my dress shoes in this damn desert") and now he moved just as sure-footed and comfortable as she did in her cowboy boots. They would help protect him against rattlers and scorpions too.

But not against Keith Hutton.

Where was he, anyway? They hadn't heard any shots, any distant engine, nothing.

She got her answer a minute later, when they caught the faint gleam of starshine off a distant windshield.

Alexa motioned to Stuart, but he had already seen it and stopped, looking around him with a tense energy visible even in the nearly nonexistent light.

She stopped too, listening for several moments. Nothing. Keith Hutton had either moved a long way from his vehicle, or was lying in wait to bag another coyote.

At least he wouldn't attack any women out here. These rural desert tracks didn't get used much even in the daytime, and hardly at all at night.

They moved forward. The pickup truck became more visible to them. It was closer than Alexa had thought. Judging distance in such poor light was difficult.

If Hutton can kill dozens of coyotes in conditions like this, then he must be a crack shot, Alexa thought.

They reached the pickup truck. No one was inside or nearby, but Alexa caught a faint whiff from the bed. Peering in, she saw something white, about the side of a coffee table book. She reached in and discovered it was butcher paper that smelled of fresh meat.

So Hutton was baiting the animals. He was clever as well as a good shot.

Alexa looked around and saw two likely routes he could have taken. One was a roughly flat area over a field of stones to a low bluff that gave a good view of the surrounding terrain. A good place for a hunter who had night vision goggles. Alexa had no idea whether Hutton had such equipment. Those didn't come cheap, and from all accounts Hutton wasn't the richest guy in the world.

The other route was a clearer area that led through an area of shrub and cacti to an area of boulders before rising into a series of hills. Alexa suspected there to be ground water close to the surface here, judging by the greater amount of vegetation. In the desert, of course, this was all relative. The "ground water" was most likely damp sand fed by a slow seep from the uplands from condensation at dawn and the occasional rainfall. And "close to the surface" meant the roots of the desert plants had to push three or four yards down to get it.

Still, plants meant animals, and animals meant scavengers such as the coyote.

Alexa moved over to her partner.

"Let's go this way," she whispered.

"I bet he's prone on one of those boulders," Stuart whispered back. "With the meat right below."

"Yeah."

I guess an ambush is an ambush, whether you're hunting coyotes or humans, she thought. *Let's just hope Hutton doesn't decide to turn his gun on us.*

Alexa felt under-armed with only her service Glock in her hands. At least Stuart gripped the pump-action twelve-gauge shotgun he always kept in the trunk. And it was two against one.

But Hutton was already set up, knew the terrain, and if they were right about him being the killer, he would fire without hesitation.

No point thinking about that now. They had a suspect to apprehend.

They headed across the open area, keeping a good ten feet between them to make a harder target. Of course, if Stuart was right and he was lying on top of one of those boulders, and with night vision goggles on, they were both going to be dead in about ten seconds.

All they could hope for was that he was facing the other direction, up toward the hills and ravines that made a jagged shadow against the starry sky. The coyotes would most likely come from that direction.

Alexa heard a soft hiss from her partner. The FBI man stopped for a second, then continued on. Despite her heart hammering in her chest and the sweat trickling down her back, Alexa had to smile. He must have brushed against a cholla. Stuart hadn't gotten used to Arizona yet.

Slowly, with infinite care, they moved forward. The boulders loomed ahead. Soon they came to them, a scattering of rough spheres washed down from the uplands from centuries of monsoon storms like some giant's child carelessly tossing a handful of marbles.

Alexa cut to her left and stopped to confer with Stuart.

"Do you see that ravine at eleven o'clock?" she whispered. "The one with the righthand side a bit higher than the left-hand side?"

His answer came so softly as to almost be inaudible. "Yes."

"Looks like it's about half a mile away. We'll head for that, keeping apart a bit so we can cover more ground."

"Splitting up in the face of an entrenched enemy is bad tactics."

"We're here to arrest him, not take him out."

"Does he know that?"

"Good point. But in this large area at night, we'll never find him if we don't split up."

Stuart shrugged, an all but invisible gesture in the starlight, and they moved out, Stuart passing around one side of the boulder and Alexa cutting fifty yards to the right before moving for the ravine. The hills to either side of it were the tallest in the region, so despite the poor light she felt confident that even a city boy like Stuart wouldn't get lost.

Whatever he might have lacked in knowledge of his new environment, Stuart Barrett sure knew how to move silently. She didn't hear a thing from him as she paced forward, eyes and ears alert, gripping her pistol. She kept a special note of the silhouettes of the tops of the boulders. Stuart's suggestion that Hutton would be lying on top of one made sense. She looked for a unusual shape on each one, but it was hard to tell if a jagged edge was a shoulder, or a humped top was a man's back.

Maybe this is a bad idea, Alexa thought.

Then a faint smell made her stop and take notice.

The smell of meat.

CHAPTER TWENTY

Alexa froze, looking all around the darkened landscape with wide eyes. Keith Hutton was close, lying in wait to fire.

Should she call out to him? Identify herself and ask him to give himself up?

No. If he was guilty, he'd shoot her dead. If he was innocent, he'd slink off into the night and they'd never catch him. Hutton had had enough run-ins with the law that he wouldn't come quietly, serial killer or no serial killer.

She had to spot him and then make him surrender.

She sniffed. Licked a finger and held it up to the air. An almost undetectable breeze blew down from the ravine. Hutton must have placed the meat a bit further up.

Alexa glanced around one more time, wishing Stuart was here. There was no way to call for him without giving away her position. She couldn't even text. Not only would the light from her phone give her away, but there probably wasn't coverage way out here anyway.

She had to do this alone.

Moving forward, step by careful step, she tested each footfall to make sure she wouldn't dislodge a rock or crackle some dried twig. Despite her caution, she knew she wasn't being entirely silent. That was impossible in the desert at night. At least for someone who hadn't spent two tours of duty doing that to stay alive. Maybe she should switch from cowboy boots to desert combat boots.

Another ten yards. Twenty. The smell of meat grew stronger.

A soft rustle up ahead and a bit to her right. She turned. A movement. Then a blinding flash as a rifle shot cracked the still night air.

The bullet whizzed by her, the displaced air brushing her cheek. Alexa hit the dirt, her arm scraping a cactus and a sharp stone jabbing at her chest.

"U.S. Marshal!" she shouted, edging her way behind a rock that was far too small for her comfort. "Keith Hutton, give yourself up immediately or I'll fire!"

Fire at what?

She had no real idea where to fire. The flash, which still made a purple afterimage hover in her eyes, obscuring her vision, had come from a boulder not far ahead and a bit to the right.

Probably. It might have been that boulder a little beyond. A brief flash in near-darkness isn't exactly easy to locate.

For a long moment she heard nothing but the ringing in her ears and the faint sounds of movement to her left. That was Stuart. Hopefully.

Keeping down behind her rock, she shouted again. "Keith Hutton, this is—"

"Is that really the law?" a male voice shouted.

No, it's Santa Claus.

"Yes, Mr. Hutton. This is Deputy U.S. Marshal Alexa Chase. I want to talk to you."

Alexa decided not to mention Stuart. He wasn't making any more noise, and Hutton probably hadn't heard his initial movements thanks to the ringing in his own ears.

She bet Stuart had been smart and rushed for the scene in the few moments after the shot when Hutton's hearing would be the most impaired. Now he had gone silent and careful again.

"Sorry, Marshal," Hutton called. "I thought you were a coyote. I didn't hit you, did I?"

Alexa tried to figure out if that note of concern was genuine or not. She wasn't sure.

"No, you missed me. Barely. Put down your gun and approach with your hands up."

"I'm on public land, Marshal, and I'm only hunting coyotes. That's one hundred percent legal. I know my rights."

"You fired at an officer of the law. It is in my rights to detain you for questioning, now drop your gun and come out with your hands up."

She had figured out where he was now. The closer boulder. As Stuart had predicted, he lay prone on top of it, a dark lump on the black mass of stone. Only the slightest of movements showed her he was not rock himself.

"I apologize for firing at you, ma'am. That was not my intention. But you shouldn't have been sneaking around in the dark like that when a man's out hunting."

"I'm not going to discuss this further, Mr. Hutton. I want you to drop your gun and come out with your hands up right this instant."

"Now, Marshal, like I said I—"

"Freeze!" Stuart shouted. "Drop your weapon!"

"Jesus!" Hutton shouted. Metal clattered on stone. "My hands are up! My hand are up!"

Alexa stood and walked over to the boulder. In the faint starshine she could see a dark shape rise on top of it, arms raised to the sky. She rounded the boulder and saw Stuart aiming his gun at him. The rifle lay not far off.

Alexa grabbed it and put on the safety. Relief washed over her.

"Get on down from there," she ordered.

"I'm sorry," he said. "I'm real sorry."

Sorry you almost shot me or sorry you missed? You sure didn't drop that gun until Stuart had a bead on you.

He scrambled down the side of the rock and landed in front of them.

"Turn and put your hands on the boulder."

He did as he was told. Alexa slung the rifle across her back, holstered her gun, and, as Stuart covered her, patted him down.

She found nothing except a large hunting knife. She took it.

"Show me where your gear is," she told him. "We need to pack up your stuff and head to Bullhead City. We have some questions for you."

* * *

The small police station in Bullhead City had a carnival atmosphere. The night duty cops had all come in to stare at Keith Hutton, and Police Chief Gregors got out of bed and hurried down to the station.

Keith Hutton sat stewing inside the tiny interrogation room while in the observation room next door, local cops were giving each other high fives and congratulating Alexa.

No one was happier than Police Chief Gregors.

"I knew he was our man the moment we nabbed him the first time," he boasted. "But those damn journalists kept whining about how we got the wrong guy. Sure, he wasn't Tyson, but he was the copycat. And now we got him."

He shook Alexa's hand for the fifth time that evening. Alexa kept her face a mask. This guy turned to the prevailing wind faster than a weathervane.

"Thank you so much, Deputy Marshal. And you too, Special Agent. You've really put Bullhead City on the map."

"I think we should go interrogate the suspect now," Alexa said.

"Suspect?" Police Chief Gregors looked confused. "Oh! The suspect."

He accentuated this last word with obvious sarcasm and air quotes.

Alexa bit her lip and didn't say the first thing she wanted to say, or the second. Instead she managed to grumble, "We need to clear some things up about this case. Since my partner and I have been in the investigation from the beginning and seen all the crime scenes, I'd like the two of us to be present."

"Of course," Police Chief Gregors said. "I'll go in too. I know him pretty well. Hell, every lawman in the county knows him well."

That got a laugh from everyone present except Alexa and Stuart. They moved out of the observation room and unlocked the interrogation room door. Keith Hutton sat sullen in one corner, his hands handcuffed to a metal chair bolted to the floor. There were only two other seats in the room. Gregors sat in one with a contented sigh. Stuart and Alexa remained standing.

Hutton was a handsome, muscular man in his early forties. Alexa judged his shoe size to be eleven, within the range of the footprints both CSI teams had found at the murder scenes, and his hair was blond and cut short, just like the hair at El Rio Park.

Alexa took a deep breath and spoke.

"So tell us again, for the record, what you were doing out in the desert at night."

"Hunting coyotes. I got some meat from Safeway that was past its sell-by date. One of the checkout girls always saves it for me. They can't sell it but it's still good enough to attract those parasites. I use it as bait."

"So why did you shoot at a marshal instead?" Gregors asked.

Hutton raised his hands as much as he could, palms outward as if to deflect the words.

"I didn't know it was a person. She didn't identify herself. All I saw was a shape sneaking through the desert toward my meat. So I fired. Thank God I didn't hit her."

"Good thing for you." Gregors snorted, crossing his arms over his chest.

Alexa made a quieting motion to him and turned back to Hutton.

"We searched your trailer and outbuilding." Hutton's eyes widened. "We found your collection of dead coyotes. Why are you killing so many of them?"

"They ate my cats," Hutton replied in hurt tones.

Laughter erupted on the other side of the one-way glass. Hutton and Alexa both turned and frowned at the wall.

These idiots didn't soundproof this place?

Alexa turned back to Hutton and said, "So you decided to kill a bunch of coyotes."

"Nothing illegal in that," Hutton grumbled, shooting an angry look at the wall again.

"Something illegal in shooting at an officer of the law," the police chief snapped.

Again Alexa raised a calming hand. She wished he would stop talking and let her carry on with the interrogation.

"Can you verify your whereabouts for the last three days and nights?"

Suddenly Hutton looked worried. "What do you mean?"

"Where have you been for the last three days and nights?" Alexa repeated, knowing he was stalling. A common technique with nervous suspects, and a transparent one too.

"Y'all know where I was the night you arrested me," he grunted.

At a late enough hour that you could have helped Robby Tyson escape and easily gotten back to this part of the state.

"What about the rest of the time?" Alexa asked.

"Hanging out," Hutton said with a shrug.

"Hanging out where?"

The suspect did not met her eye. "At my trailer. Or driving around."

"Have you been working these past few days?"

"No."

"Go to the store at all?"

"Sure. Went to the Safeway in Bullhead City."

"Anyone see you there?"

"Uh, I guess."

"You guess?"

"How the hell am I supposed to know?" he snapped, his hands jerking forward, only to get stopped by the handcuffs with a rattle. "Why you people always after me? I got my rights! This dirtbag's always had it out for me!"

Hutton glared at Police Chief Gregors, who gave him a satisfied smile.

"How about you tell us about your work at Kingman Prison?" Alexa asked.

That took him by surprise. "Huh?"

"You seem to have trouble hearing our questions, Mr. Hutton," Stuart said. "Is there a hearing aid in your trailer you would like us to get you?"

"Very funny, Fed. Why do you want to know about my work in Kingman?"

"How about you tell us about it?" Alexa said.

Realization dawned. "Oh, you're still on that whole Robby Tyson kick. First you think I'm him and you tell the world, and now you think I helped him escape?"

"We never said that," Stuart said in a quiet voice. "What makes you think that's what we meant?"

Hutton shifted in his seat, suddenly looking very worried.

"Because why else would the feds come bother me? These idiots grabbed me the night he escaped because they wanted to brag they got Robby Tyson. It was Officer Kendrick who arrested me. He's new and didn't know me. Then the rest of them, who have it out for me, decided to keep me just because they could. Then Kendrick spouted off on the radio that he had caught Robby Tyson and word spread."

Alexa looked at Police Chief Gregors and saw him blushing.

"How about you tell us about your work in Kingman?" Stuart said. "You keep dodging the question."

Keith Hutton gave a casual little shrug that did not strike Alexa as casual. "Nothing to tell. They hired me to repave parts of their driveway and parking lots. A few years ago they had hired Arizona Top Pavers. Crappy company. They do really bad work. How they got to be one of the biggest in the state I'll never know. Well, the warden sure figured out the kind of work they do. So he hired me."

"You had access inside the prison?" Alexa asked.

"Inside the buildings? No. I was inside the wall, though. All I did was work on the interior parking lot. I never even met Robby Tyson."

"You made friends with some of the guards."

Another shrug. "Sure. We hung out."

"And they never let you inside the building."

"No. Why would they? The only building I got to go inside was the guards' building right at the gate. It's air conditioned in there. I'd go there to have a coffee or my lunch. No prisoners in there."

"What did you guys talk about?"

"Usual stuff. Sports. Hunting. Not much."

"They ever talk about the prisoners?"

"Yeah. I don't remember them ever mentioning Robby Tyson, though. I remember the law trying to tie him to those killings a few years back but they never made anything of it. From what I hear, Tyson kept to himself and didn't cause any trouble."

"Oh, so they did mention him."

Hutton got flustered. "Sure. I guess once or twice. Why not? That doesn't prove anything."

Except you knew about Tyson, and you had access to guards who had access to keys.

"Who did you hang out with in that guardroom?"

"All the guys. They rotated through duties. Sometimes they'd be at the guardroom, sometimes they'd be inside or up in the tower. They rotated between day and night shifts too. So yeah, I guess I met just about all of them."

Alexa took a step forward to stand looking down at Hutton.

"Did you ever meet Robby Tyson?"

Hutton looked up at her, meeting her eyes for the first time in several minutes.

"No. I never met him and I never helped him escape."

Alexa turned to the two other men in the room.

"I need to talk with you both outside."

And you're not going to like what I have to say, she added silently.

CHAPTER TWENTY ONE

Alexa, Stuart, and Police Chief Gregors gathered outside the interrogation room, Alexa leading them a bit down the hall so Hutton didn't have a chance to overhear. That damn room hadn't been properly soundproofed.

"I'm not sure he's our man," she said in a low voice.

"What? Of course he is!" Chief Gregors exclaimed, his voice loud enough that Hutton might have heard.

"He doesn't have an alibi for any of the times of the murders," Alexa said. Out of the corner of her eye, she saw Stuart nod.

"No, he doesn't," the police chief said. "That shows he could have done them."

"Anyone who is guilty would try to think up an alibi. He freely admits he doesn't have one. All he said was that he went to the supermarket, but he didn't say anyone recognized him there."

Chief Gregors looked about to object, so Alexa went on.

"We searched his property and found no incriminating evidence."

"He had a shed full of rotting animals. I saw it myself when you told me about it. That's the sign of a sick mind."

"Agreed. But it's a big leap from legal hunting to murder. A copycat killer is a fan of the person he's trying to imitate. We saw no evidence of that there. No newspaper clippings, no violent porn, no prison gear or weapons."

"What about the knife he had on him?" Chief Gregors objected.

"Every hunter in the state carries one of those."

"What about him palling around with the prison guards? He could have gotten the key that way."

"True. And I think tomorrow my partner and I should go back to Kingman prison and interview those guards." She glanced at Stuart as she said this. He nodded.

"I think he did it and I'm holding him for further questioning," Chief Gregors stated. "I can hold him for attempted murder of a federal agent."

"He wasn't trying to kill me. If he had wanted to kill me, he would have kept on firing. We were out in the middle of nowhere. He had a decent chance to take us both out."

A little snort from Stuart told her what he thought of that tactical assessment. Alexa went on.

"Sure, at first I was suspicious, but if he was the killer he wouldn't have let himself be taken alive. He would have kept on firing. And furthermore, he tried to shoot me, not stab me. Tyson and his copycat lure unsuspecting women into a false sense of security and then stab them. If he's our man, he should have called out to me in the dark, come on over to talk, and then stabbed me by surprise."

"He probably saw Special Agent Barrett and decided he didn't have the chance."

"It was dark. Stuart moved silently and snuck up on him. I don't think he knew he was there."

"He didn't," Stuart said. "But I agree with Alexa. I don't think he's our man. Hold him, by all means. Slap a charge of illegal discharge of a firearm on him."

Chief Gregors smiled. "Now you're talking. I'll add a health violation for that shed. Maybe even cruelty to animals. And I'll fine him for that illegal satellite TV descrambler."

You're enjoying this too much, Alexa thought.

She bit her tongue. Confronting him would be counterproductive.

Stuart turned to Alexa. "I think it's a good idea to keep him in custody at least through tomorrow. Long enough for us to interview the prison guards."

"All right," Alexa said and sighed. "Let's find a motel. We won't be able to start the interviews until tomorrow anyway."

Just then her phone rang. Stacy.

"Excuse me a moment," she said, walking down the hall and into the front office.

But when she picked up, it wasn't Stacy's voice she heard. It was the slurred voice of a drunken adult male.

"Hey, is this Alexa Chase?" the voice demanded.

It took a second for her to recognize it. Stacy's dad.

Her heart sank. She didn't need this right now. And Stacy really, really didn't need this right now.

"Hello, Mr. Carpenter. How are you doing this evening?" she said, stalling for time.

Alexa hurried out of the front office and went outside. She knew this conversation was going to be a rough one and didn't want anyone to overhear.

"Pretty damn good," he bawled like it was a challenge.

"Is there a problem? I see you're calling me on Stacy's phone."

"That's because I don't have your number."

Actually Alexa had given her number to both him and his wife. They had probably deleted it accidentally or typed it in wrong.

"Well, I'm glad you called, Mr. Carpenter—"

"Like hell!"

"Is everything all right with Stacy?"

"She's fine. She's home, where she belongs. Instead of camping out in your house. Thinks she's too good for a trailer."

Alexa tensed. They had come and fetched Stacy from her house? This had never happened before. What was going on?

She decided to be diplomatic.

"Stacy does a good job taking care of my horses, Mr. Carpenter. I'm very grateful for the work she does."

"Don't worry, your little horsies are all fed and combed. We made her come right back after she was done. She's better off here with us."

Oh no, she isn't.

"I see. And why did you call?"

"Huh? Oh! Right. It's about the TV show."

Alexa felt like she had suddenly been plunged in ice water. "The TV show?"

"Yeah, the one your sister is planning. She came and talked to us. Sounds great."

"Um, Mr. Carpenter. I'm on a case right now so Melanie hasn't really filled me in. Could you give me the details?"

"Yeah. She said it was going to be a Sunday night special. You know like they do? About a girl who's an expert rider and stable girl. They'd interview us and you and Stacy, of course. Sounds pretty good. Who knows? Maybe some talent scout will spot her and put her in one of those child modeling agencies. How much do you think they'll pay us for the show? Your sister was kind of vague about that."

Alexa paused. The "Sunday night special" Mr. Carpenter was referring to was a special half-hour investigative report Action News did every Sunday. It was usually some form of negative scaremongering. If Mr. Carpenter thought it was going to be a rosy picture of a happy girl currying horses, he had obviously not watched any episodes.

And Melanie had mentioned payment? Oh God, she was playing these idiots like a fiddle.

It would be funny if Stacy wasn't caught in the middle.

"Has my sister-in-law spoken with Stacy about this?"

"Who?"

"Melanie Chase is my sister-in-law, not my sister."

"Whatever."

Pause. Had he forgotten the question?

"Has Melanie spoken with Stacy about doing this program?"

"Hell, no. that's our decision. We're her parents, aren't we? And I'm sick of you forgetting that! You always having her over, letting her stay whenever she wants, letting her have the run of the house. It's like you don't think we exist at all!"

Rage simmered in Alexa's heart. She would love to tell this failed father just what she thought of him. She'd love to mock him and insult him and tell him he was a worthless piece of dirt who was no good to anybody.

Only the thought of Stacy's welfare made her bite her tongue. She took a deep breath and said, "That's not true, Mr. Carpenter, I think you're very influential in Stacy's life." *Not in a good way.* "I'll talk to my sister-in-law about the program and get the details. Since she's family I think I can get a better deal from her."

That should keep you from calling her before I do.

"Good. You do that," Mr. Carpenter said, sounding somewhat mollified.

The door to the police station opened and Stuart popped his head out. She must have had a hell of an expression on her face because as soon as he spotted Alexa, he disappeared back inside.

"May I speak with Stacy?" Alexa asked.

The anger came back immediately. "Oh, you'd like that, wouldn't you? Cut us out of the deal! Hell, no. She's not talking to you until we get a contract with the TV station. You aren't getting more than your share."

"I'm not looking for a share, Mr. Carpenter, I'm—"

"Oh, don't get like that. Of course you are. And you'll get it. I'm sure they'll want to film in your stable and back lot. You'll get yours, but we're gonna get ours! And you're not taking it. Now get going and talk to your sister or sister-in-law or whatever the hell she is. And don't try calling Stacy until we have a signed contract."

Mr. Carpenter hung up.

Alexa leaned back against the rough stucco wall and closed her eyes, letting out a long, slow breath. Now what the hell was she going to do? Call Melanie? The reporter wasn't actually doing anything illegal, so Alexa had no way to stop her. Reasoning with her wouldn't work. Melanie saw a story and she was gunning for it. It didn't matter that a child might get hurt in the process.

Try to reason with Stacy's parents? That had even less of a chance of success. They smelled money, always in short supply since neither of them could ever keep a job for more than a couple of weeks. And what would they do when they discovered Melanie had no intention of paying them?

Alexa's eyes snapped open. Wayne. She should call her brother Wayne. Melanie's husband. He'd see reason. He was much like Dad, a practical, quiet man who enjoyed a private life and respected the privacy of others. Why he had married someone like Melanie was beyond Alexa's understanding, but if anyone could reason with her, it would be Wayne.

She called his number. After an agonizing several rings, he picked up.

"Hey, sis."

"Hey, Wayne. I need to talk to you."

"What's up?"

"Melanie has been trying to set up some Sunday special featuring Stacy."

"What?" Wayne's tone showed he knew nothing about it. But of course he wouldn't. Melanie knew he'd object.

"It's supposed to be some sort of feature about me taking care of a kid with alcoholic parents. She's even got Stacy's parents on board. They don't know what it's really about. They think they're going to get paid and Stacy will become famous."

"Jesus. I'm sorry, Alexa."

"Not as much as Stacy will be if this whole thing goes through. Can you talk to Melanie?"

"Of course! Don't worry. I'll get her to stop. She's up your way somewhere at the moment on the Tyson copycat story."

"I know. I bumped into her."

"Oh. Damn. Anyway, I'll try to get in touch. She doesn't pick up the phone too much when she's out chasing a story."

"Get in touch with her. Please. Stacy is very vulnerable and if Melanie starts wading into the situation giving her parents all sorts of false promises it could really disrupt everything."

Pause. "Alexa, maybe you should step back."

Alexa blinked. "Step back?"

"Stacy is a great kid, and you've shown her a couple of great weekends up here at the ranch, but maybe it would be better if you didn't get so involved."

"What do you mean? She needs me!"

"She needs someone, that's for sure. Maybe you should call social services."

"That would only make things worse."

Arizona's social services were stretched to the limit due to underfunding and an overwhelming need. The most she could expect would be for some social worker to show up at the trailer, give them the number of the local A.A. chapter, and do a follow-up call a month later. Stacy wasn't being completely neglected, and she wasn't being physically abused, so social services, even if they could clearly see the problem, would be powerless to intervene.

But if a social worker did show up, Stacy's parents would be so enraged at Alexa's "meddling" that they'd refuse to let their child see her anymore.

The same thing would happen if they knew she stopped the interview.

The same thing would happen if the interview went forward and, instead of being launched into their fifteen minutes of fame like they expected, Melanie presented them to the audience as bad parents like she intended.

Her and Stacy's precarious relationship had always relied on those two drunks being indifferent, even relieved that Alexa had taken over some of the expense and most of the responsibility of caring for a teenager.

"Alexa?"

Her brother's voice snapped her out of her reverie.

"I'm sorry. One of the officers was talking to me. What did you say?"

"I said that I'll get Melanie to stop trying to interview them, or at least I'll try, but you really should rethink this whole thing."

"Why?"

Wayne sighed. "Because you don't have the time to raise her. That's what you're after, isn't it? Having a kid? But you spend most of your time running around the entire Southwest chasing killers, drug dealers, and escaped convicts. How can you raise a kid, especially a needy one like her, when you're doing all that?"

"Who else is going to do it?"

"I don't know. But you don't have the time to do it right."

"What the hell, Wayne? Since when have you been against me on this?" Alexa snapped.

"I'm not against you," he replied in a calm voice. "No one is against you. All I'm saying is that you're raising Stacy's expectations, and your own, when you can't fulfill them."

"Could you just talk with Melanie and get her to lay off?"

"I will, Alexa. I will. But think about what I said, all right?"

"Fine. Whatever," Alexa grumbled. "I got to go."

"I'll try to do what I can. Take care."

Wayne hung up.

Alexa slumped against the wall, feeling ill. That stupid reporter, that plastic person who Wayne married for who-knows-what reason, was going to wreck one of the few good things in Alexa's life, and Stacy's too. Sure, Wayne would try to talk to her, but Alexa didn't give that much of a chance of success. Melanie was nothing if not persistent, and she smelled a story that might get her to the big time.

Melanie always talked about getting to a "higher profile market" like Los Angeles or New York City. And the only way to do that was to come up with some big stories that got her noticed by network management. She disliked Phoenix, calling it a "cow town," as if a metropolis of 1.6 million people was too small for her.

It was too small … for her ego. Melanie wanted the big time, and it didn't matter that Wayne had no interest in living anywhere but the family ranch. Alexa suspected that if Melanie ever achieved her dream, Wayne would get left behind. That would be the end of their marriage.

Yes, Melanie didn't care who she hurt to get what she wanted.

And hurt them she would. Because if this story went through, the Carpenters would be furious. They'd blame Alexa for being dragged through the mud.

And then what would Alexa have to come home to?

CHAPTER TWENTY TWO

That night in the motel room, Alexa couldn't sleep despite feeling utterly spent. Instead, she paced. Worries about Stacy swirled around and around in her head. The Carpenters must have come to Alexa's place and dragged her home. So the poor kid had to endure a night in that tiny trailer as her parents partied it up.

That meant not enough sleep, which meant she wouldn't be able to pay attention in school tomorrow. If she had a quiz or test, she'd bomb it. Even if she didn't, she'd get told off once again for "not paying attention."

Stacy had a reputation as a bad student, but the only reason she was a bad student was because of her bad home life.

Alexa could have intervened. Talked to the school and teachers. But if she did that, then the school might try to reach out to the parents. It would get back to Stacy that Alexa had talked to the school administration about the situation at home and Stacy would be furious at her.

And that was the major problem between them. They never really talked about the reasons Stacy kept a key to Alexa's house in her pocket every day, or how she'd linger in the back lot long after she had finished feeding and currying Smith and Wesson. Or how at least twice a week she'd sleep over, even if Alexa wasn't around.

Stacy resisted every attempt to discuss it. The girl felt deeply embarrassed about her parents. Even when their drunken bawling could be heard from Alexa's house, Stacy wouldn't say anything, she'd just turn away from Alexa and kind of freeze up.

At least nothing else was going on over there. Alexa had pushed Stacy to talk about the situation enough to reassure herself on that score. If there had been, Alexa would have intervened in a heartbeat.

But as matters stood, what could she do? While it wasn't a suitable home, social services wouldn't find enough to pull Stacy from it. As one social worker Alexa knew had told her, "In this state, you practically have to kill your kids to have them taken away from you."

And even if Stacy could be pulled from her home, where would she go? The foster care system with all its disruption and dangers?

Alexa couldn't take her in. Wayne was right about that. Social services would look at her long absences from home and reject her application. Being right next door to the parents would be another mark against her suitability.

She groaned and flopped down on the bed. What could she do? It all seemed so impossible. Checking her phone for the twentieth time, she saw no texts from the kid. Her parents had probably taken her phone out of spite.

Get some sleep, she told herself. *You have a killer to catch. Wayne will do what he can. You'll be a lot better able to deal with what happens tomorrow if you get some sleep.*

Yeah, good luck with that.

Despite the stress and worries that kept her nerves at a high pitch, Alexa forced herself to undress and get into bed. As had become her habit, she pulled out the journal Robert Powers had left her and opened to the next entry. It was the one after the bombshell where Powers revealed he had known Drake Logan.

I've been thinking a lot about Drake these past few days. I'm thinking that attraction I felt to him and his cruelty might be what launched me into a career in law enforcement. Well, not just him. Hanging out in small-town Arizona you meet a lot of thugs and weirdos and druggies. Drake Logan was just at another level.

But I was fascinated by those people. Sad to say, I admired them, even if I felt repulsed by what they did. The thought of crime thrilled me, and yet I had a conscience and couldn't live the life they lived. Thank God for good parenting!

Still, the attraction was there. I have to wonder, did I become a lawman in order to be close to criminals? My family complains that I spend more time with the dregs of society than I do with them. While that's not quite true, it's pretty damn close.

So why do I do it? A sense of justice is part of it. Those people need to be stopped. And yet I can't shake the fact that I actually identify with these scumbags a little bit. That's not entirely a bad thing. It helps me catch them, figure out their next moves. That justifies the feeling to me, I guess. It's still disturbing, though.

But I feel what I feel. And as I've written before, everyone has a dark side. Mine is just a bit darker than most. The real difference is that I turn that into something that works for the greater good.

Alexa's vision blurred with fatigue, but her mind went over what she had just read. Powers had a point there. Alexa knew she had some pretty nasty elements in her own personality, and that they could come out under stress. But her former partner was pointing out that it could be flipped into something positive.

That's what he had done, and that's what she needed to do.

Alexa set the journal aside, her eyelids heavy. Even when talking about grim things, her old mentor's writing soothed her. It was like having him still with her a little bit. She switched off the light and got under the covers.

Tomorrow was another day. Tomorrow they'd go back to Kingman Prison.

And this time, they'd get answers.

* * *

They parked in the Kingman Prison parking lot that Keith Hutton had repaved and got out of the car. The early morning sun was searing on the fresh blacktop, and Alexa could tell the day was going to be an unusually hot one. She felt grateful for her ten-gallon hat. Stuart wiped his brow as they went to the guardroom at the gate where Hutton had eaten his lunch.

Halfway there, a portly man in a cheap suit and cowboy hat came out to meet them.

"Good morning, Officers. I'm Alexander Jackson Quinnell, assistant state supervisor of prisons."

"Good morning, Mr. Quinnell," Alexa said, shaking his hand. It was cold and a bit damp. "I recognize you from press conferences, although we've never met. I'm Deputy Marshal Alexa Chase. This is Special Agent Stuart Barrett of the FBI."

"Pleased to meet you, Agent Barrett," Quinnell said, pumping his hand. "I heard you were on the case and felt much better. I read about your commendation. Bravery in the line of fire. Impressive. Very impressive."

A flicker of annoyance, quickly suppressed, darted across Stuart's youthful features.

"How can we help you, Mr. Quinnell?" Stuart asked in a level voice.

"Oh, it's not you helping me. I'm here to help you. Part of my job is to personally investigate any prison breaks. I just got here half an hour ago and was waiting for you. Let's go to the guardhouse and get out of this heat, shall we?"

"That's just where we wanted to start our investigation," Alexa said.

"Oh really, why?" the assistant state supervisor of prisons asked as they made their way toward it.

"Keith Hutton, a hunter arrested in Bullhead City at the beginning of the manhunt, is in jail again on suspicion of being the copycat. We're not sure he did it, but he had access to this guardhouse and there's a chance he stole or copied the key that freed Robby Tyson."

"Oh dear," Quinnell muttered, his soft hands brushing the front of his suit. "That would be a scandal."

They opened the door to the guardhouse and got hit with a blast of cold air. Now she knew why Quinnell's hands felt so chilly. The guards had the air conditioning cranked up to the max.

The guardhouse watched over the gate from the outer parking lot to the inner parking lot. A high chain-link fence topped with razor wire separated the two. Official cars with law enforcement ID could drive through the gate, like they had just done. All others, such as visitors for the prisoners, had to park outside and be processed through a guardhouse. A metal detector stood between the front and back doors. A desk with a computer, a police scanner, and radio equipment stood to one side. Alexa noted a series of hooks by the desk with keys hanging from them.

Two prison guards were on duty, an older white man with a pot belly and a lanky, younger black man. The older man came up and introduced them.

"I'm Sergeant Cottar. This is Trainee Officer Madison. It's his first week and I'm showing him the ropes."

"Welcome aboard, Officer Madison," Alexa said, shaking the younger man's hand.

"Should be an interesting job. I was mall security for a couple of years in Phoenix. This should be more of a challenge."

"You served, didn't you?" Stuart said. When he said that, Alexa noted Madison's close-shaved hair and erect bearing.

"Sure did. Arizona National Guard in Iraq. Those two weekends a month turned into two years."

Madison and Stuart laughed.

"I was in the Army."

"Oh, you volunteered for that? You're crazy," the prison guard said with a grin.

"You should see him drive," Alexa said.

"That's a nice car you drove in with," Officer Madison said. "I don't think the Department of Corrections is going to issue me anything like that."

"Sorry, young man," Quinnell said. "I'm afraid all my department will have you drive is a prisoner transport bus."

His laugh cut short, and he darted a nervous glance at Alexa.

Alexa gritted her teeth. He was thinking of the Drake Logan escape, where a team of his followers ambushed a prisoner transport bus, injured her and killed Robert Powers. Quinnell felt he had just made a social blunder.

He had, but Alexa didn't have time to deal with that right now. Turning to Sergeant Cottar, the older officer, she said, "We're here investigating Keith Hutton."

Cottar looked surprised. "Keith? What's he done now?"

Interesting reaction. "Does he get in trouble a lot?"

"Oh, just minor stuff. The Bullhead City police have it out for him. You know how some of these local precincts have their targets in the local community. I'm not saying Keith is a model citizen, but he's never done anything really bad."

There's a collection of coyote corpses I could show you that might make you think differently.

"So you know him?"

"Oh, sure. We all do. Well, not Madison here, he's too new, but everybody else here knows Keith. He does a lot of the repaving work and sometimes some of the guys go for a beer with him in town. I don't drink myself. I can tell you he's a good guy. Arresting him thinking he was Robby Tyson is so typical of Bullhead City law enforcement."

Alexa paused. This was a prison guard standing in front of a state prison official criticizing law enforcement. That struck her as highly unusual. Was Keith really that much of a charmer?

Tyson was a charmer too, and so is the copycat.

"We're concerned that Mr. Hutton might have aided in Tyson's escape," Stuart said.

"Why would he do that?" the older prison guard asked.

"We were hoping you might tell us," Alexa said.

"I don't think he ever met Robby Tyson. I mean, Keith never went into the yard," Sergeant Cottar said.

"But he must have known about him. He got some notoriety when he was arrested," Alexa said.

"Sure. People tried to say he was the Southwest Slasher. Maybe he was. I don't know. But maybe he wasn't. The TV is saying he didn't kill anyone after he escaped. That poor girl near Prescott National Forest was killed by the copycat. That's what you folks believe now, isn't it?"

Stuart cut in. "We don't really want to comment on an ongoing investigation. Did Mr. Hutton ever talk to you about Tyson?"

"Not that I can recall."

Alexa remembered what the Jersey Devil had said about admirers distancing themselves from their idols before starting their own murder sprees.

She decided to try a different tack.

Gesturing over to the row of keys by the desk, she asked, "What are those keys for?"

Sergeant Cottar walked over to them and started to point to each in turn. "These are for the guardhouse. These are for the tool shed in the inner parking lot. These are for the gate. As you can see, there are two copies of each."

"And what keys do you have on your person?" Alexa asked.

"Each man carries handcuff keys and keys to the guardhouse."

"Are the handcuff keys identical to the ankle shackle keys?" Alexa asked.

"No, they aren't," Sergeant Cottar replied.

"So who has access to those?" Stuart asked.

Sergeant Cottar gestured to Officer Madison.

"Care to tell us?" he asked in a teacherly sort of voice.

Officer Madison recited, "Keys to the ankle shackles are kept by the sergeant on duty for the prisoner transport, the driver of the transport truck, and the shift captain."

"And where are they kept?" the sergeant prompted.

"On the person of those individuals and in the shift captain's lockup."

Sergeant Cottar turned to them and smiled. "He's a quick learner."

"Spending two years in Iraq, he had to be," Stuart said.

"So there are no other shackle keys?" Alexa asked, her heart sinking. This wasn't going to be as straightforward as she had hoped.

"None," Sergeant Cottar replied.

"Could any have gone missing, even for just a few minutes?" Alexa asked.

Sergeant Cottar turned to the trainee, raising an eyebrow.

Officer Madison recited, “An officer’s keys are that officer’s personal responsibility and must stay on their person at all times and must never be lent to anyone else, even a superior officer. All keys are returned to and checked by the duty officer at shift change and at least once at a random time during the shift.”

Assistant state supervisor of prisons Quinnell brushed his chubby hands along the front of his suit. “So how did Tyson get one of those damn keys?”

Sergeant Cottar didn’t have an answer to that, and neither did his trainee.

Alexa thought she might, and she didn’t like the answer one bit.

CHAPTER TWENTY THREE

The interior of the prison was like so many Alexa had seen, with grim echoing corridors of concrete and steel. The space seemed to capture sound and amplify it, so that the most distant shout, the slamming of a heavy steel door, would reverberate and mix with other sounds to create a constant, hellish background noise. Even as accustomed as she was to places like this, the sounds, combined with the smell of grease on the doors and the presence of so many dangerous men, always raised the hairs on the back of her neck.

Trainee Officer Madison was leading Alexa, Stuart, and Quinnell to the east block to talk to the duty sergeant there, a man named Steve Larson. He had been the duty sergeant on the chain gang from which Tyson had escaped.

They passed along a walkway of steel grille. Beside them was a row of cells. Across an open space ran another walkway and row of cells. Above and below were two more levels of cells. The men, housed in pairs, sat talking on their bunks, or reading. As they passed, many came to their cell doors, gripped the bars, and stared.

Most of those stares were emotionless masks. Prisoners learn to hide their emotions around figures of authority. It kept them out of trouble. Alexa knew, however, that none of those hidden emotions were kindly. She felt hundreds of eyes on them.

As they passed, little sounds behind them confirmed her impression. A whisper followed by a barking laugh, or a crude sound, or the loud smack of a plastic prison-issue cup against the steel bars. That was the only aggression they could show, the only way they could express their hate. If those doors were open, Alexa felt sure, they would express their hate in far worse ways.

They came to an intersection, where another long, three-level corridor crossed their own. A slim tower rose from the center space with an observation desk enclosed on all sides by windows. Two guards sat there, staring out the windows and down each of the four branches of the east wing. A clever array of mirrors and security cameras allowed them to see into each cell.

Madison and Stuart had been swapping stories about Iraq the whole walk. While Alexa would have loved to listen in and get an insight into something Stuart had rarely talked about with her, she was too distracted by the prisoners surrounding her and ongoing questions about the Tyson escape. Worries about Stacy and Melanie intruded into her thoughts as well. She hadn't heard from either of them, or from Wayne.

Officer Madison stopped his account of getting pinned down by fire from a sniper hidden in a minaret to point at the observation tower.

"The husky redhead on the left is Sergeant Steve Larson. The smaller guy with him is Officer Donner."

"He was present at the escape too," Quinnell said.

The state assistant supervisor of prisons was sweating profusely, despite the cool, rather chilly interior. He kept looking nervously over his shoulder, as if expecting the cell doors to open and for hordes of felons to rush out at him.

They'd love to, Alexa thought, *and he knows it.*

They had to descend to the ground floor to access the door to the observation tower, which Officer Madison opened with a key card. They entered a little circular shaft taken up by a metal spiral staircase. Like the walkway, the steps were a grille, so you could see if someone was above or below you. Everything in the prison was designed for maximum visibility. Alexa mused that if someone invented transparent concrete, they'd use that for the walls and floor.

They spiraled up to the observation deck, Quinnell huffing and puffing and wiping his brow. When they made it, Alexa took a moment to pause and stare out. The entire wing stretched out on all sides, hundreds of men in orange jumpsuits stuck in cages. The desk ran all the way around, and the two officers had office chairs with wheels on them so they could move at will to look out any window in a moment. A long row of computer screens showed feeds from dozens of security cameras. Nothing could move in this wing without the guards knowing it.

When everyone stepped onto the platform, it felt cramped. There was a lot of bumping of elbows as the two officers on duty shook the visitors' hands.

"We wanted to talk with you about the breakout," Quinnell said.

Sergeant Larson flushed a little. Officer Donner looked between the newcomers and his supervisor nervously.

"I just don't know how it could have happened," Sergeant Larson muttered, looking down at the floor.

"How about you tell us what happened?" Quinnell demanded. He sounded more sure of himself now that he was confronting a subordinate. Or, as Alexa thought, he probably felt relieved to be in a more secure location.

"It was all in my report, sir," the sergeant replied.

Alexa cut in. She didn't have time or the inclination to watch a dressing down by a bureaucrat against someone standing in the front lines. "We've read your report, Sergeant. It looks like you did all you could do to avoid bloodshed and further escapees. What we want to understand is how Tyson got a key to his shackles. The report says it was a copy?"

"That's right," Sergeant Larson said with a bit more confidence now that he was speaking to someone in a uniform. "It was a copy of one of our keys. None of our keys were missing, and none have been reported missing. We checked the records as far back as two years."

Alexa nodded. That had all been in the report too. What she wanted to know was what hadn't made it in to the report.

"So you never lost any keys. That means someone had to have copied one here in the prison."

"I don't see how that's possible," Sergeant Larson said.

"Neither do I," Quinnell grumbled. He made it sound like an accusation.

"It's not too hard," Stuart said. "You get some putty and impress the shape of the key in it. Then you use that as a mold. A skilled locksmith could do it. An unskilled person could make the mold easily enough, although it would take a locksmith to pour the metal and file out the irregularities."

Quinnell stared at him. "Really?"

"Yes," Stuart said. "Are the guards searched when they go in and out of the prison grounds?"

"They pass through the metal detector," Trainee Officer Madison said. "And at random times their pockets are searched and they get a pat-down."

"But not on a regular basis?" Alexa asked.

The trainee shook his head. "No, but pretty often. If you're thinking a guard smuggled out a key mold, he would have been taking an awful risk."

Officer Donner's face turned red. "You saying one of our guys broke him out? You been here what, a week? And you're accusing—"

Sergeant Larson put a hand on his arm. "Easy there, Joe."

Alexa raised a calming hand. "No one is accusing anyone of anything. But that key copy got made somehow, and if no keys are missing …"

She left her sentence unfinished. The cramped observation tower settled into an uncomfortable silence.

After a long moment, Duty Sergeant Larson broke it.

"Well, you can check my records if you want to. Check my locker too. I don't have nothing to hide and neither does Joe here." He gestured to Officer Donner, who nodded emphatically.

I'll do that, Alexa thought.

"How well did you know Tyson?" she asked.

Officer Donner shrugged. "Me? Hardly at all. I only transferred to this wing a couple of weeks ago when another man quit. The boys pointed him out to me, but Tyson was a quiet inmate. Never talked to me and I didn't talk to him."

Alexa turned to Sergeant Larson.

The older officer nodded. "I knew him better. Been on this wing for three years. Like Donner says, he didn't talk much, to either the prisoners or the guards. I had a few interactions with him."

"Like what?"

"The usual stuff. He asked for a replacement mattress a few months back. It was getting old and I approved the request. The old mattress and the new one both got checked for contraband."

"Has he ever been found in possession of contraband?" Quinnell asked.

"No."

You'd know that if you read the report more carefully, Alexa thought, but she knew better than to say that to a state bureaucrat. Out loud she asked, "What other interactions did you have with him?"

"The usual kind of things. Instructions on the work detail. A couple of times I told him not to exercise after dark."

"Exercise after dark?"

"He wasn't up to anything. We checked. Just push-ups and stuff like that. Guys exercise a lot in their cells to let off steam. But we have a rule of silence after lights out. I didn't want him to disturb the other inmates because that can lead to trouble. After the second time he got a verbal warning and a cell search. We didn't turn up anything and he never did it again."

Alexa turned to Quinnell.

"What about the other two officers who were on chain gang duty?" she asked.

"I checked when I got here. Officer Hanson is still on sick leave. Officer Brnovich is on duty in the north wing."

"So what's Officer Brnovich like?" Stuart asked.

Sergeant Larson and Officer Donner looked at each other. The younger man's face tensed a little as he looked at his superior officer, as if trying to communicate something. Sergeant Larson gave a little wince, blink and you miss it, then turned back to them.

"Brnovich is a good man, a good officer, but he's always been a bit … chatty."

"Chatty?" Alexa asked.

"Oh, he means well and all. A real friendly guy. That's OK on the outside, but in here it's better to be a bit firmer with the inmates."

"And he isn't firm with the inmates?" Alexa thought this was an interesting detail, although she found it surprising they'd bring it up so readily.

Sergeant Larson brought up a hand. "Oh, don't get me wrong, he's not unprofessional. Everyone's got their own style, though, and I think that you should never get into conversation with the inmates unless it's about an issue that needs to be resolved."

"Did he ever speak with Tyson?"

"No, no," Sergeant Larson was quick to say. "A good man. Sorry I said anything."

"And he's on the north wing?" Stuart asked.

"The north wing has their rec time right now," Trainee Officer Madison said. "He'll be out in the yard."

"Let's go see Officer Brnovich," Alexa said.

Someone has to have some information for me. I don't think Larson and Donner did it. At least that's what my gut says, and Powers always said to "trust your gut, but check your facts."

So she'd dig a bit more into those two, and check their lockers as well. But she didn't expect to find any evidence that they had helped with the breakout.

And if they didn't do it, that narrowed the list of likely suspects down to two.

She hoped.

Because thinking a prison guard helped him escape was a hell of a long shot, and thinking one of them was the copycat was an even longer one. None of them had records, after all, or they wouldn't have gotten that job.

They headed back down the stairs and out into the ground floor of the east wing. As they walked along the corridor flanked by cells, Alexa's phone buzzed. She pulled it out and saw Stacy had sent her a text.

At least she hoped it was Stacy and not her failure of a father. Glancing to either side at the watchful eyes of the convicts, she read it, hoping it wasn't worse news than she had gotten the previous night.

CHAPTER TWENTY FOUR

"Hey," was all the text said.

"How are you?" Alexa texted back.

She got a reply immediately. "Fine. You coming home tonight?"

Alexa gritted her teeth. She would love to say yes, Stacy needed her to say yes, but the fact of the matter was that she probably wouldn't be home tonight.

"I'm not sure. I'm up in Kingman right now."

"OK. ☹"

"Sorry. How are you?"

"Fine."

Alexa paused, unsure what to say. The convicts standing at the doors to their cells stared at her phone as she passed. She hoped the kid didn't send any selfies.

"How is school?"

"I'm on break."

Alexa happened to know that at this hour she was in math class, one of her worst subjects. Usually Alexa lectured her about using her phone in class. Not today. The girl needed to hear from someone supportive.

"Miss you," Alexa texted.

"Miss you too. What's this about a TV show?"

Alexa groaned. Stuart gave her a questioning look but Alexa ignored him. She couldn't explain, not in front of all these people.

"Nothing. It's something Melanie wants to do."

"Ick. No."

"Exactly."

"My parents say it will get me on *America's Got Talent*."

Alexa rolled her eyes.

"No," was all she texted back.

"I didn't think so."

"I thought they took your phone."

"I took it back while they were sleeping."

Sleeping as in passed out, Alexa thought. "Don't get in trouble."

"They came over to your place and made me go back with them. They say it's not safe for me to stay there alone."

"I'll talk to them."

"OK."

Officer Madison led then out of the wing, having to use his key card to get through three heavy steel doors, and then into a large courtyard. Alexa's phone buzzed again.

"You coming back tonight?"

While Alexa still wasn't an expert on kids, she had learned that when they asked the same question a second time, they wanted a different answer. With a sigh Alexa texted back,

"I'll try the best I can. Just hang in there."

"Fine."

Alexa could practically hear the mopeyness in that reply.

"Hugs."

"GIANT HUGS!!!!"

"YOU TOO."

"Oh crap, gotta go."

Alexa chuckled. The "oh crap" was probably her getting caught by the teacher.

Officer Madison led them across a wide courtyard to a chain-link fence, fully fifty feet high, topped with razor wire. And identical fence stood five yards beyond that one. On the other side of that they could see a large yard. Inmates lounged around picnic benches or played basketball. Others used a track around the edges of the fenced-in rec area to run or walk laps.

Officer Madison took them to a gate in the fence. His key card didn't work on these locks. Instead he had to call out to one of the officers in the yard. This was a standard precaution. No officer had sufficient keys on his person to get from inside the prison all the way to the outside world. Thus no inmate could simply overpower or kidnap a guard and use his keys to get free. This helped keep the guards and the outside world safer.

The only flaw in that was when they were on work detail. Then only one key was between them and freedom. Whoever helped Tyson had planned the breakout well.

Once they were let through first one gate, which was locked behind them, and then the inner gate, while two guards flanked the entrance gripping rifles and ordered all inmates to stand at least a hundred feet away, they asked to see Officer Brnovich. The officer who had let them in called over to an officer on the opposite side of the yard.

Brnovich was a short, dark-haired man with heavy brows. He was in his early thirties and moved with a confident swagger through the crowd of inmates. Alexa could see right away that the prisoners looked at him with respect, at least what convicts called respect, which had nothing to do with goodwill.

He came right up to them and, with a nod to Alexa's uniform and a curious look at Stuart in his suit, turned to the assistant supervisor of prisons and said, "Good to see you again, Mr. Quinnell."

"Oh, have we met?" the official said.

"You gave me a commendation for excellent service last year."

"Oh, yes, I remember you now," Quinnell replied in a tone that showed he didn't remember Brnovich at all. "A good officer. Yes, quite a good officer."

"How can I help you today, sir?"

"Well, um, I'm here with the U.S. Marshals Service and the FBI investigating the Tyson escape. The report didn't answer all the questions we had."

Brnovich put on a face that made it look like he had tasted something bitter.

"That was a bad business. Wrenches my gut to let one of these men get out before their time."

"Do you have any idea how Tyson might have gotten a key?" Alexa asked.

"Must have gotten it copied somehow. None of our keys were reported missing. Someone must have copied it inside the prison. How, I have no idea. We have cameras everywhere."

"Do you have cameras in the bathrooms?" Stuart asked.

Brnovich cocked his head. "I beg your pardon?"

"Do you have cameras in the staff bathrooms?"

"Well, no. Oh, I see. You're thinking a member of staff went to the can and copied it there. I guess that's possible. But who?" Brnovich's face changed. "Oh, hell. It must have been one of us."

Alexa was surprised at this quick admission of potential guilt. Now she understood why he had earned a commendation. Or was he just being clever, admitting what they had already figured out in order to shift blame to someone else?

"Did you interact with the prisoner much?" Alexa asked.

"Some. I've been here two and a half years, but most of that time I've been here on the north wing. I was only subbing for someone that day because another officer who was supposed to go out with the work crew sprained an ankle. They put him on tower duty and put me on the bus instead. I didn't talk to him directly that day until he took Hanson hostage."

"When was the last time you had an interaction with Robby Tyson?"

"You mean besides that day? Oh, I guess maybe six months ago. I was subbing for someone else on the east wing. We were guarding the lunchroom as the inmates ate. We had a problem inmate and we wanted to sit him alone, so I ordered Tyson to move to another table."

"That's it?" Alexa asked.

"That's it," Officer Brnovich said with a shrug.

Considering this guy's service commendation and bearing, Alexa decided to risk a more probing question.

"Did any of the other guards on duty that day have close interactions with Tyson that you know of?"

"Um, not that I can recall. As I said, I'm not over on that wing much. Hanson used to talk about him some."

"Really? What would he say?"

"Oh, stuff like you had to watch him because he was the Southwest Slasher, and that he shouldn't be out on work detail. That sort of thing."

"I see," Alexa said. That wasn't what she had been hoping for.

"Yeah, I can see his point, especially considering what happened, but I didn't pay it much mind at the time. I always thought you should judge a man by what he's done, not what he might have done. Guess I was wrong in that case."

"So did you keep extra watch on Robby Tyson?" Quinnell asked.

"We kept a close watch on all the inmate workers," Officer Brnovich said somewhat defensively. "No way in hell he could have escaped if someone hadn't slipped him a key."

"Thank you, Officer," Alexa said, and motioned for the others to move off a bit, leaving the prison guard behind.

"So next we need to visit Officer Hanson at his home," Alexa said, remembering from the report that he lived close by in Kingman. "I'd like to visit without calling him first. Just in case. But first let's look through their lockers."

"All right," Quinnell sighed, then gave her a worried look. "Do you really think it might be one of them?"

"It could be, or it could be another member of staff. It's hard to tell at this stage."

"Oh, the scandal!" the supervisor said, wiping his brow. "I hope it isn't any of our people."

Officer Madison looked uncomfortable as he led them back out of the rec yard and toward the administrative building. Alexa felt bad for him. Here he was in his first week of work and he got stuck taking around a member of the state administration and two federal agents looking for evidence against one of his new coworkers. That would not help his reputation. Word would spread about this pretty quickly. She hoped it didn't lead to too much resentment against the new guy.

The administration building was a small concrete structure just to the left of the main gate. Officer Madison's key card got them in, but they had to pass through a metal detector and fill in a form with the officer at the front before entering the building proper.

"Lockers and changing rooms are right this way," the trainee told them.

"Where do employees park?" Stuart asked.

"Inside the wire, where you parked."

Alexa nodded. That gave an employee extra places to hide things.

Stuart must have thought the same thing because he asked, "Are the vehicles searched?"

"At random intervals like the guards themselves."

Alexa wondered how thoroughly that was done. With all the other things that needed doing, and several hundred dangerous felons to look after, looking through a coworker's car must have ranked pretty low in priority.

They came to a locker room. A small shower area stood off to one side. Because it was the middle of a shift, both rooms were empty.

"Take your pick," Officer Madison said, gesturing to the lockers. "As you can see, there are no locks. No privacy in this place, even for the guards."

Alexa paced down the lockers, each labeled with the employee's name. They weren't in alphabetical order. It appeared that new employees just got whatever locker was available.

She found Brnovich's first. Inside was nothing but a change of civilian clothes. The pockets were empty. Next she found Larson's. Inside the sergeant's locker she found his civilian clothes and a book on the famous bust of a Colombian drug cartel from a few years before. In his pockets Alexa found a ticket stub to a big action movie that was currently playing in the theaters.

Hanson's locker was completely empty. No doubt he had cleaned it out when he went on his week of sick leave after his ordeal as a hostage.

Donner's locker didn't have any civilian clothes, but it did have a leather satchel.

Alexa opened it and found a packet of cigarettes and a Chilton manual for Ford truck models from 2004–2014.

She closed the locker, feeling frustrated.

"This is getting us nowhere," she grumbled.

"Well, there's certainly no evidence that a staff member was involved," Quinnell said happily.

"We're not done with our investigation," Alexa said. The administrator's face fell. "But I think we've done all we can here. Let's go visit Officer Hanson's house."

I hope he's got something more he can tell us, because so far this investigation is getting nowhere.

And the copycat is still out there, looking for his next victim. If we don't track this guy down soon, we're going to have another dead body on our hands.

CHAPTER TWENTY FIVE

Officer Hanson's place stood on a residential street in the working class part of town. Alexa studied the small ranch house from Stuart's car, which he had parked across the street. Quinnell had not joined them, having stayed behind at the prison to speak with the warden about a press release they were working on.

The house looked unremarkable and not particularly prosperous. It was small, with a gravel yard given color only by a couple of desert shrubs. The garage door was closed and the curtains drawn. Alexa wondered if anyone was home.

Getting out, they crossed over to the house, the hot sun beating down on them. Alexa could feel it had topped a hundred.

When they got to the driveway, Stuart knelt down and touched an oil stain in front of the garage.

"Dry," he said.

"It's hot out."

"True, but oil dries much more slowly than water. If he had just gone to the supermarket or something, this should still be a bit damp."

He held up his clean fingers to make his point. Alexa went to the door and rang the bell.

Silence. Alexa rang the doorbell again.

They waited for a full minute, then knocked loudly.

"Nobody's home," Stuart said.

"You looking for George Hanson?" a voice called out.

They turned and saw a pot-bellied older man in a white T-shirt and bucket hat. In his hand he held a watering can. He stood by a mesquite tree in his front yard.

"Yes. Do you know where he is?" Alexa asked.

"Poor guy. He was really shook up about that abduction. He wanted to get out of town so he went to stay with his mother. I've been taking care of his cat."

Another cat lover, Alexa thought. *I hope this house isn't full of coyote corpses.*

"When did he leave?" Stuart asked.

"Right after the whole thing happened. You're not a reporter, are you?"

"No. I'm with the FBI."

"Oh, good. He told me not to talk to any reporters. Some of them have come sniffing around. That woman from Action News in Phoenix, whatshername, she was here just an hour ago."

Wonderful. That's just what I need.

"Where does his mother live?" Alexa asked.

"Flagstaff. He said being up in the trees breathing cooler air would do his head good. Poor guy. He felt terrible about Tyson escaping and killing that hiker girl."

"Actually that murder was committed by another man, probably the same man who killed Tyson."

"Really? I hope he heard about that. It would make him feel better. Still, he felt terrible about Tyson getting away. He was all jittery, really upset. Said he felt like a failure. I hate to see a young guy all broken up like that. I hope his boss isn't too hard on him."

"No one is blaming him," Alexa said.

"Well, I'm sure glad to hear that," the neighbor said, getting on with his watering. "He's a good guy. Very friendly, unlike some people around here. A real neighbor."

"Thank you," Alexa said. They returned to the car.

"We going up to Flagstaff?" Stuart asked.

"It's a two-hour drive away. Let's call first. No point wasting time if we don't find anything of interest."

"You talked to him on the phone already. Didn't he mention he went to Flagstaff?"

"No. But I didn't ask. After the police debriefed him, there was no need to stay in town."

"I suppose not," Stuart said, getting into the car and immediately turning on the air conditioning. "It's still a little odd, though."

"Come on. This is the guy who Tyson held at gunpoint."

"True enough. I don't see any of these guys having any motive or telltale signs. I think it's got to be someone on the prison staff. Maybe not one of the four guards, but someone working for Kingman prison."

"It might be. Or maybe it's someone else entirely, someone we're missing. I'll give Hanson a call. Maybe he's got some insights."

Alexa dialed his number. Officer Hanson picked up on the third ring.

"Hello, Deputy Marshal Chase."

Alexa raised an eyebrow. He'd put her number into his contact list. Apparently he was expecting another call.

"Hello, Officer Hanson. How are you feeling?"

"Still a bit shook up. I took a nice long walk in the pines this morning. That helped."

"Flagstaff has some beautiful mountains. I'm glad they're helping."

"Yeah, it's nice."

His reply was nearly drowned out by the sound of a game show in the background.

"Um, Officer Hanson? Could you turn the TV down? I can barely hear you."

"Oh, that's my mom. She's a bit hard of hearing. I'll move to another room."

The sound faded.

"Thank you, Officer. Now I was wondering if you could tell me a bit more about your interactions with the escapee before he made a break."

"Oh, he was bad news. You know he was the Southwest Slasher?"

"There was the suspicion that he was. He got off for lack of evidence."

"He was guilty as hell. Burned me up that he got to be on a work detail outside the wire. I warned everyone it was a bad idea. I even went and saw the warden about it. But Tyson has a slippery little lawyer that got him onto it. You know that lawyer specifically asked for him to be on an outside work crew? There are plenty of jobs inside the wire. There's groundskeeping and laundry and we have a fabrics factory that makes prison jumpsuits for the whole state. Why couldn't he have worked in one of them. But no, this guy says Tyson needs his air, that since he was such an outdoorsman before his incarceration, it would be mental cruelty to keep him locked up. Imagine that, mental cruelty! He made Tyson out like he was some sort of innocent victim, a holy man even!"

"I hadn't heard any of this," Alexa said.

"Oh, the warden didn't mention that, did he? I'm not surprised. He was the one who approved it, and now he's left with egg on his face. That guy even let that lawyer do some sort of bullshit inspection. The warden is weak. Always worried about his reputation. I'd quit if I didn't need to care for Mom."

Alexa digested this information. She wondered if the warden and Quinnell were birds of a feather. Quinnell certainly seemed to care more about a "scandal" than getting to the bottom of the case. And while he hadn't mentioned the nature of the press release he was working on with the warden, all the previous ones since the breakout had been more damage control than solid information.

Something Officer Hanson said rang an alarm bell in Alexa's head.

"You mentioned the lawyer had done a tour of inspection?" she asked. That was highly irregular.

"Yeah. Threatened a lawsuit. He said there were irregularities in how the prisoners were being treated and he claimed he was going to go to the press and the ACLU with the accusations. The warden let him do a tour of inspection just to shut him up."

"When was this?"

"Oh, I guess a couple of months ago. I can't remember exactly. I only saw him for part of it, because he came into my wing. Checked the camera system, the observation tower, the food, the toilets, you name it. Also went to examine the prison bus. Made a complaint about that. Said the seats were uncomfortable. What the hell? We're not running a summer camp here! The work crew filled his head with all sorts of nonsense and he swallowed it all."

"Wait, so he inspected a work bus with the crew in it?"

"Yeah. Delayed the crew getting to the job by a good twenty minutes. The warden gave him the run of the place."

Alexa paused, thinking. "Under guard, of course."

"Sort of. That lawyer is a nasty piece of work. Always barking at the guys, telling them to back off or he'd charge them with harassment. He sure wanted us around when he went into the cell blocks, though. Wouldn't have lasted two minutes in there without us."

"I see. Did he speak with his client when he was on his cell block?"

"No, and that surprised me. Robby Tyson is on my wing, and the lawyer passed through there to take a look at everything, but he avoided Tyson's cell. It was like he didn't want to talk with him. Probably because it wasn't an official consultation and he wouldn't get paid for it. You know how these lawyers are."

Run of the prison. Avoid Tyson. What did the Jersey Devil say? Copycats distance themselves from their idols before following in their footsteps.

Oh God, it couldn't be.

But why not? Someone who had access to the keys must have done it, and it sure doesn't seem like any of these guards would have set him free.

"Thank you, Officer Hanson. I'll talk to you later."

"You need me to come down to Kingman? I can do that if you need me to."

"That's all right."

"If you need a longer conversation, I can come down to Kingman. It's terrible about this copycat. Maybe I can help you catch him."

"That's all right, Officer Hanson. You get your rest. You've earned it."

"Well, if you need me, call me anytime. And keep me informed, will you? It sets my mind at ease to know someone capable is on the case."

She hung up. Stuart glanced at her. She had put the conversation on speaker.

"Looks like we have to dig a bit into that lawyer," he said.

"Damn right," she muttered.

CHAPTER TWENTY SIX

Sitting in a Kingman diner having lunch, Alexa and Stuart stared at the screen of his laptop as he brought up information about Damon Altschuler, Robby Tyson's lawyer.

As soon as they brought up his website, Alexa recognized him. He was the kind of lawyer who put up brightly colored billboards and had cheap homemade commercials on late-night TV.

Damon Altschuler was based in Phoenix, and despite his perfect smile and slick suit, and despite his cheesy local ads, he had a great batting average as a defense attorney specializing in big cases involving violent offenses. Searching through his website, Alexa could see that anyone answering one of his ads for a DUI or child custody dispute would be given over to one of half a dozen other attorneys who worked under him. Altschuler kept the big cases for himself.

Alexa and Stuart dug deeper, going through his CV and LinkedIn connections. Altschuler had a long history of successful defense cases including using the insanity plea or reduced capacity plea for several violent offenders. He had also written several articles for a law magazine around the turn of the millennium, when his career was just beginning to pick up speed, about the need to be more compassionate about those who had led a violent life.

These piqued their interest. As Alexa ate a Caesar salad and Stuart polished off a chicken fried steak, they delved into these articles.

Several passages caught their attention.

The violent criminal is the product of a violent society, one that glorifies violence while denying basic rights and opportunities to large sections of the population. But when oppressed individuals lash out and do the very violence that has been glorified in mass media and, indeed, in government policy, that society punishes them. We must ask ourselves—whose fault is it that this violence occurs, and who should be punished, the individual who perpetrated the violence or the society that encouraged it?

Stuart muttered something obscene under his breath.

Another passage read, *The serial killer is the epitome of our maladjusted civilization. He, or sometimes even she, is a loner, an outcast in an uncaring society. At times they function well enough within that society, even rising to positions of prominence, but deep down they have split from the rest. They cannot face the contradictions our culture gives them—preaching tolerance while people are discriminated against on the basis of race or age or gender or socioeconomic standing, preaching nonviolence while constantly engaging in foreign wars, preaching obedience to the law while raising up criminals to the level of folk heroes. Is it any wonder that some individuals crack under these contradictions and reject society with all their spirit? The violence a serial killer perpetrates is merely the bleeding knife edge of society's hypocrisy, brought into brutal reality by an individual instead of the state.*"

There were more passages like this, a lot more. After a while, Alexa stopped reading and turned to Stuart.

"These show quite a controversial train of thought. These articles sound more like the writings of some half-baked university revolutionary than an up-and-coming attorney. It's interesting that he stopped expressing these ideas after a few articles."

"Maybe some older attorney told him he was rocking the boat too much when he should have been focusing on building up his practice," Stuart said.

"Or maybe he pulled back because his real feelings were becoming too obvious."

Stuart stared at the screen and shook his head. "A defense attorney becoming a copycat killer? It sounds too crazy to believe."

"Well, someone became the copycat, and the only people we know who had access to the keys were the guards, the warden, and Damon Altschuler."

Stuart tapped on the keys, bringing up Arizona court records and searching for cases where Damon Altschuler had been the defense attorney. The majority were violent offenders, including at least three who targeted women. There was far too much material for a deep dive, but the trend soon became clear enough. He would defend anyone, and there might be a lot more women haters hidden in the files.

And then Stuart came up with the mother lode.

It took them some time to see it. The case dated to almost ten years ago, but it stuck out because the defendant was not accused of a violent crime. Instead, she was on trial for forgery. An art student at Arizona State University named Moira McKinley, recipient of numerous awards for young artists, had decided to do something a bit more challenging and profitable than painting portraits and landscapes.

Instead, McKinley learned engraving and engraved a set of plates for twenty-dollar bills. That showed smarts. Most forgers got greedy and forged larger denominations. Twenties weren't checked nearly as thoroughly.

She showed even greater smarts by even forging the metal foil thread that runs through the bill as a security measure. McKinley did this by painting a special varnish on the spot that glowed under blacklight just like the real thing. The bills were so good that she avoided detection for three years, paying for her tuition, books, apartment, and groceries with fake twenties. She claimed that she earned this cash by teaching art students, and even declared her forged bills as income on her tax returns.

Alexa started laughing.

"What?" Stuart asked.

"Declaring her income. That takes finesse," Alexa said between chuckles.

"I don't see what's so funny about a federal crime."

"Oh come on. Compared with the people we usually deal with, this is almost benign."

"Hmph. Maybe."

They read on.

And that's when it got interesting.

Moira McKinley eventually got caught through pure bad luck. An electric short in her studio while she was in class led to the fire department showing up. They burst in, doused the flames, and then saw an entire lab for making fake U.S. currency.

That landed her in prison on remand, and got her Damon Altschuler as an attorney.

Altschuler knocked down a potential life sentence to ten years by proving the girl was on the autistic spectrum and did not have full awareness of the consequences of her actions. Instead McKinley saw creating the twenties as a challenge, an artistic project, and the only way to support herself since her parents were too poor to pay for her education. Plus she was a promising young person who had never been in trouble with the law. The judge hadn't entirely bought that line of argument, but did reduce her sentence.

Alexa vaguely remembered this case. Focused as she was on grimmer crimes such as murder, drug dealing, and people smuggling, it had slipped under her radar. But she remembered there had been a follow-up story, something just a couple of years ago. She couldn't remember what, though.

"Let me dive in there," Alexa said, turning his laptop to face her more. As Stuart continued to eat, eyes on the screen, Alexa did a search for more recent stories mentioning both Damon Altschuler and Moira McKinley.

She found one almost immediately. The *Arizona Republic* had run an article a little over a year before. "Leading Attorney Takes in Forger."

Alexa read, her jaw slowly dropping.

Well-known Phoenix defense attorney Damon Altschuler is making headlines yet again, but this time it's not for keeping an accused criminal out of jail. Instead, he's taking in a recently released prisoner.

Moira McKinley, an ASU university student found guilty of forgery and sentenced to ten years in a federal penitentiary, has just been released two years early for good behavior. Her case made headlines in 2013 when it was discovered that she had made almost undetectable copies of twenty-dollar bills with engraved plates of her own design. Damon Altschuler took on her case and successfully reduced her life sentence to ten years due to mitigating circumstances.

Now McKinley has been released, and the Arizona Republic *has learned that Altschuler has taken McKinley in, allowing the convicted felon to live in his luxury Scottsdale home.*

When asked about taking in the woman, now 29, the unmarried 55-year-old attorney said, "I have no comment regarding decisions in my personal life. All I wish to say is that Moira has served her time, paid her debt to society, and deserves to live a free and private life just as any other citizen."

The article continued with details of the crime and trial that Alexa already knew. She stopped reading and turned to Stuart.

From the look on his face she could tell he was thinking the same thing she was.

She spoke first.

"A lawyer who makes excuses for the worst types of criminals and then takes in an expert forger."

Stuart said the next thing she intended on saying.

"If she can engrave plates for U.S. currency, she can duplicate a key."

"And he avoided Tyson when he visited the jail. That's suspicious."

"It's also suspicious that he's based in Phoenix, where one of the murders took place."

"Let's call ahead to find out a bit about his movements. I don't want to go all the way down there if he's got an iron-clad alibi."

"Right." Alexa went back to the webpage and found the contact number. She put the phone on speaker and dialed.

A female voice answered. "Damon Altschuler and Associates, attorneys at law. How may I help you?"

"Hi, my name is … Amanda. Um, Amanda Race." Alexa was really bad at lying, and it didn't help that Stuart was rolling his eyes. "I've been charged with stabbing my drunk neighbors and I need legal representation."

"We can certainly help with that, ma'am. Mr. Altschuler has an excellent track record in cases of your kind. You mentioned your neighbors were drunk. Were your neighbors bullying you? Threatening you?"

"Oh yes, they threatened to kidnap my child."

"That's very serious, ma'am. I'm sure Mr. Altschuler can help you. We can schedule a meeting for next week."

"Can't we arrange one sooner?"

She was hoping this would prompt some information about what he was up to. It sure did.

"I'm afraid not. Mr. Altschuler is on vacation right now."

Alexa felt like cold water had just coursed through her veins.

"On vacation?"

"Yes, until next week."

Thinking quickly, Alexa said, "Oh, but a friend said he was working just a couple of days ago."

"I'm afraid your friend must have been confused, ma'am. Mr. Altschuler has been off for the last five days."

Since just before the breakout.

When Alexa didn't say anything, the receptionist asked, "What day would be good for you?"

"Um, Tuesday."

"How does eleven sound?"

"That works. Thank you." She hung up before the woman could ask her anything more.

"On vacation. How convenient," she said.

"I heard." Stuart looked pale. "It's still hard to believe, but yeah, we need to get down there. And I'll drive faster than you've ever seen me drive before."

CHAPTER TWENTY SEVEN

Just as they made it to the outskirts of Phoenix, Stuart barreling down the highway with the siren blaring from atop his unmarked car, Alexa got a text from Stacy.

"Do I have to go home this afternoon?"

School had just gotten out, and Stacy must be about to board the bus that would drop her off at the desert road that led to the Carpenters' trailer and Alexa's home, her real home.

It was obvious the girl didn't want to go back to the trailer.

Alexa couldn't blame her. If her parents noticed she had taken her phone back, there would be hell to pay.

This wasn't a conversation to do on text. She called, first making sure she had turned off speaker mode. Stuart knew a lot about the situation, but she didn't want to embarrass the kid more than she already was.

Stacy picked up on the first ring. Alexa could hear kids laughing and talking in the background, plus the sound of an engine.

"Hey!" Stacy said. "I'm on the bus."

The way she said it told Alexa that she didn't want to talk too explicitly about what was going on. Keeping her family troubles out of her all-important social life was her first priority. Alexa wasn't sure what kind of excuses she used for never having friends over to her house. Knowing her, she had probably changed the Carpenter place from a messy trailer to a beautiful ranch home, but made the excuse that it was too far out and it was better for Stacy to come into town to hang out.

"Did your parents call you at school?" Alexa asked.

"Yeah, they were pissed."

Alexa assumed she meant pissed about the phone, and that the kid didn't want to admit within her friends' hearing that her phone got confiscated. That would break the illusion of her perfect home life.

An odd thought came to her mind. She remembered from a British movie she had seen that "pissed" meant "drunk" in England. She wondered if Stacy knew the double meaning. It probably applied in this case.

"Did they tell you to come straight home?"

"Yeah."

"Did you explain to them that you need to take care of Smith and Wesson while I'm away?"

"Yeah. They didn't care."

"They never interfered with that before."

Stuart glanced at her, then looked back at the road.

"They're saying you can do that yourself."

"Did you explain that I'm out of town?" Alexa didn't want to mention she was coming back into town. The way this case was going, she had no idea where she'd be in an hour, let alone this evening, and she didn't want to get the girl's hopes up.

"Yeah."

"Have they said anything more about the TV show?"

"No."

"Well, tell them that if you don't feed the horses, Melanie won't want to do the story. She's my sister and I'll tell her it's off."

"They'll get totally pissed."

In the American and English senses of the word.

"Tell them I'm making you. They'll be mad at me, not you."

"I guess that will work." The kid sounded doubtful.

Alexa hated to lead on the Carpenters about the show she would do all in her power to stop, but she needed to put out this brushfire fast.

Stacy caught on. "But what will they say when the show doesn't happen?"

"They'll blame me, not you."

Stacy didn't reply. Alexa could feel the kid's doubt and worry practically seep through the phone.

"It'll be all right," Alexa reassured her. She wished she could reassure herself too.

"Are you going to be home tonight?"

"I don't know."

"Where are you?"

Alexa paused. No, she wouldn't lie. That kid heard enough lies in her life.

"Phoenix—"

"Great!"

"—but I don't know how long I'll be here. I came down to interview a suspect but I might have to go right back to Kingman."

"Oh."

"Sorry."

"It's fine," Stacy said in a tone that showed it wasn't.

"I'll try to get back. Why don't you go for a ride?"

"I can't. I'll have to feed them and go straight back home. I just know it."

"OK. Sorry."

Another girl's voice squealed in the background. "Stacy! Check this out!"

"What? No way!" Stacy shouted, then laughed. "Um, Alexa, I got to go."

"OK. Talk to you soon, and I'll try to get back home tonight."

"Cool," Stacy said, then hung up, leaving Alexa to wonder if she had been speaking to her or the girl on the school bus.

Alexa smiled. Let her enjoy her bus ride. She was on the bus for forty-five minutes with a bunch of friends from school. A time to relax and be a kid before having to deal with the drama at home.

"Trouble with Stacy?" Stuart asked.

"Yeah," Alexa said and sighed, putting away her phone.

"Anything I can do?"

"Find her new parents," Alexa grumbled.

"She already did that for herself."

Alexa smiled at him uncertainly.

If only.

* * *

The offices of Damon Altschuler and Associates were located in the nicest part of Scottsdale, Phoenix's high-rent district. It was a modern glass and steel structure that sparked in the afternoon sun. On the carefully tended, water-wasting lawn out front stood one of those weird modern sculptures that to Alexa always looked like some oversized toddler's Play-Doh creation.

Alexa and Stuart didn't stop. They only passed the office because Altschuler's home address, which Stuart had gotten from the city court, was just down the street at the nearest residential district. He obviously wanted to live close to work. Damon Altschuler might have had suspicious ideas about criminal justice and a track record for getting people off lightly for serious offenses, but he certainly was a hard worker. He'd built one of the city's leading law firms from the ground up.

They passed out of the commercial street and into a quiet residential area of large houses and more water-wasting lawns. One even had a fountain. Each back yard, Alexa felt sure, had a large swimming pool. Sometimes she wished she could be dictator of Arizona. She'd have the state's water supply problem solved within a year.

They came to the address, a two-story home that looked more New England than Desert Southwest. Like its neighbors, it had a green lawn and a fenced-in back yard that no doubt contained a pool. They parked and got out.

While the garage door was closed, they could see lights on in the house.

"Let's play it cool," Alexa said. "Pretend we have more questions about Tyson."

"Sounds believable. You take the lead. He'll know escapees are more the U.S. Marshals' jurisdiction than the FBI's."

They walked up three front steps made of marble and rang the doorbell. The chimes of Big Ben sounded inside.

No reply. Alexa was getting sick of ringing doorbells and not getting any reply.

She rang again. After a moment, as the chimes of Big Ben faded away a second time, they heard the sound of approaching footsteps.

The door opened. A woman in her twenties, with black hair and very pale skin, looked at them with a pair of dark eyes that didn't quite seem to focus on them.

"I'm almost done," she said.

"With what?" The statement caught Alexa by surprise so much that she forgot to identify herself.

"With the painting. That's what you interrupted me from doing. I'd be fifteen more brushstrokes closer to finishing if you hadn't interrupted me."

The woman didn't seem to have noticed Alexa's uniform, or indeed showed any curiosity at all as to why they were there.

"I'm Deputy U.S. Marshal Alexa Chase, and this is Special Agent Stuart Barrett of the FBI. We—"

"I didn't make any."

Alexa blinked. "Any what?"

"Any tens. I was going to make some tens after I made the twenties. I didn't. I don't make money anymore. I just make art that I sell for money. It's annoying that my art can't *be* money, but that's illegal."

"We're not here about your prior conviction, Ms. McKinley. We're here to speak with Damon Altschuler. Is he at home?"

"I don't know," Moira said.

"You don't know?"

"I've been in the studio since breakfast."

Alexa glanced at Stuart. "Um, did Mr. Altschuler come into the studio and say he was going out?"

"No."

"Can we come in while you go check? We really need to speak with him."

"All right."

They stepped into a wide front hall. On the walls hung a series of beautiful paintings. Most were desert landscapes, along with a portrait of Damon Altschuler. All were done in rich oils with incredible detail and breathtaking color. Alexa and Stuart stopped and stared.

"Did you do these?" Stuart asked.

"Yes."

Moira walked off without saying another word. Her aspect hadn't changed during the entire conversation.

In a low voice, Stuart said, "I think Altschuler was right with his autism spectrum defense."

"Yeah," Alexa said, still staring in wonder at the paintings. They were museum quality.

"What concerns me is that her consent to letting us in might be disputable in court, and we're dealing with a rabid defense attorney here."

Stuart's fears proved well founded. A moment later, they heard fast, determined steps approaching. From a nearby room strode a short, trim man with salt and pepper hair and a broad face. Alexa recognized him from his local ads. The only difference was in those he was always in a nice suit and smiling. Now he was in chinos and a polo shirt, and was frowning red-faced at them.

"What the hell do you think you're doing coming onto my property without my permission?"

"We got permission from Ms. McKinley."

Altschuler put his fists on his hips, a move that somehow made him look smaller "She's not capable of giving legal consent. You must know that. You talked to her."

"That's very interesting that you admit she's not able to give consent, Mr. Altschuler," Alexa said in a flat voice.

The attorney blinked. Took half a step back. Alexa knew she had scored a hit.

It took all of half a second for him to compose himself.

"She has trouble interacting with the outside world, especially with figures of authority. But she's a genius. Just look at these paintings. If I she had tried to make it on her own as a convicted felon she would have only fallen into crime again, or been victimized. By taking her in I can keep her safe. She's building up a reputation. She'll have a show at the Tucson Museum of Art in a couple of months. And it's an honor to help her. I get to be in the presence of genius."

What else do you get to do? Alexa thought. She didn't ask it, though. She had more pressing questions to ask.

She noticed that Stuart had positioned himself slightly to the side so that if the attorney tried to run further into the house, he could cut him off. Alexa had seen him run down suspects before. As a former university football star, he was scary good at it.

"Have you been following the Robby Tyson case?" Alexa asked.

"I've already been questioned by the Scottsdale Police Department. I think it's time you left. I can get—"

"Can you vouch for your whereabouts for the past four days?"

Altschuler looked from one to the other, appalled.

"Are you serious? Are you actually serious?"

"Yes, Mr. Altschuler, we are," Stuart said.

The attorney snorted. "God, you people must be truly desperate. All right, even though you don't have consent to be on my property, come with me."

He led them further into the house. Stuart stayed right behind him, close enough to watch his every move and grab him if need be. Alexa walked a couple of steps behind the two of them, looking all around, checking every corner and doorway.

She'd had too many nasty surprises on her cases to trust this guy.

CHAPTER TWENTY EIGHT

Alexa followed Stuart and Damon Altschuler, all senses alert. She hated being in a strange place with a suspect, and this one seemed pretty sure of himself.

Of course, so had Tyson.

Despite her nerves, she couldn't help but marvel at the sumptuous paintings Moira McKinley had covered the walls with. Every one of them showed a masterful use of color and shading. Walking through this mansion was like walking through a high-end art gallery.

And there were so many of them. McKinley had an obsessive need to create. She was probably back in her studio now, finishing up yet another masterpiece.

They ended up at the back of the house in a sunny home office. There were only a couple of McKinley's paintings in here. The rest of the walls were covered in signed photos of basketball stars and a framed Phoenix Suns jersey signed by the entire team. Alexa felt a little chill at seeing that. Juana Vazquez had been wearing a Phoenix Suns jersey when she was murdered.

An oak desk ran along two walls, with a large-screen computer and stacks of files. A long window looked out over a spacious back yard with a swimming pool that glittered in the afternoon sun.

Just next to the office, a conservatory jutted out into the garden, a large space entirely enclosed by glass. Alexa wondered how much Altschuler spent on air conditioning to cool such a terrarium. Inside, Moira McKinley stood at an easel painting a sunset. The actual sunset wasn't for another couple of hours, but she had summoned up one of Arizona's natural beauties out of her imagination.

"When I'm working I can look up and see her creating," Altschuler said in a voice hushed with wonder. "She's as much of a genius with painting as I am with the law."

How modest, Alexa thought.

"What did you bring us back here to see, Mr. Altschuler?" Stuart asked with impatience, although he too kept glancing at the conservatory. Seeing true talent at work was a rare privilege.

"This," the attorney said, sitting down at the desk and turning on the computer. "I suppose you're wondering why I happened to take a vacation right when Robby Tyson escaped and his copycat killed him and a couple of other people? Because I'm the copycat, right? Jesus, you're dumb. I don't know how you got that notion into your little heads, but let me get it out of them. I was on vacation for two reasons. Here's the first."

He brought up a video file, time stamped the day Robby Tyson escaped. He started it and they saw it was a recording of a Zoom call. Altschuler and McKinley sat together in the attorney's office, speaking with a well-dressed woman in her middle age. Altschuler let the video run for a minute as they talked about plans for an exhibition on McKinley's work.

"That's the curator of the Tucson Museum of Art. I recorded it just in case she tried to weasel out of any of her promises. While it's Moira's show, she can't handle herself in this kind of situation so it's better if I do everything. Now here's the second reason."

He brought up a video clip time stamped from the night Juana Vazquez got killed. The clip was recorded off of ESPN and showed a Phoenix Suns home game. Devin Booker landed a three-point shot and the crowd erupted.

Altschuler paused the video and pointed to the front row. He was clearly visible, frozen in the act of leaping to his feet, mouth open for a cheer, fists raised over his head.

"That was a hell of a night. I got to the game early and stayed through the end. I believe that was the same night the copycat attacked that chick in the park? Oh, maybe I could have slipped away, right? Or the game was too early. Not sure I have the timing exactly right. The stadium is at the other end of town, though, and with the post-game traffic ... well. And I also have a ton of witnesses that put me at dinners, golf games, and the country club on all those days and nights. You see, Officers, I took a vacation because I've been working hard and I wanted to enjoy the game and negotiate the details for Moira's exhibition, not because I wanted to imitate Robby Tyson's alleged crimes. And they still are *alleged* crimes. For all you Keystone Cops know, the real Southwest Slasher might still be out there, along with his copycat."

Alexa stared at the image of Damon Altschuler, frozen in vicarious triumph, and felt her latest theory crumble. For a second no one spoke.

Then Altschuler stood up to his full, not very impressive height and said,

"Run along, kids. Go play somewhere else."

His mocking laughter rang in their ears as they left.

* * *

Alexa and Stuart stood next to the car, unsure what to do or where to go next. When a curtain twitched in Altschuler's house they got in the car and drove off. The last thing they needed was one of the city's best defense attorneys alleging harassment.

They drove off. Stuart glanced at Alexa, hoping she knew their next step. She didn't have an answer for him.

"That was too slick," she said after a minute. "He had all the answers right away. We didn't even have to explicitly accuse him of anything."

"We can check on the witnesses," Stuart said, although he did not sound hopeful.

"Maybe," Alexa grumbled. She pulled out her phone.

"Who are you calling?"

"The warden at Kingman prison. He was supposed to do some checking."

The warden's receptionist answered. "I'm sorry, Deputy Marshal, the warden left early today. He had a meeting with a contractor. He left me a message for you. They rechecked all employee and visitor records and couldn't find anyone who had any unusual contact with Robert Tyson. Also, they went back five years and could find no incident report of a key for leg shackles going missing, or even being temporarily misplaced."

Given the warden's and Quinnell's desperate need for damage control, Alexa wondered if that were true. She had no way to tell, however.

"Thank you," Alexa grumbled. "Anything else?"

"No, Deputy Marshal. Sorry we couldn't be of more help."

Alexa hung up without saying goodbye. "Damn it!"

"Now what?" Stuart asked.

"I don't know," Alexa snapped. "Now what?"

Stuart shrugged. "Back to digging. We still haven't had time to go through every file."

"Digging through files?" Alexa growled, her voice rising. "All that did was give us a bunch of false leads. Wasting time while the copycat goes around killing people!"

Stuart nodded sadly.

They drove in uncomfortable silence for a time before Stuart spoke.

"How about you call Hanson again? He seemed so dead set against Altschuler, maybe he has some more details that could help."

"Altschuler didn't do it," Alexa said, slumped in her seat.

"But Hanson was the one who was most convinced Tyson was the Southwest Slasher. Maybe he has some other ideas about people who contacted Tyson, people who might have wanted to imitate him."

"Another long shot," Alexa grumbled. She was tired, tired of hostile and uncooperative witnesses, tired of bad parents, tired of bad publicity, tired of everything.

Nevertheless, she pulled out her phone and dialed Hanson's number.

He picked up on the second ring.

"Deputy Marshal Chase, how are you?"

"Fine. We checked on Altschuler. There's good evidence he isn't the one."

"Oh, I'm sorry to hear that. Well, not for Altschuler's sake, but because I thought that was a solid lead. Now since talking to you I thought of another person you might want to check. I should have called you earlier but I felt sure Altschuler was the one."

What he said next got drowned out by a TV commercial in the background.

"Um, Officer Hanson? I think your mother just turned on the TV. Could you go into the next room?"

Hanson laughed. "Oh, sure. As I said last time you called, Mom's a bit hard of hearing. She wants to watch the five o'clock news. I'll move into the next room. Like I was saying, there's a guy who used to work at the prison who used to talk to Tyson a lot. He left a couple of years ago and he …"

Alexa didn't hear what he said next. She wasn't listening.

Instead she was listening to the TV, still audible in the background even though Officer Hanson had moved into the next room.

Faintly, through the words the prison guard spoke to her, Alexa heard a familiar voice.

"This is Action News at five o'clock with Melanie Chase and Rick Marston."

Melanie's voice came on. "Good evening. Our top story tonight …"

That was all Alexa needed to hear. Melanie did the five o'clock and seven o'clock spots for Action News in Phoenix. The show was not syndicated, which meant that Hanson and his mother would not be watching it in Flagstaff, which had its own local news broadcast for that network.

Which meant that Hanson had lied about being in Flagstaff. He was in Phoenix.

And Alexa could think of only one reason why he would lie about where he had gone.

CHAPTER TWENTY NINE

Prison guard George Hanson hung up the phone with a smile. He had fooled them again. That dumb chick was going to go off trying to find James Fulmoth, a guy who had been a guard at Kingman two years ago. Hanson had filled her ears with stories about how Fulmoth had spoken to Tyson several times, and had acted secretive about it.

Hanson had played it cool with the deputy marshal, acting the part of a concerned coworker. He had thought at the time, he told Alexa, that Fulmoth might have been dealing drugs to the prisoners, which was why he didn't make the connection with the copycat right away. But now, on second thought and knowing the lawyer probably didn't do it, they should really check up on Fulmoth.

What an idiot! She fell for it hook, line, and sinker! Just sat there quietly listening to everything he said. Even better, Fulmoth had moved to Alamogordo. That was across the state line. They'd have to get the New Mexico police involved, taking up more time.

And George Hanson didn't need all that much time.

Because he had his crosshairs set on the next woman he was going to charm, knock out, and cut open.

It was going to be so damn easy. That deputy marshal was even going to help him do it.

He strolled back into the living room, where they were giving the five o'clock news. His mother, a hunched little figure with curly gray hair, sat in an easy chair watching the TV through thick glasses.

"I got to go out, Mom."

"What? I haven't seen you all day. First you been on the computer and now you're going out?"

He had been on the computer tracking down Angelina Cruz and learning from her social media as much as he could about her movements. And yeah, now he was going out.

He was going to kill the bitch Robby Tyson was too weak to kill.

"I won't be long, Mom. Just got a few errands to run."

"Who was that on the phone?"

"Oh, the police. They're still looking for that murderer. I'm helping them."

"That's so good of you, honey. You were always such a good boy." His mother let out a sigh. "I just don't know why some people are so bad in this world."

George Hanson smiled at his mother. She was the one good woman among the billions of bad ones.

The prison guard went into his room, put his phone on silent, and left it under his pillow. While Mom really was hard of hearing, he didn't want to risk her hearing the ring tone if that deputy marshal called back. She was always fussing about the guest bedroom when he came down to visit.

Plus he had another reason not to bring his phone. He'd been in the Department of Corrections long enough to hear of hundreds of cases of people getting caught because their phones were traced. Only an idiot would bring their phone with them as they set out to commit a crime.

Well, the prisons were full of idiots, and he wasn't going to be one of them. No, he was smart, too smart for the police, and certainly a hell of a lot smarter than Robby Tyson.

Robby Tyson …

George Hanson's hands curled into fists and his vision grew red as he remembered.

What a disappointment that guy turned out to be! He had killed those bitches with flair, with style, and gotten away with it. He even went to trial and was found innocent for lack of evidence. That's how good he had been in covering up his crimes. Then bad luck defending himself against a drunken bully landed him in jail. Even inside, his innocent act never broke.

That was impressive. Inmates loved to brag about their crimes, and the guys respected and feared Tyson because they thought he was the Southwest Slasher. And yet he always said he was innocent of those crimes, and was just a regular guy stuck in prison because he flew off the handle one night in a bar.

Hanson knew better. He could see the predator behind the "regular guy" façade. It was obvious in the way he moved, the way he sized up a room when he came in, the way he could tell which other inmates were trouble and which were just swaggering. He had a confidence that seemed to say, "Yeah, some of you are gangbangers, some of you are lifetime criminals, but I know something you don't know."

Hanson had studied him from a distance, knowing better than to try and make conversation. Tyson was too smart to reveal anything. He'd had that confirmed by speaking with a few other inmates who had tried and failed to get Tyson to talk. Instead, Hanson had delved deep into his crimes to learn his technique, and admired the prisoner from a distance.

He had also planned, and like Tyson he had planned carefully.

Since he had chain gang duty on a regular basis, he carried a key for the leg shackles when he was on prison property. All he had to do was take a mold. No one knew that he had taught himself locksmithing, and that he had a simple shop set up in a spare locked room in his house in Kingman. He never had guests over, just in case.

Even with these precautions, he took his time. There were random key checks and random searches of his car and person. So he took care to study how well each of his coworkers did their job, and also tried to find a pattern to when people were searched.

It didn't take long to identify the guys who didn't do searches very thoroughly. While all the guards were vigilant about searching cells and inmates for weapons and contraband, even the best were less than enthusiastic about searching their fellow guards, especially when they were leaving. After all, what was there to steal in a prison?

The searching schedule was a bit harder to figure out. It was random, or at least tried to be random, and Hanson kept a calendar at home where he marked down who got searched on what days. After several months of careful note taking, a pattern emerged. What he noticed was that while everyone got searched at least once a week, sometimes it was two. Sometimes a guard was searched two days in a row, the idea being that the guard might get overconfident after the first search and wouldn't be expecting a second. That made things tricky.

Then he realized that no one ever got searched three days in a row, or two days after the first search. If you got searched on a Monday, you might get searched on Tuesday. If you weren't, then you wouldn't get searched until at least Thursday. Also, if you got searched going in, you wouldn't get searched going out that same day.

So one day, three days after being searched, Hanson cut some French bread down the center to make a sandwich, hollowed out one half, and stuck his molding putty inside. Then he covered the cavity up with a bit of bread and added meat, lettuce, and tomato. Then he made a second, normal sandwich and wrapped them up together along with some other snacks. He also brought along a gym bag filled with gym clothes, a towel, shampoo, and flip-flops to give the guys something to search through other than his lunch box. That would help distract them.

As he drove up to the gate, he felt that all these precautionary measures were pointless. He had been searched two days before. According to the pattern, he would not be searched.

"Get out of your vehicle, Hanson," the guards at the gate said. "We need to search you."

Hanson almost had a coronary. Had he miscalculated? Did they suspect him? How could they suspect him? He tried to control himself as he stepped out of his car and they went through his things.

First they searched his car, not very thoroughly. That didn't put his mind at ease. He stiffened as they started going through his gym bag, Hanson stammering out an excuse that he was going to go straight to his workout after his shift, went through his pockets, and barely looked at his lunch sack. They sure didn't open his sandwiches. They didn't even notice that they were a bit heavier than they should have been.

He let out a slow, quiet sigh of relief. He was home free.

Once inside the wire, he had to bide his time. He sweated through the first half of his shift, thinking about the putty hidden inside the sandwich inside his locker. What if the warden ordered a spot check of all the lockers? That happened sometimes. What if someone stole his lunch?

And why did they search him on the third day? They didn't seem suspicious, and the search wasn't all that rigorous. And yet they had broken the pattern. He couldn't have been wrong about that, could he? He had taken very careful notes.

Or maybe the warden had changed the schedule just this week. What bad luck!

During his first fifteen-minute break he went straight back to the locker room, only to find someone there. He had to wait.

Lunchtime arrived. The guards took lunch in shifts so that only one would be gone at a time. So when he got his half hour, he made a beeline back to the locker room and almost sobbed with relief to find it empty.

It might not be for long. He grabbed his lunch, locked himself inside a bathroom stall, and pulled out the putty. After cleaning it off, he made an impression of the key and tucked the putty back into the half sandwich, sticking it in his gym bag. Then he took the rest of his lunch and ate it in the break room, hands trembling and sweat pouring down his back, stomach clenched so tight from fear he felt sure he'd vomit.

The stress and second-guessing continued all through that day until he clocked out, handed in his keys to the duty sergeant, went back to his locker, and retrieved the gym bag. As he walked to his car, he felt sure he'd be searched on the way out. Even though it never happened, it might happen today. No, it *would* happen today. Had he acted suspicious? Had people seen he was nervous? Were his hands shaking?

And then the guys were waving him through the gate and he drove out onto the street, home free.

He couldn't stop laughing all the way back to his house. He had gotten away with it! He hadn't acted nervous at all. He was like Tyson, cool as a cucumber. No one knew what was really going on inside.

All his life he had been pulling one over on people. He had just a friendly, trustworthy demeanor. No one ever suspected that the skinned cats deposited all around his hometown were his teenaged handiwork, or that the liquor store break-ins had been done by him, or that he was responsible for knocking out that bum on the edge of town last year. A concussion and full memory loss. Never could identify his assailant, not that anyone would listen to an old wino anyway.

Yep, good old George Hanson was an upstanding member of society. Everyone trusted that guy. Now it was time for Hanson to take a step up to the big leagues.

Soon Tyson would be free, and the two of them would team up to leave a trail of dead women across Arizona.

That night he stayed up late, fashioning the little key that would set Tyson free.

Smuggling it in two days later was easy. It was too small to set off the metal detector, and he knew he wouldn't be searched two days after a random search. Much more confident now that he had proven to himself smarter than anyone else at the prison except Robby Tyson himself, he performed his duties with a calm detachment until they were out by the highway. Then he dropped the key near Tyson when the killer's back was turned and continued his rounds.

The rest had been easy. He hadn't resisted and Tyson hadn't hurt him. Hanson hadn't even been scared. The Southwest Slasher only went after women. That man in the bar had been the exception because he had attacked Tyson. As long as Hanson and the three other guards played it cool, he knew Tyson wouldn't touch him, and he had been right.

What he hadn't expected was the kind of reception he had received from Tyson when he tracked him down at his great-uncle's cabin. That had put Hanson into a rage, and set the stage for tonight's events.

Standing before the full-length mirror in his bedroom, Hanson carefully dressed in his prison uniform, complete with nightstick and handcuffs. The only extra addition was a hunting knife tucked in the back of his belt, and a loose jacket over his top. While it was too hot for a jacket, even now that the sun had set, it hid both the knife and the uniform. Now he simply looked like some guy with a jacket and gray pants instead of a prison guard.

That uniform was only for his intended victim, the next on what he hoped to be a very, very long list.

CHAPTER THIRTY

Alexa frantically called the warden's office, hoping someone was still there even though it was night. At the same time, Stuart called the Phoenix police station, asking for the address of anyone named Hanson.

They sat parked in the FBI car just a hundred yards down the road from the lawyer's house, still stunned at the discovery that Officer Hanson had lied to them about where he had gone for his sick leave.

Their calls did not bring about good results. No one answered at the warden's office, and the Phoenix police check brought back a list of no fewer than thirty-one households rented or purchased under the name Hanson.

"He mentioned a mother but not a father," Stuart said. "Maybe we could narrow it down by searching for only women. No, damn it, that won't work. The house might still be registered under the dead father's name. We could try to trace Hanson's cell phone but a court order would take ages."

"Hold on." Alexa made another call, this time to Kingman Prison's front gate.

"Hello, Kingman Prison, this is Officer Manning speaking."

"Hello, Officer Manning, this is Deputy Marshal Alexa Chase. I need the emergency contact number for George Hanson."

"Is there a problem?"

"There might be," she said impatiently. "Could I have that number please?"

"Well, normally we don't give out numbers. It's—"

"I'm a deputy United States marshal and this is a criminal investigation!"

"Ma'am, you have to understand that I cannot identify you and as a branch of the Department of Corrections, the privacy of our employees is a matter of security."

"Jesus Christ! Give me Sergeant Larson then. He knows who I am."

"He's already gone home, ma'am."

"Then Officer Brnovich."

"Gone home."

"Officer Donner?"

"Sorry, ma'am."

"Ugh!"

Alexa hung up, and only just managed not to smack her phone against the dashboard. Meanwhile Stuart was tapping away at his own phone.

"There's a George Hanson registered here in Phoenix, but he's sixty-two and works for the Fire Department. I just found his blog."

"Damn it! There's no way we can get through all these Hansons."

Stuart stared at his phone. "There's got to be some way. I have the Phoenix PD working on it. They're also looking up the warden's home phone number. We should have it in a bit."

"A bit? A bit! What if we don't have a bit? What if Hanson is taking bits out of his next victim right now?"

Alexa slammed her fist into her palm. She felt so sure it was him, and so helpless. He had been so eager to throw suspects her way, so eager to help, all the while lying to them about his location. Of course he didn't want them to know he was in Phoenix. That would put up a major red flag. So he had lied, said Flagstaff, a city far away from all the murders.

It had to be him. But they couldn't find him.

Through her anger and fear, an idea came.

"Copycats want to imitate their idols," she said, thinking out loud. "But they don't kill their idols. I've never heard a case where they did that. So what does this copycat want?"

"To be better than Tyson?"

Alexa snapped her fingers. "Exactly! Now how can he be better?"

"Well, Tyson killed allegedly three women, and got convicted for manslaughter against a man."

"Sure. So he wants to kill more than Tyson. He's already killed three. Two women and Tyson. He needs to kill at least two more. And he'll want one of those to be a woman. But which woman? When he can charm his way to anyone? Hell, he even made me believe him! I thought he was a damn hero!"

"Don't beat yourself up over that. He fooled everybody. So how can we know where he'll strike next?"

They came up with the answer at the same time.

"The victim who got away!" they shouted in unison.

"Right," Alexa said, looking out the window but not really seeing anything. "Just like Drake Logan. He went after the one that got away. Hanson will go after the one that got away from Tyson."

"Angelina Cruz," Stuart said, already pulling up her address on the GPS. He had stored it in the device's memory at the beginning of the investigation.

They tore off down the street, Alexa getting on the police radio to alert the local units, all the while having a sick feeling in her stomach that they were already too late.

* * *

George Hanson knocked on the door of the run-down house in Peoria. It was perfectly located for what he wanted. It stood on a poorly lit street in the bad part of town, a cheap structure of flaking stucco with a gravel yard. There wasn't even a fence.

The house next door looked abandoned. The one on the other side looked occupied but no one was home at the moment. Across the street, some people were having a party in their back yard. Out of sight, thankfully, but they sure made a lot of noise with their booming Latino music.

Usually Hanson hated neighbors having loud parties, but this one would drown out the screams quite nicely.

He had parked a block away and walked. A couple of people lounging on their front porches had given him a second look. He wasn't dressed right for the neighborhood or the weather.

Not much he could do about it. He didn't want them to see his prison uniform.

At least they hadn't seen much of his features, thanks to the baseball cap he wore pushed down low over his brow.

Glancing to the left and right to make sure no one was in sight, he took off both the cap and jacket. Now he needed to be seen.

He knocked on the door. Judging from the old banger in the driveway, Angelina Cruz was home. Through the Department of Corrections grapevine and his own research in newspaper articles and court records, he had learned she was a no-good druggie. Killing her would be doing the world a favor.

The door opened, although the outer door of metal mesh, no doubt locked in this neighborhood, remained closed.

A Hispanic woman in her early thirties stood there, her eyes bleary as they took in his uniform.

"Hi. Can I help you?" she asked.

George Hanson smiled. He recognized Angelina Cruz from the old newspaper photos. Another several years of drinking and drug abuse had added ten pounds to her short figure, and her face was a bit puffy, but it was definitely her.

"Angelina Cruz? I'm George Hanson. Deputy Marshal Alexa Chase sent me to talk to you. I'm helping her with the investigation."

"Oh right. She talked to me on the phone."

I thought so.

"Yes. As I'm sure you've been informed, Robby Tyson has been killed and there's somebody out there who's imitating his crimes."

Angelina shuddered.

"Yeah," she said in a quiet voice, suddenly looking like a scared little girl. Hanson felt a stirring in his chest. This was going to be good.

A male voice called from inside the house. "Angelina, who's at the door?"

Oh, crap.

"Some guy investigating the murders," Angelina called over her shoulder. She turned back to Hanson. "What did you say your name was again?"

"George Hanson."

Her eyes grew clearer. "Oh! You're the prison guard Robby Tyson took hostage."

Hanson put on a rueful face. "Yes, I am."

"Are you all right?"

Hanson hung his head. "Oh, he didn't hurt me, but I feel terrible about him getting free. That's why I volunteered to help hunt him down, and now I'm hunting down the copycat. I was wondering if I could ask you a few questions?"

A man appeared in the hallway behind Angelina. He was about the same age as her, tall and well-built, obviously a gym jock.

"Hey, man, glad you're hunting that psycho," he said.

Perhaps reassured by Hanson's uniform and the presence of her male friend, Angelina Cruz unlocked the outer door.

The man came up and shook Hanson's hand. "This isn't the kind of neighborhood where we open the door to strangers, but you're a hero, man. Good to meet you. I'm Marco, Angelina's brother."

"Pleased to meet you, Marco."

"Come on into the living room," Angelina said.

They walked down the short hallway. Hanson glanced into a side room and didn't see anyone in there. As they entered the living room, he didn't see anyone in there either. A lumpy old sofa and an armchair were the main furnishings, with a dirty coffee table between them. On it was an ashtray with a joint. The heavy smell of marijuana hung in the air.

Marco cursed and fumbled for the joint to put it away. Hanson laughed.

"I'm a prison guard, not a cop."

Marco grinned. "Right on."

"Yeah, I'm not going to arrest you," Hanson said, still laughing. That kept Marco and Angelina off guard as he pulled out his nightstick and brandished it like a big joke. They laughed too.

There's a reason they call it "dope."

Hanson smacked Marco over the head as hard as he could. The man's knees buckled under him and he felt to the ground.

Angelina screamed, but with the music from the party across the street reaching all the way into the living room, Hanson doubted the neighbors heard her.

They certainly didn't hear her groan as Hanson smacked her upside the head with his baton, knocking her out cold.

He turned back to Marco, who had risen to his hands and knees, half stunned. Hanson wound up and let him have it on the back of the head as hard as he could.

Marco fell face first onto the carpet and did not move.

Hanson hit him several more times anyway.

Tyson killed a guy too. I guess it's all part of doing business. I wonder how many more guys will get in the way.

Then he turned to Angelina's prone body lying all sexy and vulnerable.

He paused, savoring the moment. He was about to equal Robby Tyson's death toll, something he had dreamed about for years. Tyson had been a class act, a real charmer who lured his victims with a false sense of security.

Like George Hanson himself. He had always been a charmer. Even in high school he had no trouble getting girls into bed with him. As he grew older, he realized he had a real skill. He could talk his way out of speeding tickets, impress people of all walks of life, and even gain the respect of the hundreds of thugs he had to guard. None of them ever mouthed off at him or talked behind his back. The inmates actually liked him.

More importantly, they respected him.

That made it doubly painful when Robby Tyson didn't show him the same level of respect.

After waiting a suitable period of time after the breakout, Hanson had gone up to the cabin, the one he'd discovered through painstaking research into Tyson's family. As he expected, Tyson had holed up there. It took all of Hanson's charm to convince the escapee that he wasn't there to bring him in. The shocked look on Tyson's face when he revealed that he had duplicated a key and dropped it near Tyson as he worked by the highway was something he'd treasure all his life.

But what came next was something that would boil his veins the rest of his life.

"Why?" Tyson had asked, staring at him. "Why break me out?"

"Because you and I are the same. We can charm the pants off of any girl we want, but we'd rather gut them. Ever since reading about your trial I knew what I wanted to be. You showed me the way. I broke you out so that we could join forces. Think what the two of us could do! We'll paint the desert red with women's blood!"

Tyson had stared at him for a long moment, then slowly shook his head.

"You got me all wrong."

"What? Are you trying to tell me you're not the Southwest Slasher? Come on, Robby. I'm on your side. You don't have to hide from me."

Again the shake of the head. "All that time inside really made me think. I'd gone down a sick path. Gotten all twisted up inside. The time alone really helped clear my head of a bunch of stuff that had been bothering me for all my life. That's why I hardly ever talked to anyone. All those convicts would just dirty up my mind again. I can't kill anymore. I just want to live my life and be alone. Hell, I've even considered turning myself in. Maybe I can't be trusted on the outside. Oh well, I guess they'll probably catch me sooner or later anyway. In the meantime, I'll just hide out here and enjoy nature. It always was my only true friend. I wasn't meant to be a killer. I was meant to live in peace in the wilderness. People and I just don't mix."

Hanson couldn't believe his ears. Robby Tyson had gone soft?

He had no choice but to kill him then. He had smacked Tyson down with his nightstick and then cut his gut open like those women Tyson was too weak to kill anymore.

Hanson had cried when he had done it, cried for the first time that he could remember. It had felt like his entire world had fallen apart.

But no, it was only beginning.

A low buzzing from another room caught Hanson's attention. Hanson moved into the hallway and, directed by the sound, moved into the kitchen.

A cell phone lay on the counter. It stopped buzzing just as he entered the room.

Was this Angelina's phone or Marco's?

Either way, whoever called might wonder why they didn't pick up. It might not have been the first time. Stoned as they were, they might not have noticed it buzzing in the living room.

Hanson moved back to the living room.

He looked down at Angelina Cruz lying unconscious on the floor and touched the hilt of his hunting knife.

"Now to finish what Robby Tyson started. Time to be better than he ever was. But first I got to drag you outside. Tyson always made his kills outside."

He moved over to a sliding glass door looking out over a darkened back yard. He opened the door and stood listening for a moment. Other than that damn Mexican music playing across the street, he didn't hear anyone. Good, he'd be left alone.

Hanson went back to Angelina and, lifting the unresisting body up from under her arms, he pulled her out of the house.

Just then she began to stir.

CHAPTER THIRTY ONE

Alexa's hands clenched as Stuart parked half a block down the street from Angelina Cruz's house. Two other squad cars had already arrived. They had parked out of sight well down the street on either end to block off any escape by car. They had also sent a spare officer around the back of the house.

Alexa would have preferred a SWAT team, or at least a third squad car, but the Peoria police, understaffed and too stretched out to police a large area, couldn't spare any more men on the hunch of a couple of federal agents.

It was night now, the last faint traces of dusk making the otherwise black sky a deep blue to the west. Street lighting was poor in this area, leaving a lot of shadows. Plus the houses themselves obscured vision. If Hanson wanted to hide, it would be difficult to root him out.

Plus on the way over, they had discovered in state records that he was a gun owner. Alexa didn't think he'd bring a gun to something like this, but she couldn't be sure.

One of the local police called over the radio. "You want one of us to go in with you?"

"Negative," Alexa said. "Stay blocking the means of escape. Keep an eye out. He may not even be to the residence yet and if he spots a police car he'll try to leave. This guy's slippery, and if he gets away he'll take the opportunity to kill again."

Assuming he hasn't killed already tonight.

Alexa and Stuart got out and checked their guns. They could hear a loud party somewhere, the upbeat Latino music giving the dark neighborhood a surreal carnival atmosphere.

How many civilians are completely unaware of the dangers living right next door?

Most of them, I guess.

They paced down the street, spread out to opposite sidewalks. Alexa realized that during this investigation they had gotten into that habit, something prompted by Stuart's military service.

Sensitive about the war and yet as soon as he gets home he joins another one right here in the United States.

She didn't have time to think about that now. The walkie-talkie on her belt crackled.

"We've located a vehicle registered to George Hanson a couple of blocks from your location."

"Thank you."

"And we just tried calling Ms. Cruz a third time. Still no answer."

Alexa caught Stuart's eye across the road and gave him a thumbs-up. They increased their pace, looking all around them. No one was on the street. A few shadows moved behind the curtains of the party house. That was the only sign of life.

Angelina Cruz's house stood in a dark lot. Although the lights were on inside, they shone only dimly through dark red curtains. A single weak light shone just above the front door. The rest of the property lay in half shadow.

Just as they came up the walk, they heard a scream inside.

A woman's scream, muffled by the walls and the blaring music from the neighbors.

As Alexa rushed up to the door, she grabbed her walkie-talkie and shouted, "Hanson's already inside!" Then she dropped the walkie-talkie and drew her gun.

Stuart was already at the door, holding the knob with one hand and gripping his pistol with the other. The door was a security door, made of heavy metal mesh that could be kept locked while the inner wooden door could be opened for the resident to speak with any visitor in safety.

Stuart tried the door. Locked.

Another scream. There was no way to break open that door in time.

Alexa spotted a heavy ceramic pot with soil and a cactus in it beside the front porch. She holstered her gun, grabbed the pot, hefted its considerable weight, and chucked it through the nearest window.

The entire pane smashed out. Alexa hopped onto the windowsill, ignoring the bits of glass jabbing into her hand and thigh, and dropped into the darkened room on the other side.

Light and the sound of movement beyond a half-open door led her further into the house. Her gun was in her hand. She didn't remember drawing it. A thud behind her told her Stuart had jumped into the house too.

They burst into a hallway. A shape ducked into a doorway just a few feet away.

"U.S. Marshal! Come out with your hands up!"

Alexa knew Hanson had no intention of doing that, and Alexa had no intention of letting him get away. She ducked around the corner, coming low and keeping the doorway protecting as much of her body as possible.

They came into a living room. A man lay face down just beyond the doorway, his head a mass of torn flesh and blood. A broken nightstick lay next to him. She knelt by him and felt his back with her free hand. Breathing, but just barely.

She turned to Stuart. He was already on the radio for an ambulance.

But where was Officer Hanson? She darted a look all around before noticing the sliding glass door to the back yard was open a crack.

She burst out, not waiting for Stuart.

No one in the back yard as far as she could see. The whole thing was enclosed by a tall wooden fence, unlike the open front yard. The sound of a fist hitting flesh made her turn and spot a narrow path running between the fence and the side of the house. She hurried around the corner …

… and stopped.

Officer George Hanson stood in his prison uniform, a hunting knife in one hand and Angelina Cruz cringing at his feet.

"Freeze!" Alexa said, leveling her gun at him.

Hanson grabbed Angelina and held the knife to her throat, keeping her unresisting body in front of him like a shield.

"There's no escape," Alexa said. "Let her go and give yourself up."

"Put your gun down or the bitch gets it!" Hanson snarled.

"Not gonna happen," Alexa snapped.

"I heard you come in with a partner. He shows himself, this girl is dead meat."

Alexa sensed Stuart just inside the doorway to the living room. He must have heard the shouting, but he was still several paces away.

She forced herself not to look at him. She was more in the light than Hanson, who remained in shadow to the side of the house. He could see her every expression and she could barely see him at all.

"Don't move, Agent Barrett!" Hanson ordered.

Alexa couldn't hear her partner moving, but that didn't mean he wasn't.

For a second, silence reigned. Each person looked at the other, unsure what to do next.

Her eyes began to adjust to the light. The passage between the side of the house and the fence, which was above head level, measured about five feet wide. Hanson and his captive were about ten feet away from her, close to the front of the house. Beyond Hanson she could just make out where the wooden fence turned to meet the house, sealing off the back yard from the street. Although she couldn't see it, she knew there would be a locked gate there. Pretty standard for Arizona homes. No way Hanson could open that without Alexa getting a shot off.

He was trapped and he knew it.

Angelina let out a soft moan. That seemed to break the spell.

Hanson gave Alexa a devilish grin. "You're not going to stop me from achieving my dream."

When he said that, something Thornton had said clicked in her mind.

Copycats may love their idols, but they want to be better than them too.

And that gave her an idea.

"You're never going to be better than Robby Tyson," Alexa said.

Hanson glared at her. "Like hell I'm not."

"Tyson killed three women and one man. What have you done? Two women and one man."

"Two men," the prison guard corrected.

"That guy inside is still alive, and an ambulance is already on its way."

"Doesn't matter." Hanson gave Angelina a shake. She moaned. One of her arms moved half up to her chest before falling down again. "I'm going to kill the one that Tyson let go."

Alexa forced herself to laugh.

"Yeah, but he never got caught. You just did. Even if you kill her, you're still never going to be half the man Tyson was. And that man lying back in the house? The one that's going to pull through? You got him by surprise, didn't you? Tyson stood face to face with the man he fought. No tricks. No surprises. Just up and killed him. Like a real man."

Even in the dim light, she could see Hanson's face darken.

"He was weak!" he shrieked. "When I talked to him in his cabin he said he wanted to give it up. He wasn't a real killer. He didn't have it in him!"

"And you're nothing compared to him," Alexa went on relentlessly. She wanted to goad him, taunt him until he did something stupid. Because not only did she want to save Angelina, she wanted to fight this son of a bitch. "You couldn't even match his numbers. You'll spend the rest of your life in prison knowing you never quite made the grade. Unless …"

Alexa holstered her pistol.

"What are you doing?" Stuart and Hanson asked at the same time. Stuart had gotten a lot closer to her than she realized.

"Giving you a chance," she told Hanson. "Think you can take on a woman who knows how to fight back? Or are you too much of a wimp to try?"

"What the hell is this?" Hanson asked.

"You got a knife," she said through gritted teeth, the heat rising up in her. "I got my gun, but do I have a chance to draw it in time? Let her go and take me on."

"Yeah, right! Your partner will shoot me if I take a single step."

"Damn right I will!" Stuart shouted. "Now let Ms. Cruz go and surrender, or you're going out in a body bag."

Hanson brought his knife up close to Angelina's throat and ducked down behind her.

"Think your aim is good enough?" Hanson called to Stuart, still out of sight to him around the corner.

"Let's find out," the FBI man snarled.

"No, Stuart," Alexa said. "Put your gun away. This is the only way to save Angelina, by giving this chickenshit a chance to prove himself."

The captive moaned, stirred. Her eyes fluttered open.

Angelina didn't say anything, just stayed stiff and unresisting in Hanson's grasp.

"Make the FBI guy move away and we have a deal," Hanson said.

"I'll do you one better." Alexa stepped into the darkened little space beside the house. One step. Two. Three. She was now just five feet away from Hanson, almost within reach.

"Better?" she asked in a mocking voice. "No way Stuart can get around the corner in time, and even if he does, I'll be in the line of fire. So make your play, Hanson, if you think you got it in you."

She could see Hanson hesitate.

"If you get a cop, you'll be better than Tyson. Way better. But do you have the guts? Do you have the guts to go up against two holstered guns with a knife?"

He paused, just for a moment. A grin started to spread across his face, slowly, tentatively at first, then grew like the Cheshire Cat's, the teeth clear in the dim shadow. His eyes sparked with a fanatical gleam.

With a loud howl, he shoved Angelina aside and rushed for Alexa.

Angelina fell hard on the floor, but pushed herself up immediately.

"Bastard!" she shouted, grabbing at his foot.

Hanson was stronger and wrenched his foot away, but the move made him stumble, made him pause for a crucial half second.

Long enough for Alexa to draw her gun.

She got off two shots. Two bullets pierced his chest. Hanson jerked like a marionette.

A moment later he slammed into Alexa, his weight and the force of his charge knocking her down.

The back of her head struck the fence. Stunned, her gun fell away, and she lay for a moment helpless as Hanson fell on top of her, then slid to the side. Whether by accident or design, he had put her body between himself and Stuart's line of fire.

Face twisted in rage and pain, Hanson raised the hunting knife. Alexa gripped his hand and they struggled. Hanson jerked his hand away. He still had strength. The shock of the two shots hadn't come onto him yet. He still had time to kill.

Stuart cursed, rushed over, and tried to grab Hanson's knife arm. The prison guard slashed at him, cutting his forearm. The FBI agent cried out and took half a step back.

Alexa planted a fist in Hanson's face. His head jerked back, thumping against the ground. Alexa punched him again, then grabbed at his knife hand and twisted.

The shock was getting to him now. His blood soaked both their uniforms. He resisted, the last of his strength making them struggle for a couple of moments, then she twisted the knife out of his hand.

Hanson roared, got to his knees, and got a kick to the head courtesy of the FBI. The killer flopped down on the ground. Alexa gave him another couple of punches, snarling with rage, and then cuffed him, leaning hard on the small of his back with her knee.

The sound of footsteps made her look up. Two Peoria police officers burst around the corner.

"Get your first aid kit and call an extra ambulance," Stuart said.

Don't call an extra ambulance, Alexa thought as she stood up. *This guy doesn't deserve it.*

She didn't say anything, though. If she had learned anything from Robert Powers, it was that what you felt didn't matter, it was what you did.

CHAPTER THIRTY TWO

Alexa sat slumped on Angelina Cruz's front porch, utterly spent. She barely saw the police officers and EMTs rushing all around her, going in and out of the house, taking statements and collecting evidence. She was done. Hanson had been caught. Others could pick up the pieces.

A siren cut the night air as an ambulance pulled away with Hanson under heavy guard. Another ambulance had already left with Angelina's brother.

Stuart walked over to her, a bandage wrapped around his wrist.

"The EMTs told me it looks like Marco Cruz will pull through. Severe concussion and probably a fractured skull, but he should be fine after a long hospital stay."

"And Hanson?" Alexa asked.

"Looks like he'll live," he said.

"A pity," Alexa grumbled. "He'll probably get a lethal injection eventually."

"Yeah, eventually."

With the trial and appeals, that might not happen for another ten years. Meanwhile, two innocent people, murdered just because a weak man wanted to be big.

But it was over. Alexa wanted to go home.

Stuart looked down at her, sympathy showing in his face.

"I know what you're thinking. Why is he alive and those two women dead? That's not justice. But we don't get to bring justice to the world, not as much as we like anyway. Because once the crime is committed, you can never really balance the scales. We do what we can. That's all we can hope for."

Alexa nodded. She hoped Hanson would suffer in prison. A prison guard turned convict? The other inmates would not look kindly on him.

Stiffly she rose, the dried blood on her uniform crackling with the movement. She wouldn't even try to get it cleaned. She'd burn it tonight. Hanson's blood made her feel sullied.

"How's your wrist?" she asked.

"Just a scratch. No stiches. Stings like hell, though. Like fifty bees lined up on my arm and stung me all at the same time. Annette is coming to pick me up." He grinned. "I'm staying over at her house tonight. She said she'll take tomorrow off and give me the spa treatment."

"The spa treatment?"

"I don't know what that is either. I'm looking forward to finding out."

Alexa managed a smile. Stuart grew serious.

"I'm sorry I blew up at you before."

"I shouldn't have read up on you. I was being nosy."

"No, you were being a cop. It's just that … I don't like people looking into all that stuff. It doesn't matter."

What doesn't matter? Your FBI commendation? Your military service? Your girlfriend getting murdered? Any of it?

And am I really supposed to believe none of it matters?

Alexa had no answers to any of that. Stuart Barrett remained a riddle to her.

"Enjoy your time off," Alexa said.

"You too."

Alexa put a hand on Stuart's shoulder, and then headed over to one of the squad cars, hoping to hitch a ride home. Unlike her partner, she wouldn't be going back to anyone.

On the other side of the police tape she saw Melanie and the Action News truck. Her sister-in-law rushed up to her.

"Oh my God, are you OK?"

"It's not my blood," Alexa said, passing Melanie by and knowing that wouldn't shake her. When the reporter followed, Alexa said, "You got here quick."

"I have a good friend in the Peoria Police Department."

That reminded Alexa of something Melanie had said over one drunken Thanksgiving dinner. "I don't have friends. Only contacts." That statement perfectly summarized why Alexa hated her.

"Where are you going?" Melanie asked.

"Home."

"Do you need a lift?"

A lift would mean an interview. Melanie didn't have sisters-in-law, only contacts.

"No."

"Come up to the ranch this weekend," Melanie said. "You need a rest. It did you a ton of good after your last case. We'll go riding."

Alexa stopped, studying her sister-in-law. Melanie hardly ever went to the ranch, and she hated riding. She was only saying that hoping that Alexa would bring Stacy up.

Rage began to simmer in her chest, the same rage as when she was fighting Hanson. Alexa looked around. Too many people.

"Let's go for a walk," Alexa said.

"All right." Melanie sounded like she had just been offered a present.

They went past the crowd and the cars until they got out of the lights. The street seemed dark by contrast. The neighbors who were curious were all clustered around the scene. Those who didn't want to get involved, even as spectators, had shut their doors and drawn their blinds. After walking a block, Alexa and Melanie were alone.

Alexa turned and squared up on her, making Melanie stop short, jerking back a bit in surprise.

"I'll make a deal with you," Alexa said.

"A deal?"

"You inadvertently helped me solve this case. I'll tell you how if you promise to drop the story about Stacy and leave her alone from now on."

"But—"

"That's the deal and you're taking it."

Melanie blinked. Even Alexa was surprised at the force with which those words came out.

"You are not going to interfere with me and Stacy. You are going to call the Carpenters and tell them the schedule is filled up for this season."

"We don't have programming seasons in the news business."

"They won't know that."

"And I thought you wanted the show canceled."

"If you cancel it outright, they'll get mad and take it out on Stacy. And me. Us. I can't have that. String them along. Maybe they'll forget about it."

Alexa knew that kicking your problems down the road rarely solved them, but she couldn't see any better way out.

Melanie studied her for a minute. Even in the half-light of the dim street, Alexa could see the calculation in her eyes.

"So what's this about me helping you find the murderer?"

"I was talking to Hanson on the phone and he was giving me names of people I should investigate. Trying to send me on false trails to buy himself time. He had told me he had left his house in Kingman to stay with his mother in Flagstaff. I had no reason to doubt him so I didn't check. But then I heard the Action News five o'clock theme come on, and your voice."

Melanie took a deep breath, eyes sparkling.

"That's wonderful."

Wonderful. Three people are dead, a woman is traumatized, my partner has a new scar, and she calls it wonderful.

"So there's your story. Run it and leave Stacy alone."

"That's great! I'll put it on the eleven o'clock spot, and the morning show. Would you be available for an interview?"

"No."

"I understand. I can fill in the background. But you might want to reconsider the Stacy story."

Alexa's hand went to Melanie's throat. The reporter took in a sharp intake of breath. Alexa didn't squeeze. Her fingers barely touched skin. But she held her hand there.

"That's the deal. You leave my girl alone. You understand?"

Melanie, stiff as a board, didn't dare nod. She only whispered, "Yes."

"Now get out of my sight, you parasite."

Alexa turned and walked down the street, reeling at what she had just done.

She had threatened violence toward her own family.

To protect her own family.

What had Stuart said? *Family is what you make of it.*

Melanie wasn't family. Not really. While Stacy, who wasn't related to her at all, was closer than anyone in her biological family. And Melanie had been way out of line.

Touching someone else in anger is way out of line.

For a moment she thought of going back and apologizing, but that would make Melanie think she could go back on their arrangement.

And, truth be told, she did not feel sorry, more like shocked at the depth of her anger, and that it could leak out to someone she was related to.

A shudder ran through Alexa's body. She had walked around the corner now, and the lights of the emergency vehicles were now just a pulsing glow over the rooftops. She'd walk a while, then catch a cab.

While this wasn't the kind of neighborhood where a woman should walk alone, she was a woman in a U.S. Marshals uniform soaked with a murderer's blood. No one was going to mess with her.

And no one was going to mess with Stacy either.

She took a deep breath of the warm night air, and smiled.

Her anger had gotten a bit out of hand back there, but as Powers wrote in his journal, it could be a force for good.

And scaring the crap out of her sister-in-law to protect a vulnerable child counted.

* * *

Three days later, Alexa and Stacy rode a couple of her father's horses north of the family ranch. It was one of their favorite trails, a narrow ravine cut between two steep, red-rocked cliffs on which clung cacti and a few hardy desert shrubs and wildflowers. Alexa pointed to the ridge top, where a javelina and her young were snuffling about looking for food.

To Alexa's surprise, Stacy did not pull out her phone and take pictures. Riding in the countryside seemed to have a magical effect on her. She sometimes didn't bring her phone at all. Back in Phoenix it was practically glued to her hand.

Here she enjoyed a deeper, more enduring happiness.

Enduring as long as she's here, Alexa thought with regret.

Alexa, on the other hand, had been on edge since the wrap-up of the case. Melanie had boasted about "the surprising role of Action News" in catching Hanson on the air for several days running, adding to and elaborating the story with each retelling. She had not called Alexa or Stacy and had not come up to the ranch this weekend. She had also not mentioned their altercation to Wayne. Her brother was too forthright not to say something if she had.

Stacy hadn't said anything either.

All this silence, especially Melanie's silence, had Alexa worried.

While it was an unspoken rule never to talk about Stacy's parents when they were riding, Alexa couldn't help herself.

"Did your mom and dad say anything about that show?"

Stacy's face darkened. "No. Well, they said it would be next year and that I should help at the stable more to make a better story. They were also saying a camera crew will come up here."

"Wait. They said that or Melanie?"

"I think that was their idea. I thought you were going to stop all this."

"I'm trying, kiddo."

"Oh, look!"

A hummingbird the color of turquoise flitted across the path, hovered in front of Stacy for a moment, and was gone.

"Let's take the east fork," Stacy said, pointing to where the ravine divided up ahead. "We saw some hummingbirds there last time, remember?"

"All right," Alexa said, glad a bit of Arizona's wildlife had turned the girl's thoughts to happier things. The desert had a way of doing that.

After a minute, the horses' hooves clattering on the loose stones of the ravine, Stacy asked,

"Why didn't Stuart come up this weekend?"

"He's with his girlfriend." She decided not to mention him getting hurt. Stacy had enough to worry about.

"He's got a girlfriend?"

"Is that so surprising?"

"I guess not. I thought he liked you."

"He doesn't like me."

"Yeah, he does."

"He hasn't said anything, has he?"

"No. I just notice these things."

Oh, the expert in romance. Alexa managed not to smile.

The next thing out of Stacy's mouth surprised her even more.

"Who's that girl in the picture?"

"What picture?"

"He's got an old photo in his wallet. Some girl. Looks about sixteen or seventeen."

"Oh," Alexa said, her voice going quiet. "I haven't seen that."

"I don't think I was supposed to either."

"It's someone he lost. A long time ago."

"His sister?"

"No … a girlfriend. He doesn't like talking about it."

Maybe that's why he doesn't like looking at his past. It's all tied up with thoughts of her. Him getting angry at me reading about his FBI work was really him being angry about his unresolved grief. Poor guy. He's carrying a lot of weight.

After a minute, in which Stacy looked deep in thought, she asked quietly,

"Was she murdered?"

Alexa looked at her in surprise. *Maybe you really do have some insight.*

"Yes. Please don't mention it to him. It would only upset him."

"I won't," the girl replied as they headed into the narrow east fork. A cluster of bushes stood up ahead, their roots sunk deep in the ground to tap into hidden water. If they were lucky, they'd see some more hummingbirds over there. "Did they catch the guy?"

"No," Alexa admitted.

"Are you trying to find him?"

"It was a long time ago, Stacy."

"Yeah, but he's your partner. And you catch murderers, right? Maybe you can find him."

Alexa didn't reply. The case was almost two decades old, and Stuart didn't want her to pry. She should just leave it.

But as she thought this, she knew she couldn't. That nagging feeling she always got at the beginning of a case, that mixture of excitement and determination, was beginning to rise up in her. She needed to help her partner, she needed to give him some peace, some closure.

He deserved that.

As terrible as Robert Powers's murder had been, Alexa knew she would learn to live with it, precisely because the killer and his accomplices had been caught and punished. Stuart didn't have that, and he deserved it.

"Look!" Stacy cried, pointing a slim arm toward the nearest bush.

Three emerald hummingbirds hovered around the bush, searching for nectar to suck from the tiny peach-colored flowers. Alexa and Stacy brought their horses to a stop and watched, entranced, at this little miracle of the desert.

Yes, I'll look into that murder. Maybe, even after all this time, I'll find something the local cops missed. A lot of local forces are a bit sloppy, or undermanned or don't have the latest equipment. I certainly had that driven home in this last case. So yeah, I'll see what I can find.

"They're so pretty!" Stacy said.

But not until next week. This weekend is for Stacy. I have another important job on my hands right here next to me.

THE KILLING POINT
(An Alexa Chase Suspense Thriller—Book 4)

When U.S. Marshal Alexa Chase arrests gang-members in a routine drug seizure, she thinks nothing of it—until she realizes there's far more to the drug-killings than meets the eye. A member of their gang has gone off the rails, morphed into a psychotic serial killer, and Alexa will have to navigate the treacherous gang-world to find him and save the next victim before it's too late.

THE KILLING POINT (An Alexa Chase Suspense Thriller—Book 4) is book #4 in a new series by mystery and suspense author Kate Bold, which begins with THE KILLING GAME (Book #1).

Alexa Chase, 34, a brilliant profiler in the FBI's Behavioral Analysis Unit, was too good at her job. Haunted by all the serial killers she caught, she left a stunning career behind to join the U.S. Marshals. As a Deputy Marshal, Alexa—fit, and as tough as she is brilliant—could immerse herself in a simple career of hunting down fugitives and bringing them to justice.

But with her recent work a big success, the FBI and the Marshals have decided to make their joint-task force permanent. Alexa, reeling from her own traumatic past and her PTSD of hunting serial killers, has no choice: she will now have to work with an FBI partner she dislikes and hunt down serial killers whose jurisdiction intertwines with that of the U.S. Marshals. Alexa finds herself forced to confront the thing she dreads the most—entering a killer's mind.

As Alexa dives deeper into the case, she realizes that she's not the only one who wants this serial killer stopped: the gangs, too, want him brought under control. But she'll have to navigate the treacherous gang underworld to find him, and the people leading her may be the people she can trust least of all.

Is she just leading herself deeper into danger?

Or will the killer come for her next?

A page-turning and harrowing crime thriller featuring a brilliant and tortured Deputy Marshal, the ALEXA CHASE series is a riveting mystery, packed with non-stop action, suspense, twists and turns, revelations, and driven by a breakneck pace that will keep you flipping pages late into the night.

Books #5 and #6—THE KILLING FOG and THE KILLING PLACE—are also available.

Kate Bold

Debut author Kate Bold is author of the ALEXA CHASE SUSPENSE THRILLER series, comprising six books (and counting); and of the ASHLEY HOPE SUSPENSE THRILLER series, comprising three books (and counting).

An avid reader and lifelong fan of the mystery and thriller genres, Kate loves to hear from you, so please feel free to visit www.kateboldauthor.com to learn more and stay in touch.

BOOKS BY KATE BOLD

ALEXA CHASE SUSPENSE THRILLER
THE KILLING GAME (Book #1)
THE KILLING TIDE (Book #2)
THE KILLING HOUR (Book #3)
THE KILLING POINT (Book #4)
THE KILLING FOG (Book #5)
THE KILLING PLACE (Book #6)

ASHLEY HOPE SUSPENSE THRILLER
LET ME GO (Book #1)
LET ME OUT (Book #2)
LET ME LIVE (Book #3)

Printed in Great Britain
by Amazon